LOSING HER INHIBITIONS

LINDA FAUSNET

This book is dedicated to women everywhere.
May we support each other and lift each other up no matter what
paths in life we may choose.

My books contain steamy sex, bad words, and human beings of all sorts, include gay people. If you're not a fan of those things, you may want to stop reading now. If you're cool with that stuff, come take my hand and join me on this journey…

Published by Wannabe Pride 2018

Editing by Linda Hill

Cover Design by Chuck DeKett

FIRST EDITION.

Library of Congress Control Number: 2018904920

ISBN: 978-1-944043-27-8

❀ Created with Vellum

CHAPTER 1

$\mathcal{I}$ walked out to the center of the stage, closed my eyes, and drew in a deep breath. I loved the smell of the theater. The scent of the paint and wood and the smell of hairspray, wig glue, and makeup. The sensory overload filled me with anticipation of the world that came alive when actors stepped onstage. I also loved the whole *feel* of the theater. The crackle of electricity in the air. The feeling anything and everything was possible here in the land of make-believe.

As a 6'2", broad-shouldered, muscular guy who worked as a maintenance manager during the day, nobody ever expected me to be a theater geek. But that was me. I tolerated my regular job, but the theater was where I really belonged. Even now, alone on the stage, I felt the magic in the air.

"Hi, Mr. Rannells!" shouted Anthony, one of my theater students, as he jumped out from behind the curtain and scared the bejesus out of me. He giggled when I jumped half a mile into the air.

"Hey, hey! What's the big idea?" I said in my best 1950s greaser accent, putting up my dukes to do mock battle with the little guy. I played Danny in *Grease* once, and I loved old-timey lingo.

The door to the auditorium opened and a few more of my students trickled in. Teaching acting and voice lessons to underprivileged kids at The Creel Foundation for the Arts was just a part-time gig, but I loved it. It was a hell of a lot more fun than unclogging toilets and changing lightbulbs like I did in my day job. My dream was to perform on Broadway, but it was always a thrill for me to work in any theater. If only I could teach theater and go on auditions full time. That would be sweet.

The door opened again and in walked my teaching partner, Susie Peters.

"Hey, Luke," she said with a smile, and I saluted her in return.

Now *she* got to do theater full time, that lucky so-and-so. Susie was awesome. I had a blast working with her and the kids. We recently did the show *School of Rock,* where I played Dewey and she played the principal. We also ran lines frequently to prepare for auditions and often bonded over our failures when we didn't get the parts we wanted. She was one of my closest friends in New York.

She also happened to be gorgeous. Shoulder-length brown hair and blue eyes, and the girl had legs for miles. Susie was a terrific dancer, which was why she had a killer body. Like every other girl around here, she was taken. She was crazy in love with her boyfriend, David Groff, a wealthy businessman who wore suits that cost more than most people's rent. A pretty powerful guy, he probably had the connections to get me rubbed out should I look at his girl the wrong way. He came across as gruff, but he was a nice guy once you got to know him. It seemed to bother him a little that me and Susie were close friends, but he wasn't a jerk about it. David had nothing to worry about: Susie was totally devoted to him, and I would never chase after another guy's girl anyway.

The other gorgeous girl who worked here at The Creel Foundation, Rosemary, was *way* off limits. Her boyfriend was the big boss, Johnny Creel himself. He was cool and laid back, and he paid me a ridiculous amount to work here part time doing what I loved.

Working alongside beautiful women I wasn't allowed to touch was incredibly frustrating. Too bad I wasn't in any shows, except for the ones I worked on with the kids. When I was in a show, I could usually find at least one actress to hook up with during the run. I liked dating actresses; most women outside of the acting world either thought I was gay or were kind of embarrassed by me because of my love of the theater. They didn't think that being a musical theater actor was exactly macho. It'd been way too long since I'd had sex, so it was almost worth putting up with a woman's scorn to get a little action. Almost. I tried not to think about it, and instead focused on the job at hand.

"Okay, let's do a warm-up song before we get into rehearsing for the show," I said to my students. Our next production was *Willy Wonka and the Chocolate Factory.* We were still in the early stages of rehearsal for it.

"Come on, everybody," Susie said in her best teacherly voice. She taught high school in Washington D.C. for years before moving to New York and knew how to handle an unruly mob of eleven-year-olds. "Gather around and let's get started. What should we sing first?"

I looked at Felicia, who was one of the best students in the class. "How about 'Guns and Ships'?"

Felicia grinned excitedly. That song was her chance to shine and she knew it. "Guns and Ships" was a song from *Hamilton* that featured a lengthy rap sequence from the character Lafayette. I loved doing songs from *Hamilton* with my students. They were inspired by African-American and Hispanic people who looked just like them, serving in such leading roles on Broadway. Felicia, with her dark brown skin and deep soulful eyes, knew the fast-moving rap sequence cold. It was a joy to see her in her element.

Susie did the part of Aaron Burr, I was George Washington, and we all joined in to sing the chorus parts. As always, Felicia was perfect. Not only did she get all the words right, she had incredible stage presence. She had no qualms about giving it her all in front of everybody.

When the song was over, I grinned proudly at my little guys. "Fantastic job, everybody. Felicia, way to tear it up!"

We all applauded loudly, and Felicia smiled with pride. Damn, was this the best job on the planet or what? I got to do what I loved and help a bunch of great kids feel good about themselves in the process.

"All right, let's get to work on *Willy Wonka,*" Susie said. "Anthony, front and center."

Anthony, our Charlie Bucket for the show, stepped up. I knew I wasn't supposed to have favorites in my class, but Anthony was my man. Eleven years old and slightly short for his age, he had light brown skin and light brown eyes. Anthony was unbelievably talented. This wasn't just some after-school program for him. He wanted to do this for real. I'd talked to his parents to get a feel for how supportive they were, and got mixed results. His father was a stand-up guy who worked a bunch of jobs to support his family. Sadly, Anthony's mother was a drug addict, and unreliable to say the least. She frequently showed up late to pick him up, and I worried constantly about her getting him home safely. I told his dad I would be willing to take Anthony to auditions any time I could, and he seemed open to the idea, so that was a start.

"Oh hey, before I forget," Susie said with a happy smile,

"Mr. Groff had a fun idea for the show. He suggested we give out real chocolate to people as they come in the door. And, of course, there would be enough for all the actors, too. What do you think?"

The kids cheered. I loved seeing their enthusiasm. David seemed to have a soft spot in his heart for kids, so his generous offer didn't surprise me.

"Sounds groovy to me," I said. "Okay, ladies and gents, let's get to work. How about we run through Veruca's song first?"

Maaria, a sweet girl whose family came to the U.S. from Pakistan just a few years ago, stepped forward shyly. A quiet one most of the time, Maaria magically transformed into the brattiest character of the show when the music started. It was fascinating to watch.

The rest of the night's class went well. Anthony was terrific as always, and the other kids seemed excited about being in the show. As usual, I hated to see the evening end. Tomorrow was another working day, but I knew it wouldn't be long until I came back. To do what I loved most.

* * *

DEALING with exhaustion by 10am was the norm in my job as head of maintenance for a fifteen-story building in Manhattan. There was always something to be fixed in a hurry, adding to my stress level. So far I'd had to deal with a blown fuse, several leaky sinks, and worst of all, a burned bagel had set off the fire alarm. I'd had to act quickly to determine the cause and send the all-clear before the whole damned building got evacuated. Fortunately, I had a terrific group of five guys working under me. I supervised them, and they in turn supervised other guys. We made a terrific team, doing our best to keep everything running smoothly while

5

staying out of the way of The Very Important People who worked in the building.

The Very Important People, both male and female, wore expensive suits and rushed around acting like they were in charge of saving the Universe. I had no idea what most of them did for a living. Among the many businesses in this building, one company, Wicket Professional Technologies, took up more than half the building's space.

"We havin' fun yet, Luke?" asked Manuel, one of my favorite guys on the team.

"You know it, Manny. Hey, nice job on the Great Bagel Debacle." Manny had been the one to track down the cause of the fire alarm in enough time to call off the fire department. With expressive brown eyes, Manny was rather short and unimposing. He was light on his feet and instinctively seemed to know how to fix anything.

"That was a close one," he said, shaking his head.

It certainly had been. When there was a problem, we were supposed to swoop in and fix it while still being as invisible as humanly possible. The Very Important People looked right through us. We ceased to exist until we were needed. Had the whole building been evacuated, The Very Important People's Very Important Work would have been disrupted, and the dirty, sweaty maintenance guys would have been to blame. Never mind that it was one of The Very Important People who can run the business world but couldn't figure out how to heat up a bagel without burning the place down.

Roger, one of my other favorite guys, came walking up to us. "Okay, fixed the bank of lights on seven, Twinkletoes."

"Good deal. Thanks, man," I told him, ignoring his mocking name for me. The guys teased me relentlessly for being a theater actor, but it was all in good fun. I'd quit explaining years ago that I was mainly a singer and an actor and not a dancer, but they still called me Twinkletoes, Fred Astaire, and Baryshnikov, among other things.

Roger nodded. He was cool. Unfortunately for him, Roger had more trouble being invisible than the rest of us. He was a 6'6", built black dude. Oh, he was visible all right. People tended to back away when they saw him coming, which pissed me off. He was hardworking, honest, and a fun guy all around, but people treated him like a thug because of the way he looked.

A particularly attractive Very Important Person with light blonde hair pulled back and out of her face, and pretty blue eyes rushed past us. Like most businesswomen, she wore a suit that covered up most of her body. At least her suit had a skirt instead of pants, so it showed off her shapely legs. She wore incredibly high heels that looked sexy as hell.

I had seen her before. She never smiled, but unlike most Very Important People, she actually looked at us when she passed. She would nod a greeting in her rush to get to wherever, but at least she acknowledged our presence.

Even better, I could have sworn she glanced at my biceps, which were partially visible under my tight T-shirt.

Roger, Manny, and I stared at her as she rushed down the hall.

"How long do you think it's been since that woman had sex?" Roger asked bluntly.

I burst out laughing at his question. It was just so unexpected.

"A woman like her got no time for sex," I told him. "That's what vibrators are for. Quick and easy. She can take care of her needs fast and get right back to work."

Roger chuckled. "No doubt."

"You know," Manny said, scratching his chin as if deep in thought, "I bet for her, getting laid would be good for business."

7

"How do you figure that?" I asked.

"Well, think how tense she must be. Would *you* be able to concentrate if you hadn't gotten laid in forever?"

Once again, I tried not to think about how long it had been for me. There was an actress who played opposite me in an off-Broadway show two months ago. Nothing since then.

"If you're all wound up, how you gonna be able to concentrate on your job?" Manny asked.

"Ain't that the truth," Roger said. He was happily married and had a terrific sex life. Or at least that's what he always told me. "That woman needs a good hard pounding to clear her head."

I chuckled. "Can you imagine what it would be like to be the first guy she's had in a long time? God, that would be fun. Mess up her hair and wipe the uptight expression right off her face."

I conjured up all kinds of delightful images of me with Blonde Lady. Her hair finally free from its tight clasp, her legs wrapped around me as I gave her what she desperately needed. I got rock hard just imagining all the sounds she would make. Her cries of passion as I satisfied her long-ignored sexual needs. The moans, the screams, and hearing her cry out my name when I made her come.

I bit my lip. "Oh man. I could give her just what she needs."

Manny and Roger laughed heartily.

I raised an eyebrow. "Are you questioning my manly abilities, gentlemen?"

"You could never get a high-class girl like that, ya dirty bastard," Roger said. "Look at you."

He gestured toward my sweat-stained shirt and pants, which were dirty due to having crawled under the sink up on twelve to fix a leak. Roger had a point. A classy, well-educated Very Important Person like Blonde Lady would want nothing to do with me. Not that I really cared. I didn't have much interest in snooty businesswomen, anyway. I knew her kind. She worked all the time and had no life outside of the office. Ate takeout for every meal. Spent her whole life at a soulless job, always trying to make more and more money. A humorless, uptight businesswoman. No, she wasn't my type either. Still, I liked to think I could get a girl like her if I wanted.

"Okay, so I'm not her usual kind of guy. That doesn't mean I couldn't get her into bed."

The laughter from the two buffoons was much louder this time. It stung my pride.

"Hey, I could make it happen," I insisted. "Like you said, it would do her a world of good. It would be a work of charity on my part. Take her to bed and make her feel like a woman before her lady parts turn to dust."

"Okay, smartass. You think you can seal the deal with Blonde Lady? Put your money where your mouth is, Luke," Roger said. "A hundred bucks says you can't bag her."

"Hey, hey," Manny said. "I want in on the action. I match your hundred bucks. You got two weeks."

"All right, wait. Hold on there," I said. "I didn't agree to that."

"You scared of a little challenge there, Romeo?" Manny asked, knowing full well it was the perfect tactic. I loved a challenge. If there was an electrical or plumbing problem nobody else could solve, I made it my mission to figure it out no matter how long it took. I didn't make it to head of maintenance for a prominent Manhattan high-rise by backing down from a challenge. And if trying to make it to Broadway wasn't the ultimate challenge, I didn't know what was. Besides, my manly pride was at stake here.

"Of course I'm not scared. I guarantee you I can nab Blonde Lady and give her a night she'll never forget, but I need at least a month to thaw the Ice Queen. It'll take a least a few weeks to get that stick out of her ass."

Roger and Manny chuckled.

"Okay, okay. Fair enough," Roger said. "We'll say a month."

Manny nodded his agreement.

"Today's July sixth, so you got exactly one month to fuck her brains out, or you owe us each a hundred big ones," Roger said.

I caught a glance of Blonde Lady herself from down the hall, and a sliver of guilt sliced through me. She seemed like she was a nice enough woman, and I felt kinda bad about talking about her like she was a piece of meat. Still. If I could charm my way into her bed, I knew she'd be grateful to me for satisfying her womanly needs.

"Deal," I said, sealing the agreement with a firm handshake.

This wasn't going to be an easy bet to win, and the clock was ticking. There wasn't a moment to lose, so I figured I'd get started right away. Start subtle. A friendly smile in the hallway would be a good beginning.

Blonde Lady was walking toward us.

"Elyse!" someone called to her from the hallway.

Okay, so at least now I knew her name. Elyse paused in the hall for a few moments, chatting with some guy in a suit who looked as uptight as she was. Roger, Manny, and I puttered around, trying to look busy, killing time until Elyse made her way back down the hall. Suit Guy finally let her go, and I took in a deep breath.

At the exact moment Elyse got close enough for me to shoot her my best boyishly handsome smile, my radio crackled.

"Hey Luke," came Paul's voice. Paul was another one of my best guys. "We got a situation on seven. Somebody took a huge dump in the men's near the supply room. Toilet overflowing all over the joint. It ain't pretty. You better get here quick."

Elyse winced, having overheard every word about the next assignment in my glamorous job. She avoided my gaze as she rushed past us.

I closed my eyes and let out a breath, trying to tune out the howls of laughter from my "best guys."

I opened my eyes, glared at Roger and Manny, then headed to the seventh floor to deal with my latest challenge.

Okay, so it was a rocky start. Who cared? That would just make it all the sweeter when I won the bet.

Elyse.

She was a beautiful woman, that was for damned sure. She might not know it yet, but she needed me. She needed me to end her sex drought and satisfy her wildest desires. Once I was done with her, she'd be totally relaxed and content, and maybe that would make her able to concentrate on her Very Important Job even more.

Oh yeah.

That's what Elyse needed.

A guy like me to take control and fuck her senseless.

CHAPTER 2

I let out a sharp cry of pleasure as Brad pounded me hard.

"Are you close, Elyse?" he asked breathlessly.

"Yes, God yes, I'm close," I moaned.

"Good, 'cause so am I," he said with his sexy boyish grin.

Brad was a terrific lover. He always made sure to satisfy me first, though sometimes it was a close race to the finish line.

"Faster," I cried. "Faster!"

He planted his hands on the mattress and thrust into me harder and faster, hitting just the right spot. I dug my nails into his back and cried out one last time as I reached an intensely pleasurable orgasm.

Brad chuckled deep in his throat. "That's a good girl."

Closing his eyes, he shifted into a slightly different rhythm to maximize his own pleasure. He plunged in and out of me for mere seconds before he found his own release, letting out a sexy, masculine groan as he came.

He panted for a moment, then opened his eyes and grinned down at me.

Pushing my hair out of my face, I smiled back. "That was amazing. Oh God, I really needed that."

Brad kissed me on the cheek and then rolled off me and collapsed onto the bed.

"Rough week?" he asked.

"Yeah. Not bad, just crazy busy."

He nodded. He lay there for a few moments to catch his breath, then got up to leave.

Brad Seymour was the ideal friend-with-benefits. He satisfied me sexually, and he never wanted to stay overnight. It was a win-win. We dated briefly a few years ago, but we didn't have much in common, so we broke up. Now, he served as the perfect booty call when I was between boyfriends. Brad was always just a text away when I needed to relieve my sexual tension, which was quite frequently. I enjoyed sex, and Brad was a reliable and safe way to have a good time. He was clean, and I was on the pill, so I never needed to use a condom with him.

As he started getting dressed, I reached over to my purse on the nightstand and took out my wallet. This part of the night was always a little weird for me. I felt like I was paying a gigolo for services rendered, but it wasn't like that. My wealth allowed me to give Brad a hundred bucks for "cab fare." Money was tight for him, and I never minded tossing him a few extra dollars.

"Here you go, hon. Get home safe," I told him.

Brad smiled at me, then bent down and kissed me on the cheek. We only kissed on the lips during foreplay.

"Thanks, Elyse. Take care, and don't work too hard."

"I won't."

"Yes, you will," he said with a smile. He finished getting dressed and headed out.

I lay back on the bed and let out a sigh of sheer sexual relief. There was no feeling in the world that could

13

LINDA FAUSNET

compare with the contentment and relaxation from having great sex.

After resting for a few moments I got up, pulled a night-gown on over my head, then padded to the kitchen. I opened the fridge and grabbed a Red Rooster Ale, a beer from Heart-land Brewery, one of my favorite microbreweries in New York. I *loved* microbrews. Every time I had a work reception or business dinner, I drank wine instead. I didn't even like wine, but that was what women were expected to drink. Either wine or some super-sugary fruity kind of cocktail. The male executives at my company would be intimidated if they found out I knew more about beer than they did. Men's egos could be fragile, and I knew how to adapt my habits to conform to what they expected. It was the only way for me, or any woman, to advance in this business.

I loved my job, but it always felt good to let loose a bit on the weekend. Smiling at work was considered unprofes-sional, especially if you were a woman. It implied weakness. Outside of work, random men had the nerve to tell women they should smile *more.* You couldn't win sometimes.

After grabbing a beer, I scanned my fridge for food. I spied some leftover seafood alfredo I thought I'd finished already. "Sweet!"

I grabbed the Tupperware container and poured its contents into a bowl, then put it in the microwave. I loved to cook, but I worked such crazy hours that I rarely had to time to make meals during the week. I usually prepared a few entrees on the weekend and froze them so I could eat well during the workweek. Trying new recipes was one of my favorite hobbies, so when I moved into my apartment, I splurged on an enormous kitchen with fridge and freezer to match. I could spend hours in this kitchen trying out new recipes, even though I was only cooking for myself. Sometimes I froze stuff and gave it to family members, but other than that, it was just for me.

I enjoyed living alone, and I was grateful to have the means to hire help for anything I didn't want to do myself. My housekeeper, an older lady named Norma, came in three times a week to keep things tidy and do my laundry. My assistant, an NYU student named Kelly, picked up my dry cleaning and ran other errands. Best of all, Kelly did all the "essential" grocery shopping. The boring stuff. I got to do the fun part, like shopping for cooking ingredients at specialty shops in Chelsea and places like that. I was so lucky not to have to waste time doing boring errands on the weekends. I worked hard all week, so I enjoyed my time off.

I put my beer and seafood alfredo on a tray and carried it into my bedroom. Crawling into my super-comfy king-sized bed with satin sheets, I settled into bed with my snack in front of the TV. I usually checked out the late-night shows to see if they had any good guests on. If not, I'd go to Netflix for some good stand-up comedy. I relished having this time to myself, and I was looking forward to having a relaxing weekend. My plan was to sleep in, and then my sister and brother and I were going to a microbrew festival in New Jersey in the afternoon. We always had a blast at those things. I'd hired a limo so the three of us could get totally plastered and not have to drive anywhere. Angelica and Leo would crash here tomorrow night, which was always fun. We'd order pizza and stay up late, like a grownup sleepover.

As much as I loved chilling out and having fun on the weekend, I was usually eager to get back to work on Monday morning.

I nearly choked on my beer during Conan's opening monologue. Giggling, I wiped my mouth with a napkin.

Life was good.

CHAPTER 3

I'd been so damned busy all morning, I barely had time to look for Elyse. My plan had been to start slowly. Begin with a friendly smile to get her to notice me. Well, I was pretty sure she had noticed me before, when she checked out my biceps. Made me wonder if she'd ever stopped to check out my ass when my back was turned.

She worked up on ten but, unfortunately, I hadn't had any maintenance calls up there today. Plenty everywhere else, it seemed. Knowing Manny and Roger, they were deliberately making sure things were running fine and dandy on the tenth floor, in order to sabotage our bet.

Cockblockers.

I could hardly blame them. I'd have done the same thing in the spirit of healthy competition. I finished tending to a security alarm that wouldn't stop beeping on the eighth floor and took the stairs up to ten, to see if I could track down Elyse to start my mating dance.

And who should I see in the stairwell on the tenth floor? It was Blonde Lady herself, leaning against the wall.

She looked like death.

It was startling to say the least. Her eyes were closed, and she was ghastly pale.

"Hey, are you all right?"

Elyse gasped and her eyes flew open.

"I'm sorry, I didn't mean to scare you," I said as I walked toward her.

"That's okay," she said in a weak voice. "Yes, I'm fine."

"You don't look fine. I mean, you look *fine*, but you also look sick."

She laughed softly, which surprised me.

"I'm all right, really."

Elyse drew in a deep breath, then stood up straight. She was clearly trying to pretend nothing was wrong, but she looked like she could pass out at any moment. Wouldn't be the first time I'd dealt with a medical emergency on the job. I always hated seeing people in pain, but it was especially jarring to see someone like Elyse suffering. She always seemed so in control.

"The hell you are. You look like you need an ambulance. What hurts?"

"Nothing. I said I'm *fine*."

Lots of people who insisted they were fine wound up in the hospital. I was no doctor, but I needed her to tell me what was wrong.

I realized it might be something embarrassing, like bad diarrhea or stomach cramps or something. I wanted to get her to trust me so I could help her.

"What's your name?" I already knew her first name, but she didn't know that.

"Elyse Pippin."

"Okay, Ms. Pippin, what—"

"Elyse. Call me Elyse," she said with a weak smile.

"Fine, Elyse. I'm Luke Rannells," I said, then added sternly, "You can call me *Mr.* Rannells."

That got another soft chuckle from her.

"Since you're sick, you can call me Luke."

"Well, that's very sporting of you."

"Elyse, please tell me what's wrong. I want to help you." I meant every word. I wanted to turn on the charm, but this had nothing to do with trying to win the bet. I was legit worried about her.

"I'm okay, Luke. If you'll excuse me, I really have to get back to work." She drew in a deep breath and straightened out her suit jacket. My guess was she planned to get through the rest of the day without anyone else knowing she was sick. That's why she was hiding in the stairwell. So she could quit pretending for a minute.

"You're obviously not well. What is it? Food poisoning? Stomach cramps?"

Elyse groaned, closed her eyes, then leaned back against the wall. My muscles tightened, ready to pounce into action. I was fully prepared in case she slid down the wall and collapsed onto the floor. She looked that bad.

Her pretty blue eyes opened again, and I saw pure agony in them. "It's my period, okay? It's not something I can share with my male co-workers. They like to pretend periods don't exist, and they expect us to do the same. It's just something I have to live with."

"Wow," I said. I'd admit to being a bit like her co-workers. A tad squeamish talking about such things. I was sure it was uncomfortable for her, too. Still, I couldn't believe a menstrual cycle could cause this much agony. Elyse looked like she was *dying*.

"I mean, I know it's supposed to hurt, but is this normal? It's not supposed to be *this* bad." I'd had several girlfriends who usually gave me a heads-up when they were on their period, which meant no sex for a few days. Sure, they'd had some cramps, but I'd never seen anything like this.

Elyse sighed. "No, it's not normal for most people. But I've always had it bad. Ever since I was twelve, I—" She laughed suddenly. "I'm sorry. Why I am telling you all this?"

"Because I asked, and I'm concerned," I said.

"Thank you, Luke." Her eyes softened, and she looked truly grateful. Now that she'd confided in me, maybe she wouldn't have to suffer alone.

"Can I get you anything? Do you need some Tylenol or Advil or something?"

Elyse smiled. "I took my medication. It's stronger stuff my doctor prescribed. Just takes a while to kick in, that's all. I'll be okay, really."

She reached out and took my hand in hers. She squeezed it and said, "Thank you for your concern. It's very sweet of you."

Elyse looked me in the eyes and suddenly she wasn't Blonde Lady any more. She wasn't even A Very Important Person. She was just a person. Vulnerable, like anybody else.

She smiled at me, then straightened up and took another deep breath. The transformation was amazing. It was as if nothing was wrong. Elyse Pippin looked like a well-coiffed, professional business woman who had Very Important Work to do. You'd never know she felt sick.

Unless you looked into her eyes. You could still see the pain in those blue eyes of hers. In that moment, I would have given anything if I could just convince her to go home and rest in a comfy bed with a heating pad over her midsection. Stubborn lady like her would never give in and go home. Never.

"Well, I hope you feel better," I said. The words seemed so inadequate, but what else could I say?

"Thanks," she said before she slipped out the door.

I thought about Elyse all morning long. I pictured her trapped in business meetings, suffering in silence and hiding her pain. Maybe she was meeting with clients and had to put on a brave face for them. She was probably used to it, but I felt so bad for her. I wished there was something—*anything* I could do to cheer her up.

Then I got an idea. It was a little weird, but I still wanted to try it. Elyse had shared a personal secret with me, and I wanted her to know I was thinking of her. And that I cared.

I usually grabbed lunch with my guys, but I told them I had an errand to run instead. I went to the drug store and got some stuff to put together a care package for Elyse. I bought her a heating pad, some chocolate, and some chamomile tea. I also got her a small bottle of pain medication, made just for menstrual pain. I doubted she would use it since she had stronger stuff from her doctor, but it was the thought that counted. I also found a little teddy bear with a heart on its chest, with the words "Get Well Soon." I thought long and hard before buying the little guy. I figured it might be a bit over the top.

Then I pictured Elyse's agonized face when she was slumped against the wall in the stairwell. I grabbed the damned bear.

I found a cardboard box down in storage, arranged all the items inside, and headed up to ten. I scribbled a note on the top that read "A gift from Mr. Rannells." I hoped she wouldn't be in her office so I could drop it off and let her find it later.

No such luck. She was in her office, hard at work. I stole a glance at her, trying to see if it looked like she felt any better. I couldn't see much of her face because she was at her computer. Oh well. It was go time.

I walked over to her office and stood in the doorway. She looked up and was quite surprised to see me. I spoke before she had a chance to say anything.

"Got a package for you." I popped into her office long

enough to put the box on her desk, then hightailed it out of there. Not the smoothest way I could have done it; she probably thought I was nuts.

I headed out to the hallway and then carefully peeked around the corner so I could watch her reaction without her seeing me. Understandably, Elyse appeared bewildered and a little wary as she opened the box. My stomach tightened, and I started second-guessing myself. What if she got embarrassed or offended by my gift? It could be considered harassment. What if she reported me to HR? I could lose my job. What the hell was I thinking?

Elyse opened the box and peered inside.

Then she burst out laughing. I watched her take out the chocolate and the tea, and set them on her desk. She pulled out the bottle of pain pills, which got another chuckle out of her. Then she pulled out the teddy bear and smiled fondly at it. She set him down on the desk and put a hand over her heart. Good God, Elyse was beautiful when she smiled. It made me feel good all over that I had managed to make her feel better.

She glanced up, probably looking for me. I ducked back into the hallway and dashed toward the stairs.

I couldn't help smiling as I jogged down the steps. Elyse already seemed way cooler than I had given her credit for. She clearly wasn't always a no-nonsense business woman with a stick up her ass. I found myself looking forward to getting to know her better, and not just because of the bet.

I was tied up for the rest of the day with one stupid maintenance issue after another, and I never made it back to the tenth floor.

I finally got a chance to stop by the next day. I peered around the corner and saw Elyse at her desk. I didn't want to stride right up to her; I wished there was a way I could casually run into her. I walked past her office, hoping she would see me. She didn't.

I felt like an idiot, walking down the hallway for no reason. Fortunately, nobody was behind me, so it was easy for me to reach the end of the hallway and turn back around. I caught a break on the way back. My radio crackled just as I went past Elyse's office, and the noise made her look up.

At least this time it wasn't a gross bathroom emergency. It was Paul giving me a heads-up that the air conditioning unit on three was fixed.

I slowed my roll as I walked down the hall and soon became acutely aware that Elyse was behind me.

"Luke!" she called out.

Yes!

I turned around. She had her hair tied up in a bun as always, and she wore another boring business suit, but there was a softness in her eyes. Her sweet expression didn't match her all-business exterior.

"I wanted to thank you for the gifts you got for me yesterday. That was incredibly thoughtful of you," she said.

"Happy to do it." I lowered my voice a bit, since she clearly didn't want anyone else knowing about her problem. "How are you feeling?"

"Much better," she said, letting out a soft breath. She did look much better. The agony was gone from her eyes, and all I saw now was relief. "First few days are the worst. I'm almost done now, thank God."

I nodded, honored that she would confide such personal details to me. It was awful to think she must go through this torture every month without letting anybody know she was hurting.

"The chocolate really helped," Elyse said with a pretty smile. I was tempted to tell her she should smile more often, but then I realized how condescending that would sound.

"I'm glad," I told her.

Elyse glanced up at the clock on the wall. She appeared genuinely grateful for my gesture but didn't seem all that interested in me otherwise.

I decided I would ask her out anyway. The worst she could do was shoot me down, and at least Roger and Manny weren't around to witness it. I opened my mouth to ask her if she would like to grab a drink or something after work. Then the door to the office next to hers burst open and A Very Important Guy in an expensive suit dashed out into the hallway.

"Elyse! We got the conference call with the Japanese company in three minutes."

She nodded. "Headed to the conference room right now." Elyse looked at me and said quietly, "Thanks again. It really did make me feel better."

Elyse gave me a much smaller smile this time, and her expression was proper and businesslike. It was funny; she had looked like a completely different person when I saw her open my gift. She didn't know anyone was watching, so she had laughed and smiled freely. My guess was you had to act like A Very Important Person at all times at work when you were in, well, whatever business she was in.

She rushed past me and headed to her meeting. I sighed as I walked toward the stairwell. Her thanking me for my present was the perfect opening for me to ask her out. It would be much harder to strike up another conversation with her. What could we possibly have in common?

I spent the next few days making every effort to run into Elyse, but it wasn't easy. After all, I was in charge of keeping things running smoothly on all fifteen floors of our high-rise, not just on the tenth floor where she worked. And she was every bit as busy as I was. I lost track of how many times I tried to casually walk past her office, only to find she wasn't there. The worst part was Manny catching me doing it twice in one day.

"How's it goin' with the girl, Twinkletoes?" he asked.

"Never you mind," I told him. "I got this under control. I'm gonna take good care of her."

"You got to find her first."

Tell me about it.

She found me once later in the week, though I knew she wasn't actually looking for me. We passed in the revolving door in the lobby as I was headed out for lunch. She had two Very Important Suit Guys with her, including the same jackass who'd blown my chance the other day. *Hope the Japanese company meeting was worth it, asshole.*

I caught her eye and smiled. She gave me a tiny, nearly imperceptible smile in return. She looked uncomfortable, glancing at the Suit Guys walking with her.

Unfortunately, Roger and Manny were with me. They cackled loudly as Elyse and her co-workers rushed past.

"Oh, yeah," Roger said in that deep voice of his. "She wants you *bad.*"

"Don't you worry. I'm just wearing her down, little by little."

"Only got three weeks there, homie. Can't take too long," Manny said with a grin.

As far as my guys knew, I hadn't made any progress with Elyse at all. They weren't aware of my earlier interaction with her. As much as I wanted to tell them she and I had made a personal connection, I couldn't betray her confidence. She clearly wanted to keep up her businesslike front at work, and her reputation was obviously important to her. She was wound tight all right, which made me want to relax her all the more. Once I finally got her away from the office, I wondered if it would be tough to convince her to go to bed with me, or if she would be so horny she'd be eager for a long-overdue roll in the hay.

I finally caught up with her again the next day, and this time we were alone in the hallway. It was no accident: it finally dawned on me I could check the conference room schedule and find out when Wicket Pro had a meeting. I looked to see when Elyse would be in there and planned my visit for when she came out. Her co-workers dispersed to their respective offices, and I managed to get her alone, more or less. People hurried past us, but nobody paid us any attention.

This time, Elyse gave me a real smile. There was also a hint of apology in her expression, like she knew she'd acted differently around me when her co-workers were around. That bit of snobbiness on her part made her slightly less attractive to me. And yet, it also made me look forward to having sex with her all the more. I'd wipe the snobby look off her face once I took charge in the bedroom. I wanted to do things to her that would make her blush when she saw me the next day at work.

"Hey," I said.

"Hey."

I tried to figure out a way to ease into the conversation, but then I thought, fuck it. If I hemmed and hawed any longer, she might rush off to another Very Important Business Thing, and I'd never get to ask her out.

"I was wondering if maybe you'd like to go out for a drink or dinner sometime."

Elyse blinked in surprise. The old "deer in the headlights" cliché was the only way to describe the look on her face. She looked utterly trapped with no way out. I'd asked women out dozens of times in my life, and naturally some of them shot me down. Normally, it wasn't a big deal. Elyse looked slightly horrified, and her reaction stung. Was I *that* hideous to her?

"I get it," I said, forcing a smile. I glanced down at my dirty, maintenance-guy pants and shirt. "I'm not exactly your type."

"N—no," Elyse stammered, her face turning pink. "It's not that. I—I just ... uh ..."

Of course it was "that." Elyse probably only dated Very Important Suit Guys. She must not have been dating one now, though, or she would have used it as an excuse.

"You don't have to explain, Elyse," I said, feeling slightly annoyed. She didn't think I was good enough for her. Fine. Fuck the bet. Somewhere out there was a woman who wouldn't look down on me for being the blue-collar type. "I'm glad you're feeling better. See ya."

I swallowed my wounded pride and turned to leave.

"Wait," she said, her pretty blue eyes full of apology. I could see she hadn't meant to make me feel bad. "I mean, how do I know if you're my type? I don't really know you."

I nodded.

"But I'd like to," Elyse said softly. I got the distinct impression she was humoring me. Maybe she didn't know how to get out of going out with me without hurting my feelings, so she figured she might as well just go. That was good enough for me. We could go out for a quick dinner and, if things went well, we might wind up in the bedroom. She would find out a blue-collar guy was lot better in bed than her stuffy Suit Guys.

"Give me your number and we'll figure out the details later."

Then again, maybe not. I knew a brushoff when I heard one.

I snorted. "Yeah, okay."

"I mean it, Luke," Elyse said, looking me in the eye. "I have to run for now, but give me your number. I'll text you later so you'll have my number."

Whatever. I almost said it out loud. I fished a fast food receipt out of my pocket and scribbled down my number.

"I'll talk to you soon," Elyse said earnestly, still trying to convince me she wasn't blowing me off.

"Okay," I said with a smile, still not believing her.

"I'm looking forward to getting to know you better, Luke," Elyse insisted.

I nodded, then headed back down the hallway.

Yeah right. Elyse was looking forward to getting to know me better. She already looked down on me for being a maintenance worker. Wait 'til she finds out I'm also a theater geek.

I tried to put the whole Elyse situation out of my head for the rest of the day, but it was hard. She seemed so sweet when she opened the care package I gave her. She looked so pretty when she smiled. I'd hoped she would turn out to be different from all The Very Important People who looked through me every day, but it turned out she was just like the rest of them. She was ashamed to be caught smiling in my direction; she'd probably never want to be seen in public with me. Instead of forgetting the whole thing, I spent the rest of the afternoon working myself into a snit of righteous indignation.

Who the hell does she think she is? What a snob. Thinks she's hot shit just because she —

Then I got a text from her late in the day.

Good afternoon, Mr. Rannells.

She even added a smiley face after the words. Typical. She would only smile at me in secret. I tried to stay mad at her, but I found myself grinning like an idiot.

How about dinner this Friday night?

I stared at my phone, hardly believing my eyes. She could have gotten away with meeting me for a drink on a weeknight. Or worse, she could have suggested meeting for a

27

quick coffee during the workday. No. She went straight for dinner on a Friday. Date night. Wow.

I forced myself to wait a full half hour before responding, so as not to appear too eager. Finally, I wrote back.

Sounds great.

CHAPTER 4

 sat a table alone at Smokey Joe's Pizza Place in Manhattan, not far from the building where Luke and I both worked. I chose the place because it wasn't too expensive. Most men insisted on paying, at least for the first date, and I didn't want to put him in a financial bind.

I was nervous about going on a date with Luke. I was sure he thought I was a terrible snob, but he really wasn't my type. Not that I knew what my type was, but it likely wasn't a maintenance guy. Luke was probably a lot like Brad: hot and sweet, but rather simple. What in the world would we talk about?

My heart skipped a beat when I saw Luke walk in, and my reaction caught me by surprise. He looked incredibly handsome, clad in tight jeans and a dark-blue button-down shirt. And he wasn't only cute, he also happened to be a nice guy. The care package he put together for me was so thoughtful, and it truly made me feel better. It must have been awkward for him to go shopping for those things, and I found it touching that he'd gone to all the trouble.

I waved at him from my seat at the table, and he caught

my eye and smiled. Luke took a seat across from me and glanced at my outfit.

"You look nice," he said with a grin.

I had my hair down, which was how I usually wore it outside of the office. My light blue dress was also different from my work attire. Less severe, and much more feminine. Luke glanced at my cleavage as quickly as he could get away with while still seeing the goods, then he glanced back up at my face. It was adorable.

"You look nice, too," I told him, though "hot" would have been a better word.

We stared at each other for a moment. It was awkward. I had no idea what to say to him. Most of my dinners out were work meetings to discuss business matters. We usually launched into a discussion about whatever project we were working on, having little time for small talk. I rarely dated businessmen. Actually, I rarely dated at all. It wasn't a conscious choice. I loved my life the way it was, enjoying my alone time outside of working hours. Occasionally I met someone who caught my interest and we'd date for a while, but I hadn't had an actual boyfriend in quite some time.

"What would you like to eat?" Luke asked, finally breaking the silence. "You don't have to get pizza if you don't want to. There's lots of other things on the menu."

"Pizza sounds great to me," I said. "You like meat lover's pizza?"

"Yeah. Do *you*?"

"It's my favorite."

"Really?" Luke asked, clearly surprised. "I had you pegged for a dainty salad girl."

"Guess again," I said with a smile. "I usually behave during the week, but I like to eat real food on the weekend."

Luke grinned back, and I felt a flutter of renewed attraction. So, we had meat pizza in common. That was a start. Even if it turned out to be the only thing we had in common, that would be okay. I found myself already wondering what Luke would be like in bed. It was exciting to think about having sex with someone other than Brad. It had been a long time since there had been anyone else. I'd see how the rest of the evening went with Luke, then I would decide whether to invite him back to my place.

The server arrived, and she inquired about our order.

"We'll take a large meat pizza," Luke said. "Elyse, what do you want to drink?"

I turned to the waitress. "What do you have on tap?"

"We've got Bud Light, Miller Lite, Sam Adams seasonal, Yuengling, and we've got the Owl Farm Milk Stout Nitro."

"Oooh, I'll take the Nitro. Thanks!"

"Bud Light for me," Luke said. "Thanks." After the server walked away, he said, "Nitro, eh?"

"Let me guess. You had me pegged as a wine girl."

"Sure did."

"Surprise," I said with a smile.

More awkward silence.

"So," I began, suddenly remembering why I never went on dates. First dates were the worst. I pictured my comfy bed and rather wished I was home, drinking beer and watching stand-up comedy on television. "What do you like to do for fun?"

"You mean when I'm not fixing toilet clogs?"

"I ... uh. I really don't know what I'm supposed to say to that."

Luke chuckled. "Well, I do work crazy hours, so I don't have a lot of time for fun. I'm not only a maintenance guy, you know. I'm director of maintenance for the whole building."

"You are? I didn't know that. That's impressive."

"Well, I do more than just replace lightbulbs and fix leaky sinks you know," Luke said defensively.

Once again, I had no idea what I was supposed to say to that, so I said nothing.

Luke's expression softened, and he laughed uncomfortably. "I'm sorry. I don't know why I'm giving you such a hard time. Lots of people who work there, you know, on the business side, treat me and my guys like we're beneath them."

I nodded, hoping I'd never made him or his co-workers feel like that. If I had, I certainly hadn't meant to.

The server arrived with our drinks. I sipped my beer.

"Oh, that is so good," I said. "I've never had Owl Farm's Nitro brew before."

"You like microbrews, huh?"

"I love them. My sister and brother and I visit microbreweries all the time."

"What's a 'nitro,' anyway?" Luke asked.

"It means they use nitrogen instead of carbon monoxide to make the beer bubbly. Makes for a smoother pour." I took another sip. "Mmmm. That is smooth."

"Cool," Luke said, sounding genuinely interested.

"You know," I said, putting on my most haughty expression. "I know you don't want me to look down on you, but I have to say I'm judging you pretty hard for drinking that cheap domestic beer."

Luke laughed heartily, and I felt my body relax a bit. He'd had me feeling super defensive for a while.

"Fair enough."

"So, what *do* you do when you're not fixing clogged toilets?" I asked, figuring I might as well be blunt.

Luke smiled again, his eyes sparkling with amusement. Just when I thought his defenses were finally down, he seemed to tense up again. "Well, to be honest ..."

"What? Do you have a secret life I should know about?"

"Kinda. Well, as much as love my glamorous day job, it's not really what I want to do with my life."

I paused, giving him time to continue when he was ready. He seemed self-conscious about whatever he was trying to tell me. That made me quite curious.

"I'm actually a singer. Well, actor and singer."

I stared at him. "You're kidding."

"Nope. I'm a total theater geek."

"Theater," I said slowly, letting this information sink in. "Theater as in ... *musical* theater?"

"Yep."

"That is so *cool!*" I exclaimed, much louder than I had intended.

Luke laughed. "People have lots of words to describe my theater life. I don't think anyone's ever called it cool."

"You mean, like ... you can sing?"

"I like to think so, yes. Sing, act. Dance, occasionally, if the show calls for it."

"Wow, that's amazing," I told him. "Oh, I *love* musical theater. It's one of the best things about living in New York. I go to see pretty much everything that comes to town."

"Seriously?" Luke asked. "What's your favorite show?"

"Oh, that's tough. There are so many good ones. I'm definitely a fan of the lighter ones, you know? The funny, upbeat ones."

"So, you love *Les Miz* and *Miss Saigon*, right?" Luke asked, naming some of the most depressing shows out there.

I laughed. "Yeah, right. Let's see. I love *Avenue Q* and *Spamalot. Young Frankenstein.* Oh, and for sure *The Book of Mormon.*"

"Oh, that one is the best!" Luke exclaimed. "Definitely a favorite of mine."

"I got to see it with the original cast," I boasted.

"Ah, you lucky *bitch!*" Luke blurted out.

I threw my head back and laughed. Luke seemed surprised and pleased I wasn't offended at being called a bitch. After all, *The Book of Mormon* was an incredibly irreverent show. Certainly not one for the easily offended.

The server brought over the delicious-smelling pizza. Luke served me a slice. I was starving, but I was far more interested in his life as a musical theater actor. I'd been smug about his misjudgment of me, but I was way off about him. I'd never in a million years have guessed he was a performer.

"So what shows have you been in?" I asked.

"Oh, gosh. Tons of them over the years. Started in high school. Then I did lots of shows in community theater back in Pennsylvania where I'm from originally. And I've done some off-Broadway stuff here."

"Really? That's impressive. I would think getting any part in New York would be tough."

"Oh, it is, believe me. The best part I've ever gotten was playing Andrew Jackson in *Bloody Bloody Andrew Jackson.* You know that one?" Luke asked, before biting into his slice of pizza.

"I've heard of it, but I've never seen it."

"Oh, it's so cool. It features Andrew Jackson as this emo rock star."

"And you were the lead?"

"Yeah," Luke said, his eyes lighting up with excitement. His passion when he talked about his theater life was an incredible turn-on for me. The flicker of attraction I had felt for him was building to a flame. Luke was handsome, thoughtful, *and* he could sing? Holy hell, where had this man been all my life?

Right under my nose at work. I probably ignored him like everybody else on the "business side," as he put it.

"I got pictures of me in the show. Wanna see?"

"Yes!"

34

Luke grinned and then fished out his cell phone from his pocket. He thumbed through some pictures until he found the right ones.

"Here," he said, handing it to me. "I got a whole album in there with pictures from the show."

I wiped my hands on my napkin and took the phone. My heart fluttered when I saw the first photo of Luke onstage, in costume.

He was decked out in black jeans and a tight white T-shirt that showed his muscular body in all its glory. He wore dark eyeliner around his eyes and his mouth was curled in a sexy sneer. *Good God, did he look hot.* Luke appeared to be an entirely different person in the photo, which was a testament to his skill as an actor. I was suddenly dying to hear him sing. He must have an incredible voice to land the lead in an off-Broadway show.

"Wow," was all I could say as I thumbed through the rest of the images.

"I had so much fun doing that show." I could hear the joy in his voice.

"Damn, you looked *hot* in that outfit," I told him as I handed back the phone. "I mean, you always look hot, but *wow.*"

Luke grinned at me. "Thanks. I also played Danny in *Grease.* Wanna see pics of me in my leather jacket?"

"Yes, please."

He laughed, then flipped through more photos until he found the *Grease* album. He gave his phone back to me.

I stared at the photo of Luke with his brown hair slicked back, sporting a sexy leather jacket and another tight T-shirt. My heart fluttered once again, and desire tingled between my legs. That flame of desire was now a full-fledged bonfire. I could flip through the pages of a men's fitness magazine if I wanted to look at hot guys, but this was different. Luke's unmistakable charisma burst forth from the photographs. Stage presence, they called it. I'd seen enough shows on Broadway to recognize talent when I saw it. And I hadn't even heard him sing yet.

"Well?"

I glanced up to see Luke grinning at me.

"I need a napkin to wipe the drool from my mouth."

Luke laughed again. He seemed impressed at how unabashed I was. I found Luke incredibly attractive, and I wanted him to know it. Speaking up about negative things was harder for me, which was why I'd accepted Luke's invitation in the first place.

Thank God for that.

To think, I nearly turned down a chance to go out with this incredible man.

"Okay, okay. Enough about my life. Tell me more about you," Luke said.

"What do you want to know?"

"Well, what do you do when you're not … what is it you do, anyway?"

A ripple of pleasure went through me. I loved talking about my job, and I was glad he had finally asked me about it.

"As you know, I work for Wicket Pro. It's a global technology company with offices all over the world. Japan, Taiwan, the UK, Australia, and we're expanding all the time. I work in sales strategy and operations. We try to land important clients, and my job is to teach companies about how our tech services and products can help them."

Luke nodded, listening carefully to what I was saying. It was nice telling somebody new about what I did for a living.

"We offer all kinds of technology services. AI, SDN, cloud computing, big data and analytics, IOT, Agile Systems development, service-oriented architecture, imagery and LIDAR data analysis, things like that."

Luke's brow furrowed, and I laughed. "Am I losing you here?"

"A little. I mean, I'm interested, I just can't quite follow all of it," Luke said with an adorable smile.

"It's okay. I have an MBA, of course, but I also have a bachelor's degree in computer science."

"*Really,*" Luke said. He sounded impressed, which was exactly the reaction I wanted.

"Yeah. It's cool because pretty much everybody I work with has an MBA, but I'm the only one with a computer science degree. It means I can understand a lot of the technology stuff the other guys can't."

"That *is* pretty cool. What got you interested in computer science?"

"For one thing, I love a challenge. I knew it would be difficult, so I wanted to try it."

"Nice," Luke gave me a sexy grin. I was pleased to see he wasn't threatened by my intelligence.

"And I love how exact computer science is. Same thing with mathematics. There's usually a clear, black and white solution, you know? Not like the rest of life, which can be so messy."

"Makes sense. I like challenges, too. Like figuring out electrical wiring and stuff. But loving computer science and math? I'm afraid we are total opposites in that regard."

"Well," I said seductively. "You know what they say about opposites."

"Oh, I'm attracted all right."

I laughed, and so did Luke.

"I can't even imagine understanding all that technical computer stuff," Luke said, shaking his head and reaching for his beer.

"Yeah, well I can't imagine being brave enough to get up onstage in front of all those people and do what you do. I love all the techy stuff that comes with my job, and I even enjoy the high pressure of it all, but sometimes I need a break. Turn my brain off for a while. That's why I love going to theater shows. N—not that I'm saying what you do is *brainless*. I—I mean—"

Luke laughed good-naturedly without a trace of his earlier defensiveness.

"No, I get it. That's one of the reasons I do what I do. I think of theater as escapism, too. And I'm like you; I like the lighter shows. The fun, feel-good ones that make you laugh."

"Exactly."

Luke looked at me curiously for a moment.

"What?"

"It's funny. I always thought you hated your job."

"Why would you think that?"

"I don't know. You're always rushing around the place looking stressed, and you never smile. At work, anyway."

I smiled at him now.

"You're so pretty when you smile, Elyse," Luke said, and I could hear the tenderness in his voice.

"Thanks. I love my job. It's challenging, yes, but really rewarding. I am a bit of a workaholic, but it's only because I get so excited about what I'm doing. Learning about the latest developments in technology and the exhilaration of landing a huge sales deal. I know it sounds totally nerdy."

"Not at all," Luke said. "Nothing wrong with a little ambition."

"Oh, it's more than a little. I've got my eye on a huge promotion. My boss is leaving soon to work in the London office, so his job will be vacant. Right now, there are four of us in the department, so it will be either me or one of the other two guys."

"Nice. What's the job?"

"Senior Vice President, Worldwide Sales Strategy and Operations."

"Wow."

"Yeah, wow. Oh Luke, I want this job so bad."

"I hope you get it. Good luck. To you and your new promotion." Luke held up his beer glass and he clinked it with mine. We drank to my successful future.

"Anyway, that's why I never smile at work. I've worked hard to gain the respect of my peers. I never talk about my personal life in the office. They need to think I'm totally focused on work and don't have any outside distractions. Especially with this big promotion on the line."

"So I guess that's why you look so different at work?" Luke asked.

"Yes. If you want to know the truth, I hate most of the business suits they make for women. They're just so *mannish*. But I have to wear them if I want to be taken seriously."

"You always look nice at work, Elyse. But you look even better now. You look so pretty with your hair down."

"Thank you, Luke. That's very sweet."

"I gotta say, you're a lot different than I thought you were."

"Is that so? Well, I could say the same thing about you. I would never have guessed you were a theater guy. I thought you were one of those types who sat around drinking beer and watching football."

"I *do* like beer and football," Luke said. He lifted his beer glass and tilted it at me. "Though I prefer baseball."

"Me too!" I exclaimed. "I love baseball. I like going to ball games almost as much as I like going to the theater." I narrowed my eyes at Luke. "Who's your New York team?"

Luke narrowed his eyes, too. "You first."

"On three," I suggested. "One ... two ... three. Yankees!"

"Mets!" Luke said.

We stared at each other.

"Oh, how will we raise the children?" Luke wailed.

Not to worry. I'm not planning on having kids. Ever.

Of course, it was far too early in our relationship to talk about that sort of thing, so I let Luke's comment pass.

"My sister-in-law is expecting, and I've already bought Yankees gear for the little tyke."

Luke's expression was grim, and he shook his head. I laughed, which made him break character and smile.

"Will there be anything else?"

I jumped. I hadn't even seen the waitress arrive at our table. Luke looked at me, questioning, and I shook my head.

"I'm good."

"Me too," Luke said. "We're ready for the check."

The server nodded and placed the check on the table. We both reached for it.

"I got this, Elyse."

"I really don't mind, Luke. I can pay for it."

"So can I."

"I know that. Of course, you can."

Luke grinned at me. "I make six figures, you know."

"You do?" I couldn't hide my surprise.

"Low six, but yeah. I told ya, I'm in charge of the whole building. To do that, you gotta know electrical systems, HVAC, and plumbing. You also gotta know all the building and safety codes. Plus, I'm in charge of all the housekeeping and grounds staff. I even have my own office."

"Is that so?"

"Yes. It ain't exactly a corner office with a window, but it's all mine."

We stared at each other for a moment, both of us still holding on to the check.

"You're gonna let me pay, see?" Luke said in a hilarious

imitation of a cop from an old movie. "I'm not about to let some dame pay the dinner bill."

I laughed heartily but still didn't let go of the check.

"Please, Elyse? Lemme pay this one time?"

I lifted my hand from the bill and sat back in my chair. "I have the feeling you get away with a lot of stuff by being charming."

Luke batted his eyelashes, getting another laugh from me. The server arrived and picked up the check. Luke paid in cash, so we were ready to go.

"Thank you for dinner, Luke."

"My pleasure."

We looked at each other for a moment, not quite sure what to do next. It was funny; things were already a lot less awkward between us. We were still feeling each other out, getting to know each other, but I was starting to feel comfortable around him.

"So, what do you want to do now?" I asked, hoping Luke felt the same way as me. I didn't want the evening to end.

"Well, we could … I mean, would you want to …" Luke began.

I smiled encouragingly at him. He was awfully cute when he was nervous. If he asked me to go back to his place, it would be a definite yes.

"Would you, you know, maybe want to hear me sing?"

I giggled. "That's not what I thought you were going to ask me."

Luke laughed, too.

"And *yes*, Luke. Yes. I would absolutely love to hear you sing!"

"Cool," Luke said, looking relieved.

"So, what do we do? Go someplace that has *karaoke* or something? Or do you want to go to your place? Or mine?"

"I've got the perfect place in mind," Luke said. "I work

part time teaching underprivileged kids. I teach voice lessons, acting. Stuff like that."

"Wow," I said, my heart melting even more. He was full of surprises.

"Yeah, so if the theater space is open, we can go there. I work at this place called The Creel Foundation for the Arts."

"Creel?" I asked. "As in Walter Creel, the famous attorney?"

"Yep, that's the one. Well, I don't work with him. I work for his son, Johnny."

"You work with Johnny Creel?" I asked with astonishment. Johnny Creel had been an infamous playboy. As Walter Creel's spoiled heir, he'd been a constant feature in the gossip rags. He'd been a notorious partier and womanizer, until Walter Creel suddenly had his assets frozen. His partner had apparently been involved in all kinds of illegal activity, and it took a while to clear Walter's name. During that time, his spoiled son had had to fend for himself for the first time in his life.

"Oh, yeah," Luke said. "Johnny's a great guy."

That's what I'd heard. *Now* Johnny was a nice guy instead of a pompous ass. The story was Johnny had reached out to his former secretary for help, and they fell in love. Once Walter Creel was cleared of wrongdoing, Johnny was rich again and started falling back on his old ways. He must have royally screwed up with his girlfriend, because a video of him apologizing to her went viral. He actually *sang* to her, and she sang back. First, she sang a brief medley of angry songs, before segueing into a song of forgiveness. It was like a scene from a movie.

"Is he still with that girl?"

"Rosemary, yeah," Luke said with a smile. I could hear the fondness in his voice. "She's a real sweet girl. A good friend of mine. If you ever meet her, though, don't bring up the video."

"Why not?"

"She's a little sensitive about it. I mean, don't get me wrong. She loves Johnny with all her heart. But she's a terrific performer, and she's worked incredibly hard to get where she is now. Hell, she's even been on Broadway."

"Yeah, I think I heard something about that. It was in the news because Walter Creel was at the premiere. And Johnny, too, of course."

"That's just it," Luke continued. "She's amazing in her own right, and she's not crazy about being known only as Johnny Creel's girlfriend."

"That makes sense," I said. I respected Rosemary for that. Some people were happy to ride to fame on someone else's coattails. Not her: she sounded like a strong woman.

"Lemme just text Johnny and make sure nobody's using the auditorium now."

By the time we headed out the door to look for a taxi, Johnny had responded and given us the all-clear.

The Creel Foundation for the Arts was farther away than I had expected, but that was fine by me. I had more time to spend with Luke. We laughed so easily together, and we had fun simply riding around New York in the cab.

We arrived at the foundation, which was in a terrible area in Brooklyn. I couldn't begin to imagine what it was like living here. Those poor little kids.

"I know it's kind of a rough neighborhood," Luke said after observing my expression when we got out of the cab. "But the inside is really nice."

I paid the driver and was pleased Luke didn't argue about who would pay this time. He punched in the security code to the front door, then led me inside.

"Wow, this *is* nice," I said as I looked around. The reception area was clean and bright, with a desk area for the receptionist and plenty of chairs for people to sit in and wait. It resembled a friendly pediatrician's office, designed to make the kids feel comfortable.

Luke put his hand on my back and led me down the hallway. I loved that he already felt comfortable touching me like that.

There were framed photographs on both sides of the long hallway. Lots of pictures of the kids onstage. They looked so happy and excited, it made me smile just looking at them. I stopped to gaze at a photograph of Luke onstage with a bunch of kids.

"That's from *School of Rock*," Luke said proudly.

"Oh, such a fun show!" I exclaimed.

"Let me guess. You got to see it with Alex Brightman, right?"

I nodded.

"Not fair," he pouted.

I laughed and gently punched him in the shoulder. "Stick with me, kid. I'll get you into the best shows on Broadway."

"Sounds peachy-keen," he said, making me laugh again. "Oh, here. Here's Rosemary."

Luke pointed to a photograph of a pretty, red-haired girl in 1960s garb onstage.

"Oh, wow. That's *Hairspray*, right?"

"Yup."

"One of my favorites. Talk about a feel-good show. She looks beautiful."

"Yeah, that was something. Seeing her onstage. *I* got to go to opening night for that one," Luke said, then stuck his tongue out at me.

"Well, I saw the revival twice, so *nyah*," I bragged.

Luke laughed and then led me down the rest of the hallway to the auditorium.

"Right through here," he said as he opened the door for me.

"Wow, this is lovely," I said, surveying the theater. The stage was gorgeous, with beautiful red velvet curtains. There were several thousand seats in the auditorium. What a thrill it must be for those kids to perform in such a place.

"Yes, it is," Luke said with reverence. I could see how affected he was by simply being inside this beautiful theater. He looked like a completely different person here than when he was at work. Like this was where he belonged.

We walked toward the front, and Luke headed straight for the stage.

"Sit anywhere you're comfortable," he told me.

I chose a seat a few rows from the front and sat in the middle where I could see him best. Luke paced back and forth on the stage for a few moments, performing vocal warmups. He looked so commanding onstage. I was already impressed.

"Okay," Luke's voice boomed from the stage. "Any requests?"

I thought for a moment. "How about "I Believe" from *The Book of Mormon?*"

He laughed and clapped his hands. "An excellent choice."

Luke walked to the side of the stage to fiddle with the sound system. Soon, I heard the familiar beginnings of one of the best songs from one of my favorite shows.

A ripple of excitement went through me. Luke looked incredible, and I could hardly wait to hear him sing. He had a deep and sexy speaking voice, so he must be an incredible singer.

The song started out slow, with the main character, Elder Price, questioning himself and his mission. Then he begins to feel stronger as he sings, reaffirming his beliefs, hence the title.

"I *believvvve*," Luke sang out, loud and strong.

A literal shiver went through me. He sounded *wonderful.* I couldn't help but laugh as Luke sang about all the crazy things Elder Price believed in, including God's plan to give him his very own planet. The song was a terrific one for a singer to belt out, but its lyrics were hysterical. Luke managed to grin at me from the stage while singing. He wasn't offended I was laughing; it meant he was doing it right.

I leaned forward, enraptured, as Luke sang his heart out. When he got to the line about believing Satan has ahold of you, he pointed directly and accusingly at me. I laughed so hard I was wiping tears, just as I had when I saw the original show on Broadway.

The song built to a strong finale, and Luke ended it by waving his arms with hysterical, over-the-top religious fervor.

"I *BELIEVVVVEEEE!*"

I stood up and applauded, and Luke took a dramatic bow. He locked eyes with me from the stage, and my heart thumped wildly. Luke was a *star*, and I felt honored to be on the receiving end of his attention.

"That was amazing, Luke. Just amazing. More! More! I want more!"

Luke shot me a sexy smile and my knees went weak. "You got it, little lady. What do you want to hear?"

"How about something from that Andrew Jackson show you were in?"

Luke's handsome brown eyes lit up, and I knew he was pleased with my request. "Good idea."

He walked back over to the sound system, which gave me ample opportunity to check out his ass. He looked terrific in blue jeans, but my mind kept going back to the photos he showed me at dinner. Those tight black jeans he wore in the emo-rock version of Andrew Jackson, with his hair wild and the black eyeliner around his sexy eyes. I had a sudden, vivid fantasy of Luke fucking me hard against a wall while wearing that outfit. Fully dressed, with only his jeans unzipped to free his cock so he could give me what I needed.

I drew in a deep breath, grateful Luke was onstage and too far away to hear my panting. I always did have an active sexual imagination. I used it frequently when I was with Brad. But this Luke-in-costume fantasy was more exciting than anything I had conjured in quite some time.

It was delightful.

Rock music started blaring, and Luke stalked across the stage, already in character as an angry Andrew Jackson. He shot me the same sexy sneer from the photograph, which set my heart to pounding again.

The song he chose was a furious and loud, yet surprisingly funny song. It was all about how his life sucked, and he was Andrew-fucking-Jackson.

I loved it.

I clapped like crazy when it was over. Luke stayed in character, standing still onstage. Another song began, and he launched right into it. The first song contained lyrics about how Andrew Jackson was "not that guy," and now this new song had lyrics saying, "I'm *so* that guy," asserting that he was going to fight back on behalf of his country. I knew from high school history class that he killed a bunch of Indians, and I felt a bit guilty about being aroused by the song. It wasn't like I was hot for the actual Andrew Jackson. But Luke looked so damned sexy up there on the stage, rocking out and looking angry and determined.

Luke paused again onstage, and I bit my lip in anticipation of what might be coming next. The next song began with lyrics asking why a girl wouldn't go out with him when they were in school. Luke sneered at me in the audience as if

47

I'd been the one to reject him. I moaned aloud, turned on beyond all reason by his smoldering look. Good thing the music was far too loud for him to hear me.

The song went on to sing the praises of populism, and at one point, Jackson sang about filling you with "popula-jizzm." Naturally, he looked right at me when he sang that part, causing me to burst out laughing. I caught the hint of a smile on Luke's in-character sneering lips. The next song he did had a line asking if I wanted to see his "stimulus package," and of course he looked at me. I mouthed "Yes," and he laughed slightly as he sang.

Luke finished up the song and then walked over to turn off the music. I stood up and applauded, and his handsome face broke into a full grin. It was fascinating to watch as he transformed from Andrew Jackson back to Luke Rannells, right before my eyes. He was one hell of a performer.

Which, of course, got me wondering about his other performance abilities.

I walked toward the stage, and Luke held out his hand to help me up. We sat close together on the stage, our legs hanging off the edge. He was sweating from the exertion of his performance, and I could practically feel his adrenaline pumping. The stage was clearly where he came alive. I stared at him.

"What?" he asked.

"I am totally fangirling over you right now."

Luke laughed modestly, which made him even more attractive.

"I mean it. You were fantastic!"

He searched my eyes for a moment, like he was trying to figure out if I meant what I'd said or if I was only humoring him. If he had any idea how close I was to jumping him right there on the stage...

Luke smiled softly and seemed pleased with what he saw

in my eyes. "Thanks. And thanks for, you know, coming here and indulging me. I guess I figured if you really wanted to get to know me, this was the best way to do it. This here," he said, turning around and gazing at the stage. "This is who I am."

It was a highly personal thing to say, and he didn't look at me as he said it. He hesitantly turned back to me.

"Who you are is wonderful, Luke."

He smiled at me, then seized this perfect moment to kiss me for the first time. He dipped his head down and pressed his lips to mine. I moaned softly and wrapped my arms around him. His body felt hard and strong, and I found I loved the smell of his manly sweat. My bonfire of attraction was now a full-fledged wildfire, burning out of control. I had never been so turned on by anyone in my life. I forced myself to resist the urge to lie down right there and pull him down on top of me.

When he finally lifted his head, he said, "I think you're wonderful too, Elyse."

A delicious thrill went through me, just hearing him say my name in his deep, sensual voice. I was so mesmerized by him, I couldn't speak for a moment. I could only hope he was half as affected by me.

"So," I said when I finally found my voice. "Is this what you want to do?"

I glanced at center stage where Luke had stood while giving his electric performance.

"Yes," he said without hesitation. "I consider myself lucky as hell that I get to perform as much as I do now. Here at the foundation, and when I'm lucky enough to get cast in an off-Broadway show. I've already racked up a bunch of hours on union shows, so I'm getting closer to being eligible to join Actor's Equity. That's the actors' union."

"And then what happens?"

"Well, once you're in the union, it gets a lot easier to audition for shows on Broadway."

The way he said *Broadway* made me smile. He said it with such reverence; I could see how much it meant to him.

"I've seen a lot of shows on Broadway, Luke. And after seeing you perform tonight, I can easily imagine you on a Broadway stage."

Luke looked at me doubtfully.

"Okay, I'll level with you here. I think you're an awesome guy, not to mention smokin' hot, so I would tell you what you want to hear just to make you feel good. But in this case, I also happen to be telling the truth. You're an incredible performer, Luke. I really mean it."

Once again, Luke searched my eyes for the truth. I loved when he looked at me like that. It felt like he was gazing right into my soul. He could search all he wanted; all he would find was sincerity. I was blown away by his talent, and not only because I was hot for his body.

"Thanks, doll," he said with a wink. "You've seen me in my element tonight. I feel like I should return the favor. Watch you in the board room or something."

I laughed. "Oh, please. You'd be bored stupid. It'd put you to sleep if you had to listen to me do a technology presentation."

"Not necessarily," Luke said, tracing my lips sensually with his finger. "I think it's so hot that you're smart. Say something computer-techy to me."

I thought for a moment. "Wicket Pro can help you simplify and automate your IT operations management through our hyperflex systems and Intersight cloud-based platform."

"Hmmm, so sexy," Luke said, then he kissed me again. "You're gonna make the best Vice President of Strategy and Whatever there ever was."

I laughed, pleased he'd remembered most of what I said about the promotion I desperately wanted. "Senior Vice President, Worldwide Sales Strategy and Operations."

"Mmm, say that again," Luke said, pulling me close for another kiss. I laughed as he tried to kiss me, which made him kiss me harder.

I wasn't laughing anymore. Luke wrapped his strong arms around me as we kissed hungrily for several moments. I wanted him. Badly.

"Luke," I managed to say breathlessly after breaking off our kiss. "Do you want to come back to my place?"

With the sexy grin that drove me wild, he said, "Thought you'd never ask. Let's go."

CHAPTER 5

I had never dreamed any woman would look at me the way Elyse did when I sang. She seemed enraptured. It was such a thrill to get up onstage and impress her with my performance on our very first date. Usually, it took an enthusiastic audience of hundreds of people to get my adrenaline pumping like that.

It was hard to tell if Elyse's rush to get back to her place was because she wanted *me* so badly, or because it had been God knew how long since she'd gotten laid.

She lived in a seventh-floor apartment in an impressive neighborhood on the upper east side of Manhattan. Elyse pushed me against the wall of the elevator and pressed her lips to mine. I was already hard and had been during the whole cab ride over. I could hardly believe I was about to get lucky. Elyse moaned softly as my tongue brushed against hers. Yes, she was definitely horny as hell. It wouldn't take long to make her come, that was for sure. Maybe I'd even get to have sex twice tonight. The first time to relieve her pent-up sexual frustration, and then we could take our time on the second go-around.

The elevator door opened and Elyse led me by the hand to her apartment.

I took a deep breath when we walked inside. "Wow, very nice."

You could fit my whole apartment into her living room. Elyse's place was much warmer and inviting than I had expected. There was one of those fake fireplace things that run on electricity, a large-screen television mounted on the wall, and two comfy-looking soft, brown couches with a matching recliner chair.

"Come here. I want to show you my kitchen," Elyse said. I wanted to head straight to the bedroom, but I figured we'd get there soon enough.

Elyse flipped on the light and stepped back so I could take a good look. Her kitchen was nearly as big as her living room. There was a large refrigerator and a separate freezer beside it. Lots of counter space, loaded with every kind of appliance you could think of—blender, mixer, cappuccino machine, Cuisinart, and more.

"Wow, *very* nice."

Elyse smiled proudly. "Thanks. It's my second-favorite room in the house."

My cock twitched in my pants. I hoped her favorite room was the same as mine.

"I love to cook."

"Yeah?" I asked. Elyse was full of surprises tonight. She was nothing like the uptight business executive I had thought she was. Not an over-stressed, miserable woman who lived on takeout, but warm and kind, loved her job, and she could cook.

"Yep. I don't have much time to cook during the week, but I spend hours on the weekend trying out new recipes. I'll have to make you something sometime."

"I'd love it. I can't cook worth shit."

Elyse smiled, then cocked her head seductively. "Wanna see the bedroom?"

"Yes, please."

She laughed, then led the way.

Elyse's bedroom was as warm and comfy as the living room, not to mention super girly. The curtains were a dark pink, and the carpet was a lighter shade of pink. Her bedspread had a rose pattern on it.

"Huh," I said.

"Huh, what?"

"It's very *pink*. Not what I pictured at all."

Elyse smiled. "Yes, Home Elyse is a girly-girl. Work Elyse is not."

"I see." The difference between Home Elyse and Work Elyse was astonishing. Like she was a completely different person. She walked over and wrapped her arms around me. I gazed down at her. "You're shorter than I thought."

"Work Elyse wears heels all the time," she said. Wasting no time, she stood on her tiptoes to kiss me. For so long, I'd been fantasizing about satisfying her needs, and I was grateful she was finally letting me do it.

Her kiss was aggressive, and I pressed my hard length against her. She moaned again.

"I need you."

God, she *was* desperate.

"Been a while, has it?" I said before I could stop myself.

Elyse blinked. "What?"

"I'm just saying you seem pretty eager to get down to it, so I'm guessing it's been a while since you … you know."

She narrowed her eyes. "Let's see. It's been four … five … six … Yes. Six days."

I opened my eyes wide. "Six *days?*"

"Yup," she said. Elyse let go of me and took a small step back.

"Wow."

"I like sex," she said bluntly.

As much as I liked hearing her say that, I was still processing the news that Elyse had been with somebody else less than a week ago. Did she have a boyfriend? Was she only interested in sex and not in a relationship? With most women, that would have been a dream come true for me. Just sex, no commitments, no pressure. It was different with Elyse. Even after one date, which technically wasn't even over yet, I knew I wanted more.

"I'm not seeing anyone," Elyse said softly. She could see I was kind of freaking out. "It's just a friends-with-benefits kind of deal. I don't date a lot, so I call him when I feel like having sex."

"You don't owe me an explanation."

She smiled. "Thank you for saying that. Most men would demand one. I don't mind explaining it to you, because I want you to know there's nobody special in my life right now."

Relief washed over me. I still felt weird about her sleeping with another man, but that was my own hang-up. She was a grown woman with sexual needs. Her having a friend-with-benefits was no different than me having a one-night stand with an actress from one of my shows.

As if reading my mind, Elyse said, "It's really no different than when a man picks up a woman in a bar for a one-night stand. It's lot safer, especially for the woman, to call on a guy she knows and trusts. I certainly don't want a lot of strange men knowing where I live."

"Good point."

"And I want you to know I'm never with two men at the same time. Even if I've only had one date with a new guy, I stop calling Brad until I know where the new relationship is going." Elyse tenderly stroked my cheek. "And I don't know about you, but I definitely want to see where this is going."

"I do too. Right now, I want to see it going to the bed."

"Hmm, now who's eager to get down to it? How long has it been for you?"

My face got hot and she grinned. She had me right where she wanted me, and she knew it. Worst of all, it was my own damned fault. I'd been so cocky about satisfying her needs, and yet I was the one who was hard up.

"Do I really have to answer that?"

"No," she said with a gentle laugh.

"Okay, I admit it. It has been a while, and I want to get you into bed as soon as possible, but not *only* because I'm super horny. It's also because you happen to be strikingly beautiful," I said, punctuating my words with kisses. "And super smart … and funny … and sexy as hell …"

Elyse wrapped her arms around me. "Hmmm. Those are good reasons."

She pulled me toward the bed and let go so she could lie down. Then she reached out. When I took her hands, she pulled me forcefully on top of her.

"I like a girl that knows what she wants," I said breathlessly.

"I want *you*." She unbuttoned my shirt and rubbed my naked chest. "You're pretty ripped for a theater geek."

I slipped my hands up her dress and ran them over her trim frame. "And you're pretty toned for a desk jockey."

She laughed, and I marveled at how much fun I was having with her.

Elyse pulled me in for a kiss. "If you perform half as well in bed as you do onstage …"

I loved that she said it, and I loved the *way* she said it. Like she thought my being a theater performer was sexy. I sat up and pulled her into a sitting position so I could slide off her dress. She wore a fiery-red bra and panty set underneath. Reaching around her back, I unclasped her bra while she pulled off my shirt. She unbuckled my jeans, and I helped her tug them off me, pulling my underwear off with them to save time. I grasped her red lace panties and slid them off, stifling a groan of desire when I was finally treated to the full view of her naked loveliness.

Elyse gazed into my eyes as she grasped my rock-hard cock with her hand. Her eyes flashed. "Hmmm, very nice."

I groaned as she stroked my cock. The sharp bolt of pleasure was intense and was yet another painful reminder of how long it had been since someone other than me had touched it.

"I'm on the pill, by the way," she said seductively, managing to make the not-so-sexy yet important matter of birth control sound hot. "So nothing needs to come between us."

She didn't have to tell me twice. Grabbing her left leg, I opened her up wider. She gasped, watching me with anticipation. I forced myself to wait for a few agonizing seconds, then slid myself inside her.

We both moaned together, relishing our mutual pleasure. I wrapped my arms around her neck and pressed my lips to hers as I began thrusting in and out of her. Oh God, it felt so good.

I broke off the kiss, but only because I was panting too hard to keep my lips on hers.

Elyse closed her eyes and threw her head back. "Luke, oh Luke," she said, moaning my name at first. The harder I thrust, the louder she cried. "Luke! Luke! *Luke!*"

I loved how loud she was during sex and how *into* it she was.

I gazed down at her; she looked up at me tenderly. "Luke," she said, softly this time.

In that moment I felt a powerful connection to her. Not only were our bodies joined together, something in her pretty blue eyes told me we were truly meant to be together. And the sweet way she looked at me made me know she felt it, too. This was no one-night stand for either of us.

My whole life, I'd thought the idea of soulmates was ridiculous. Until now.

"Elyse," I whispered before tenderly pressing my lips to hers again. I slowed my thrusts and, instead, made love to her with a gentle yet pleasurable rhythm.

"Oh, Luke," she moaned after several moments of slower lovemaking. My heart pounded and my cock throbbed. I could hear her pleasure growing as I stroked her. "Oh, Luke, oh God ..."

I heard the desperate need in her voice. She needed release, and she needed it *now*.

"Luke, oh, God. Faster, faster!" she begged.

I planted my hands on the mattress to gain better traction and pounded her hard. She threw back her head and cried out so loud, I thought she had reached orgasm. Then she leaned forward again and dug her nails into my back. She pleaded with her eyes for me to keep going.

"Luke, oh God, just like that ..."

I watched with fascination as her pleasure intensified. "Oh, Luke ... oh ... *LUKE!*" Elyse *shrieked* my name when she came. Good Christ, it was so hot. Seconds later, I gripped her shoulders, and shuddering, emptied myself inside her. I let out a deep groan as I reveled in the most pleasurable orgasm I'd ever had. It wasn't only because of my sex drought. It was because of *her*. Sexy, smart, sensual *Elyse*.

I panted hard, still on top of her.

"Oh, Luke," she whispered as she wrapped her arms around my neck.

I had never felt so good in my entire life. I was completely sexually satisfied and utterly fulfilled in every possible way.

I rolled off her, then pulled her close to me. Holding Elyse in my arms felt natural and perfect and *right.*

After we caught our breath, Elyse turned to me with a wonderful, sleepy, satisfied expression on her face. Oh yes, this woman knew what she wanted in bed, and I had given it to her.

"You perform even *better* in bed than you do onstage, and *that* is saying something."

I smiled at her. That was probably the best compliment any woman could have given me after sex. "Well, they say you're only as good as your scene partner."

I pulled her in for another kiss, hardly believing how incredible she was. This woman had watched me sing and act, then sat on the stage and talked to me about my theater dreams. I had listened to her talk animatedly about her job, and watched her eyes light up when she talked about the promotion she wanted. I wanted her every dream to come true, and I knew in my heart she felt the same about me.

Elyse lay flat on the bed, and I shifted to my side so I could look at her. She was beautiful, and she seemed incredibly relaxed, exactly the way I'd imagined her looking after having sex with me. But I could only take partial credit for her look of calm. As it turned out, Elyse Pippin was not the high-strung, sex-starved, uptight executive I'd assumed she was.

I gazed at her tenderly, just enjoying being close to her. I couldn't remember the last time I hadn't wanted to hightail it out of there after sex. With Elyse, I never wanted to leave.

"You have such pretty hair." I reached over to run my fingers through her blonde tresses.

"It's fake. I mean, the hair is real. The color is not."

I burst out laughing. "I love that you're so honest about

59

such things." Her eyes sparkled with amusement. "You got pretty eyes, too. You don't wear colored contacts, do you?"

"Nope. And my boobs are real, too."

I laughed again. "Good to know."

We looked at each other for a moment. The silence between us didn't seem awkward anymore, not like when we were tentatively getting to know each other.

"It's funny," Elyse said softly. "I feel like I've known you so much longer than I have."

"I know, right?" I said, thrilled she had put into words the way I had been feeling all night. "It's weird. And awesome."

"Yeah," she said, snuggling closer to me.

We held each other for a while longer, and then I spoke up. "What time is it, anyway?"

"Gotta be after one by now," Elyse said. She picked up her cell phone from the nightstand and glanced at it. "Two-thirty."

"Shit. I gotta go."

"Do you have to?" Elyse asked, a sad smile on her face. I was glad she wasn't mad or offended that I was leaving.

"Yeah. It's not that I want to go, believe me. It's just I've gotta teach a class of nine-year-olds in the morning."

"Oh," she said. "Had it been anything else, I would have tried to guilt you into blowing it off so you could stay."

"Had it been anything else besides teaching my little guys, you wouldn't have had to guilt me." I stroked her face with my finger. "I really am sorry I have to go."

"I understand," Elyse said, sounding like she meant it. She wasn't one of those girls who said "It's fine," when they really meant "I'm pissed off at you." She got up and began getting dressed, and then helped me on with my jeans. It was a simple gesture, but I appreciated it. It made me feel less guilty about leaving than if I'd had to leave her naked in bed while I got ready to go.

Once we were both dressed, I smiled at her and asked, "Would I sound needy and pathetic if I asked to see you again tomorrow night?"

"You would *not*," she said definitively. "But I can't. Oh, I wish so much I could, but I have plans with my brother and sister-in-law. She's due to have her baby in less than a month, so we're doing some last-minute baby shopping. They've got most of the essentials already, but I want to buy a bunch of teddy bears and blankets and stuff like that. I plan to spoil my niece or nephew from day one."

"Nice," I said, pulling her close. Elyse sounded both regretful that she couldn't see me and excited about being with her family. It was kinda sweet.

I kissed her softly and she wrapped her arms around me. It was crazy how hard it was to let go of each other already. I lifted my lips and sighed heavily.

She nodded. "I know. You have to go."

"Yeah," I said, still not releasing her.

"Hey, how about Sunday?" she asked. "You busy Sunday?"

"Nope." I felt a surge of euphoria at the thought of being with Elyse again.

"Perfect. Why don't you come over here again, and I can cook for you?"

"That sounds wonderful."

I bent down to kiss her again. It was only slightly easier to think of leaving, knowing I would see her again so soon.

"Okay, I'm really leaving now," I said with a laugh. I headed out of the bedroom and she followed me to the front door.

"Bye, Luke." She smiled sweetly.

"See you soon."

She nodded, and I reluctantly left, shutting the door behind me.

Two seconds later, I knocked on the door.

Elyse opened it with a quizzical look.

"I need one more kiss," I said as I grabbed her. I kissed her adorable laughing mouth one more time. "Okay, I'm leaving now. I mean it!"

Elyse laughed again, and I forced myself to leave for real this time.

That woman was like crack to an addict. I'd never get enough of her.

I smiled to myself. What a wonderful problem to have.

CHAPTER 6

*M*y stomach tingled with excitement. Luke would be here any minute. It was slightly scary, how hard and fast I was falling for him. That had never happened to me before. I hadn't cared this much for a guy since my college boyfriend, Alex. And even with Alex, it had taken a while for me to get to know him and develop feelings for him. Corny as it sounded, with Luke it felt like I'd been shot right in the heart by Cupid's arrow. I was *crazy* about him.

We texted back and forth on Saturday once he was done teaching, and he'd told me Mexican food was his favorite. He'd informed me that he liked his food like he liked his women; hot and spicy. That gave me the perfect chance to try out a new spicy enchilada recipe I'd come across a few weeks back. The kitchen smelled heavenly, and I couldn't wait to show off my cooking skills for Luke.

Most of all, I simply couldn't wait to see him again.

The doorbell rang, and my heart lurched. I laughed and shook my head. I was acting like a lovesick teenager. But what was wrong with that?

Straightening my hair, I headed to the front door. I opened it and my heart flipped again. Luke was standing there with his sexy grin, wearing tight jeans and a blue-and-white checkered button-down shirt.

He took a full step back and looked me up and down. I, too, wore tight jeans, along with a black blouse.

"Dammmmn. I've never seen you in jeans before."

I smiled. "No, I guess you haven't."

"You look *great*." Luke stepped forward and kissed me. I ran my fingers through his soft brown hair.

"Is it crazy that I missed you already?"

"No. It should be, but it isn't," Luke reassured me. "I missed you too."

He took a deep breath. "Whatever you're making smells amazing."

"You hungry?"

"Starved," he said seductively, clearly talking about more than food.

"Me too," I said, matching his tone.

Luke arched his eyebrow and smiled slyly at me. It was almost enough to make me forget food altogether. *Almost.*

"Come on in. Lunch is about ready."

I took his hand and led him to the kitchen.

"I really love your place," Luke said, looking around. I had a table and two chairs pushed right up against the kitchen window. The table was set for two.

"Thanks. Have a seat."

He sat at the table and gazed out the window. "Wow."

I loved how affected he seemed by the gorgeous view of New York my kitchen window offered. He loved the city as much as I did.

Luke grinned up at me as I set a bowl of tortilla chips and salsa in front of him. "Thanks."

"Extra hot salsa," I told him.

"Perfect."

"You want a beer?"

"Definitely. I bet you've got some great microbrews on hand."

"You know it." I opened the fridge and surveyed my beer selection. "Okay, do you like stout, IPA, APA?"

"Umm, I don't know."

I glanced over at him, then said in my snootiest voice. "Oh, right. You drink cheap domestic stuff."

"Why don't you pick something for me, your highness?"

I giggled. "Okay, I will. I'll start out gentle." I made my choice, then walked over and placed the bottle in front of him. "Try this. Metropolitan Lager by Flagship Brewing. Nice and smooth. Do you want a glass?"

Luke shot me look that made me laugh again. "Right. Of course not."

He took a healthy pull on the bottle. "Mmmm, that is smooth." He dipped a chip in the salsa and sampled that as well. "Damn, this salsa is *dialed in.*"

I smiled, pleased he liked it.

Luke took another sip of beer. As promised, the salsa was super spicy.

"Where'd you get this stuff?"

"The salsa? I made it."

"Seriously?" Luke asked, sounding impressed.

I grabbed an IPA from the fridge and joined him. "Yup." I dipped a chip in the salsa and ate it with enthusiasm. "This is one of my go-to late-night-snack recipes."

"Nice," Luke said, grabbing a handful of chips and putting them on his plate.

"Don't fill up on these, though. Got enchiladas coming."

"*Very* nice. Thanks. It was real nice of you to cook for me."

"My pleasure," I said, putting the emphasis on the last word. The effect was not lost on Luke. He smiled.

"I love Mexican food. My buddy at work, Manny? He's Mexican, and his mom makes this Mexican bread pudding that is out of this world. It's got, like, pineapple and raisins and walnuts in it. Plus, you know, a ton of butter and sugar in it."

"That does sound good," I said, dipping another chip in the salsa. "I think I've seen him at work. Him and that other really tall guy."

"The black guy," Luke said.

"Yeah. Him. He's not bad-looking."

"Whaddya trying to say there, gal?" Luke asked.

"That I think your tall friend is hot," I said bluntly, not backing down.

"Oh," he said glumly. Luke balled up his fists and put them on his cheeks, his elbows resting on the table. He looked like a little kid throwing a tantrum.

I burst out laughing.

"You're much hotter, Luke."

"Okay!" he said cheerfully, dropping the act and stealing another chip. I laughed again. I adored his sense of humor.

I brought over two plates of steaming-hot—both in temperature and spice—enchiladas. Luke leaned over his plate, taking a deep breath.

"Heavenly," he said.

"Taste it first before you say that."

"Happily." Luke grabbed a fork. I watched with great anticipation as he took his first bite. His reaction did not disappoint. He closed his eyes and let out a deep, satisfied groan, not unlike the sound he'd made Friday night while having an orgasm. "Again, I say, *heavenly.* This is delicious, Elyse. You're one damn fine cook."

"Thanks," I said.

"Manny's mom makes enchiladas, too, but I gotta say yours put hers to shame."

"Wow. Thanks. So, are you close with the guys at work? Like, are you friends with them outside of work?"

"Yeah, I am."

"Manny, and what's the others guy's name? Or should I call him Hot Tall Guy?"

"No, you should *not*. And how dare you objectify him in that manner," Luke said firmly. "He has a *name*."

"Which is ..."

"Roger," Luke said brightly, making me laugh again. It was quite entertaining to see how quickly he could jump in and out of characters. His students must adore him.

"Yeah, Manny and Roger are good guys. They love to bust my balls for being a theater performer, though. Insist on calling me Twinkletoes, even though I'm really not that much of dancer."

"That doesn't sound very nice."

"Ah, you know how guys are. It's their way of showing they care. They're just messin' with me. They come to all my shows, though."

"Really? That's cool."

"Yep. They don't even heckle me during the show. They save all their comments for after."

I laughed. "Oh, I'm sure they do."

Luke had already polished off his enchilada and was back on the tortilla chips.

"I like a man with a good appetite."

"I feel the same way about women. I mean, I understand you all want to try to keep your girlish figures, but there's something super sexy about a woman who's not afraid to throw back a few beers and eat more than salad."

"Work Week Elyse eats salad. Weekend Elyse cuts loose."

"Ooh, I do like that Weekend Elyse. But let's talk about Work Elyse. What is she working on right now for Wicket Pro?"

It made me happy that Luke asked about my work. Most people outside the business thought what I did for a living was boring, but he seemed genuinely interested.

"I'm working on a proposal for a clothing retailer in Finland."

"That sounds pretty cool."

"Yeah, it would be a big deal if I managed to snag this company as a client. Finland is one of the countries we haven't made much headway with yet, and the company I'm courting there is huge. Only one of us from my department will get to go to Finland to give the presentation, and I really, really want to go."

"That would be quite an adventure to go to Finland," Luke said, munching on a chip. "You like to travel?"

"I do. What about you?"

"I like it. I don't get to do it much, though. My day job certainly doesn't call for work travel, and my dream job is to perform right here in New York."

I nodded, impressed as always by the passion in Luke's voice when he talked about performing.

"What's this proposal all about?"

"It's our company's hyperconvergence technology. It combines software engineering and networking. The bottom line is it maximizes efficiency, data storage, and stuff like that."

"Cool. I understood most of those words," Luke said with a grin.

I smiled back. "The three of us in our department are each putting together our own proposals for the Presko Group—that's the retailer in Finland—and whoever has the best presentation gets to travel to Finland to present it."

"So, who decides who wins?"

"My boss, Owen Bialystock."

"He's the one who's leaving. And his job is the promotion you really want, right?"

"Yes," I said softly. It was such a simple thing, but it meant a lot to me that he remembered. It meant he was listening to me.

"Do you like giving presentations like the one you're working on? Isn't that kind of scary, getting up in front of important people like that?"

"Oh, I love it," I said, feeling a flutter of excitement in my stomach just thinking about it. "I find it exhilarating. I get excited about new technology, and I think it's fun to talk about. I really believe in what my company does, and I'm genuinely excited about the product we're selling."

"The hyperconvergence thing?" Luke asked.

"Yes. That. I think it's great. Wicket Smart Hyperconvergence Technology is what it's called, though I tried like hell to talk them out of going with that ridiculous name for it."

"What's wrong with the name?"

"It's Wicket Smaht," I said in my best Boston accent.

Luke cackled. "Oh, I see your point."

"At least in Finland they won't be familiar with a local accent like that."

"True," Luke said, his eyes sparkling with amusement. "Well, I think you're wicked smart, Elyse Pippin, and that is sexy as hell."

"Thanks."

"I mean it. Hearing you say all them fancy technology book-learnin' terms turns me on."

"Really," I said seductively.

"Oh yeah."

"Our hyperconverged infrastructure is available in hybrid or all-flash systems, and can scale virtual desktop resources, will reduce provisioning time, and can rapidly deploy VMWare view."

Luke fanned himself with a napkin. "That sure gets my hard drive going."

I laughed heartily. "Yeah, well, I get just as hot for you when you're performing."

"Really?" Luke asked so earnestly, it melted my heart.

"Yes. Really. You're always attractive Luke, but you never look hotter than when you're singing."

Luke raised an eyebrow, then sang the first few lines of "The Song That Goes Like This" from *Spamalot*. I laughed softly. It was kind of a parody of love songs, and Luke sounded great.

I got up from my chair and held out my hand to him. "I cannot resist you when you sing, Luke Rannells."

"Hmmm, good to know," he said as he accepted my hand and stood.

Luke dipped his head and kissed me. Good God, was he a terrific kisser. I put my arms around his shoulders, reveling in how big he was. Big and tall and strong.

"God, I want you," Luke said in a deep, sensual voice that reduced my legs to jelly.

"I want you too," I breathed between passionate kisses.

Luke untucked my blouse from my jeans and slid his hand over my breasts. He pressed his erection against me and I moaned out loud. I was about to say we needed to move this party to the bedroom *now*, but it seemed Luke had other ideas.

He gently but firmly pushed me down on the kitchen floor. He slipped his hand under my head to protect it from the hard ceramic floor. Luke gazed into my eyes questioningly, as if making sure I was okay with this. I glanced over at the huge windows. They only had side curtains, for decoration mostly, and there was no way to close them.

My breath caught in my throat. The thought of openly having sex on the kitchen floor in plain view was impossibly exciting. I started unbuttoning Luke's shirt, and a slow, sexy grin spread across his face. He climbed off me, but only so he could get his jeans off faster. Luke was naked before I knew it, and the sight of him in all his rock-hard glory made me gasp.

"You're *gorgeous.*"

"And you," Luke said, pressing his lips against mine, "are the most beautiful and exciting woman I've ever known."

He pulled off my blouse and unhooked my bra in record time. My jeans and panties were also history in no time flat. I lay naked on the floor, hardly feeling the coldness of the tiles. My body was overheated with desire.

Luke's brown eyes flashed with raw passion. He grabbed ahold of my left leg and spread me wide open, just as he had done the last time. I *loved* it.

I gasped again. He looked down between my legs and then back up at my face. It was excruciating, yet thrilling, to have to wait for him.

"So beautiful," he said, admiring the view.

He lowered himself, pressing his hard cock against my opening, rubbing the outside, making me crazy.

"Luke," I pleaded.

He grinned, loving that he was making me insane with desire. Finally, he rammed himself into me. I closed my eyes and cried out, the intensity of my pleasure magnified by his teasing. Luke was one hell of a lover.

It was dangerous and exciting, having sex on the floor in broad daylight, in front of the windows. Being flat on my back allowed Luke to penetrate me much deeper than in bed. It was so good, all I could do was cry out his name in ecstasy.

"Luke ... Luke ... Oh God ..."

I was close to coming already but I didn't want this incredible experience to end yet.

"On your back, Luke," I panted. "I want you on your back."

"Anything you say, baby," Luke said in a husky voice. He gripped me tight and rolled over onto his back, still managing to stay inside me.

I took a moment to catch my breath and force myself back from the brink of orgasm. Luke smiled up at me from the floor.

"So beautiful," he said again.

As I looked down at him, I felt the same powerful connection I had the first time we had sex. It was like we belonged together, fit together like perfect pieces of a puzzle. I loved that we could have wild, frenzied sex but still take a moment to simply adore one another in the middle of it.

I leaned back, putting my hands behind his knees, and began to ride him. We both moaned with the pleasurable friction of my motions. I could feel his eyes on me, watching me as I raised and lowered myself on him.

"Elyse," he moaned, and the tingling vibrations of bliss between my legs magnified at the sound of his voice. I rode him faster, both of us needing release.

"Not yet," Luke croaked. Then, in a louder and more commanding voice, "I want you on your knees."

"Yes," I said, though I had been so close to orgasm that it was painful to stop. I climbed off him and got on my hands and knees on the floor. In no time, Luke was behind me and then inside me.

I cried out again at the sweet invasion of his cock.

Three positions. I can't remember the last time I was in three different sexual positions during one encounter.

My heart pounded with adrenaline, and I was still very aware of the windows. I wondered if anyone was watching. The thought was so exciting, it pushed me closer to the edge.

"Luke, Luke ..." I cried as he pounded me harder and

harder. He kept at it long enough to make me almost come, then he pulled out.

"Luke!" I screamed in frustration.

"I'm sorry," he said, panting. "I want to see you. I need to see you. Turn over."

I lay back down on the floor as quickly as possible, and then flung my legs wide open. "Please, Luke. *Please.*"

His expression of total adoration made this last bit of waiting worth it. And then I understood why he had stopped. He wanted to look into my eyes as we finished. It was so lovely and sweet and perfect.

Luke straddled me and plunged inside, pounding me hard immediately.

"Luke, Luke, Luke …"

I had a sudden mental flash of Luke dressed as emo rock Andrew Jackson, with wild hair and black eyeliner. The mere thought was enough to push me over the edge.

"*Luke!*" I screamed as a powerful orgasm slammed into me and rocked me to the core. My whole body convulsed with sheer bliss, and I dug my nails into his back as I rode wave after wave of pleasure.

I opened my eyes to find Luke mid-orgasm. His eyes were squeezed shut and he let out the familiar sexy groan that was fast becoming my favorite sound ever.

We gazed into each other's eyes for a moment, panting and catching our breath.

"Luke," I said softly. His name was all I needed to express how I felt, because I knew he was feeling the same way. Satisfied. Happy. Connected.

"Elyse," Luke said. It was the perfect response.

Luke kissed me tenderly before lying down beside me. He slipped his arm under my neck to protect me from the floor.

"That can't be comfortable," he said.

"But it is. I'm very comfortable."

He smiled and pulled me closer. We lay there for a few moments.

"That was fucking incredible," Luke said.

I let out a deep, satisfied sigh. "Yes, it sure was."

"I don't ever want to get up," Luke said. "I'm full of delicious food, completely sexually satisfied, and holding onto you. It doesn't get any better than this."

I snuggled up closer to him, feeling as comfortable with him on the floor as I would be in my own bed.

"Can't believe we did it in front of the window," he said.

I laughed. "I know, right? Now every time I cook in here, I'll think of you."

"Cool," he said. He sounded a little down.

"You okay?"

"Yeah. It's just tomorrow's Monday. You know how it is. Back to the grind."

"I really don't mind going to work."

"Nerrrrrd."

I laughed, and he chuckled along with me.

"I really am a nerd. I'm grateful, though, that I have a job I love. It's exciting and challenging and fun. By the end of the week, I'm ready for a break, but by Monday I'm usually more than ready to get back to it."

"That's good," he said, still sounding bummed out.

"I guess you're not thrilled with your job, huh?"

"It's not a *bad* job. Keeps me busy and on my toes all day. It can be challenging, believe it or not. Pays well enough, and I like the people I work with. I can't complain, I guess. But it always feels like I'm killing time to be done with work so I can go do what I really love."

"Theater."

"Yes."

"Geeeeeek."

We laughed together. I shivered a bit from the cold.

"We gotta get you dressed," Luke said. He gingerly slid his arm out from under me, and then held out his hand to help me up. He pulled me in for a wonderfully warm naked embrace before letting me get dressed.

Luke put his jeans and shirt back on, then got to work clearing the table.

"You can just leave the dishes. I'll get to them later."

"You sure? Don't wanna leave you with a mess."

"No problem. Thanks, though. Come sit with me." I headed toward my living room and he followed. I sat down on one of the couches, and he sat next to me. I hadn't bothered to put my shoes back on, so I draped my legs over Luke. He started rubbing my feet.

"Mmmm, that feels good," I said, feeling totally relaxed. I felt so at ease with Luke. It was funny the way we'd fallen into a smooth rhythm already, as if we'd been dating for months.

"Do you have a busy day tomorrow?" he asked as he massaged my feet.

"Kinda. Got an 11 o'clock meeting. We're working together to develop a sales presentation for a new network security technology we're rolling out."

"And who's we?"

"Me and those other two guys I work with. Hunter Higgins and Keith Foster. The three of us work together on lots of projects."

Luke arched an eyebrow. "I've seen them two around you. Pretty good-lookin' fellas, eh?"

"Yes, they are," I said with a smile. "And we work long hours together. I get the feeling Keith has a thing for me, too."

"Really?"

"Yeah. I mean, I don't really know. It's just a vibe I get from him lately."

75

"Why, I oughtta ..." Luke mock-threatened, letting go of my foot long enough to make a fist. "That guy's cruisin' for bruisin', I tells ya."

I laughed. "You have nothing to worry about. He's a good guy and nice to look at, but I'm not interested in him. Besides, I'll bet you work with a lot of gorgeous actresses."

"I suurrrre do. Ones like Johnny Creel's girl. Talk about cruisin' for a bruisin'. He's got the dough to have me sleepin' with the fishes with one phone call if I so's much as look at his gal."

"You're such a goofball," I told him. I thought for a moment. "Can I ask you something? Promise you won't think I'm needy and pathetic?"

"I promise," he said, looking up at me with his sweet brown eyes.

"I know it's really soon, probably too soon, but ..."

"Of course I'll marry you, Elyse."

We shared a laugh together, which eased the knot of anxiety in my stomach and made it easier to say what was on my mind.

"Well, I'm not ready to take that step quite yet. But what do you think about you and me being ... exclusive?"

Luke's eyes opened wide. "You mean ... *go steady?*"

"Yes," I said with a smile.

Luke's expression softened, and he dropped the silly act for a moment. "I would love that. The idea of you being with somebody else already makes me crazy."

He leaned over and kissed me. I felt the same way about him. There would be no more friend-with-benefits visits from Brad while I was with Luke, and I wouldn't have to worry about him seeing other women.

I lay back on the couch and looked over at him, knowing the hard part wasn't entirely over with yet.

"There's one other thing," I began cautiously.

"You want to see other *women?*"

I smiled. "No. That's not it."

Luke looked at me expectantly, and I saw a hint of worry in his eyes.

"It's nothing bad, really."

"That's what people say just before they say something bad."

"Look, *please* don't take this the wrong way. And it's *nothing* personal, but at work, you know ..."

"You don't want people to know you're dating the janitor."

"*Luke.* That's *not* what I'm saying. I don't want people knowing I'm dating anyone. I keep my work life and private life completely separate. In the corporate world, people want to believe you're totally focused on the job without any outside distractions."

"Got it. Work Elyse doesn't have a personal life."

"Right," I said, putting my arms around him. "But Home Elyse has a new boyfriend who she's totally crazy about."

"Okay," Luke said, kissing me. "I'll take what I can get."

He seemed disappointed, which broke my heart. I felt horribly guilty. It pained me to have Luke think for one second that I was ashamed to be with him. On the contrary, I was proud to be his girlfriend.

"I'm sorry, Luke. But especially now, with this promotion on the line ..."

"Hey, it's not like I want anybody knowing I'm dating one of the hoity-toity business types, either," Luke said, pushing his nose up with his finger, indicating I was a snob.

"Fair enough."

"Seriously, Elyse. I understand. I know how much you want this promotion, and I'm happy to do whatever I can to help."

"Thanks."

Luke sighed heavily. "Well, I guess I better go home and rest up for tomorrow."

I got up from the couch and Luke stood with me. I put my arm around his waist as we walked to the front door together.

"I hope your Monday goes by fast. Have fun at the foundation tomorrow night."

Luke smiled and ran his fingers through my hair. "Thanks. I will. I always do."

He kissed me once more before heading out the door.

CHAPTER 7

I timed my visit to the tenth floor to catch Elyse
headed to her 11am meeting, and just seeing her
lifted my spirits. Four of my guys had called out today, and
I'd been dealing with problems left and right. A particularly
bitchy Very Important Person locked herself out of her
office, one of the elevators got stuck, and it seemed like half
the sinks in the building had sprung simultaneous leaks.
None of that mattered anymore the moment I laid eyes on
Elyse.

She was in the hallway, outside her office, talking animatedly with her co-workers. Elyse didn't smile, but I could see
the enthusiasm in her eyes as she spoke. It was funny how I'd
always thought she probably hated her job, but now I could
see how excited she was by it.

All the warm feelings I'd experienced over the weekend
with her suddenly washed over me again. I recalled her soft
skin, her gentle touch, and the way she took such an interest
in my performing. Asking me questions, hearing me sing,
and simply understanding that my work at the foundation in
the evening meant more to me than anything I did in my day

job. And she laughed so easily when I was being goofy, instead of rolling her eyes at me. That was no small thing. I was a performer, so I tended to be "on" most of the time. Elyse seemed amused and entertained by me, which made me feel good all over. Not only was she officially my significant other, she was also my biggest fan. And I was hers.

I watched proudly as she talked with Keith and Hunter about the new tech presentation they were working on. The Hunter guy was okay-looking. Brown hair and brown eyes like me, but shorter and scrawnier. That Keith guy, though. He was a looker. Keith reminded me of Superman—dark hair, bright blue eyes, and muscular. But he wore a boring business suit, so in that sense, he looked more like Clark Kent.

Elyse rattled off a bunch of technology words I could hardly follow, which really turned me on.

"Whew, is it getting hot in here?" I said loudly, fanning my face.

Elyse looked up, noticing my presence for the first time. A thrill of pure delight rippled through me when I saw her eyes light up. Cue the warm feelings again. She visibly had the same reaction to seeing me as I did when I caught sight of her.

"Whew!" I said again, fanning myself harder.

She turned away, and I found it amusing to watch her try not to laugh. It was going to be tough for her to act like Work Elyse with me around.

Average Guy, Superman, and Elyse started walking down the hall toward their meeting. Elyse glanced up at me and flashed me a brief yet beautiful smile. We were both enjoying our secret relationship at work. Though I wasn't crazy about keeping my gorgeous girlfriend a secret, it was rather exciting.

Besides, there was no way in hell I was going to tell Roger

and Manny about me and Elyse. As it turned out, I'd bagged Elyse in less than two weeks: half the time I thought it would take, but none of that mattered now. Let them think I'd lost the bet. Let those guys have their money and their fun and tease me mercilessly. I'd gotten something far better out of the deal.

I'd met the woman of my dreams.

I texted her later in the day.

Hey, Nerd.

Hey, Geek, she responded a short while later.

How'd the meeting go?

Great. We're making good progress on the tech proposal.

Cool. That Hunter guy seems nice. I hate Keith, though.

Why??

He's hot. He looks like Superman, so I don't like him.

Lol. Damn, he DOES look like Superman!

If he even looks at you funny, Ima give him a knuckle sandwich.

Haha. You have nothing to worry about, Geek. I only go for goofy, sexy theater types. Speaking of which, I really wanna come hear you sing again.

I grinned at my phone like an idiot. I still couldn't get over how supportive she was of my theater dreams. The actresses I'd dated weren't impressed, because they did the same thing. My non-actress exes tolerated my performances but didn't seem thrilled with them.

Soon. I promise.

Cool. Gotta get back to work. Later, Geek.

I grinned again. I put my phone away and starting humming to myself as I headed toward the elevators.

"Hey, Nightingale!" Roger called as he jogged down the hallway toward me. He smiled.

"What?" I knew a smile meant he had something unpleasant to say.

81

"Somebody stuffed some of them feminine hygiene things in the toilet in the ladies on six. Good luck with that!" He punched me on the shoulder.

"No problem. I'm on it." I sailed past him, singing "Green Finch and Linnet Bird" from *Sweeney Todd*. It was the only song that came to mind with the word "nightingale" in it. I heard Roger chuckle behind me. Seeing Elyse had put me in such a good mood, I didn't even mind dealing with an unholy mess in the bathroom. It was still turning out to be a shit day when it came to work stuff, but I'd get to teach my kids tonight, and I had an amazing, if secret, girlfriend.

It didn't get much better than this.

CHAPTER 8

*W*alking to my 11am meeting, I was a little disappointed that Luke didn't put in an appearance, like he had done several times this week. He was probably having a busy morning, and I couldn't very well expect him to make it to the tenth floor at the same time every day. Luke's job seemed to keep him running in all directions, all day long.

Keith looked up at me and smiled when I entered the conference room. His whole demeanor toward me seemed to have shifted. We'd worked together for more than a year, but about a month ago he mentioned something in passing about having broken up with the girlfriend he'd had for most of that time. I genuinely liked Keith, but only as a co-worker, albeit a gorgeous one. If he was starting to think of me as something more, I sincerely hoped he wouldn't act on his feelings. It would be incredibly awkward, having to shoot him down and then have to work with him every day. I wouldn't have been interested in him anyway, but now I had Luke in my life, there was no way I'd go out with Keith.

Luke.

Just thinking about him made me happy. If I allowed myself to smile at work, I would, every time I thought of him. He was everything I never knew I wanted in a man.

"Okay, I think we're making some great headway on the network security sales presentation," I said. I always tried to speak first when in a meeting, especially since I was the only woman. Fortunately, Keith and Hunter were good colleagues. I had worked with more than my share of misogynistic men who resented the presence of a woman in the boardroom. Old habits died hard, and I was always careful to stay on my toes. I didn't get where I was today by letting my guard down.

"Yeah, I think so, too. I think Wicket SecurePro is gonna be a good seller for us," Keith said, making eye contact with me.

"With all the hacker stuff in the news these days, we couldn't be rolling this out at a better time," I said. "The trick is to use those security threats as a sales tactic, but not as a scare tactic, if you know what I mean. It's a tricky line to cross."

"I dunno," Hunter said. "Scare tactics tend to be successful. Once you make a company aware of what they stand to lose if their systems get compromised, it's easy to reel them in."

"True. And for sure, we need to play up all the security threats hitting companies these days. My point is, you can do that without a hard sell," I said.

"I'm not so sure that's a good idea," Hunter argued. "I like the hard sell tactic."

"But then you run the risk of coming across as a snake oil salesman," I countered. "Trust me. You can do a softer sell while still discussing the security threats. Make it convincing by showing them you're on their side, and you can do it in a positive light."

"I get what you're saying, Elyse," Keith said. "Make it more casual and friendly. As in 'Hey, if this happens to your systems, this is what Wicket SecurePro has to counter it.'"

"Yes, exactly! And we really do have everything these companies need to ward off most threats," I said excitedly. It certainly helped that I believed in our company's products. They worked well and provided strong security that could save companies months of heartache, and even from going under.

"I think we can easily make our case by simply discussing the threats, showing clients that we are fully aware of the serious security issues out there, and that we have the solutions," Keith said. "Make them feel they can't live without our services by showing them we have what they need, without making all-out dire threats about what will happen without Wicket SecurePro. The whole 'you really need this technology, even if you don't get it from us' routine."

"Yes," I said simply. Keith smiled at me again, gazing at me longer than was appropriate.

Oh Lord.

I wasn't sure why I hadn't been interested in Keith even before I met Luke. He had incredible blue eyes and he was smart as well as a nice person. He was a great catch, just not for me.

Hunter was still hemming and hawing over the hard sell tactic.

"Look, why don't we try out the softer approach on a few smaller clients. Feel it out, see how it goes. Then we can tweak the presentation accordingly, or even do a total overhaul and go the scare-the-hell-out-of-them route if the first way isn't working," I suggested. "Deal?"

"Two against one," Keith reminded him.

"Fine," Hunter said. Then muttered, "I wanted to scare people. Tell you what. You guys work on the proposal the way you want to, and then I'll come up with my own and present it to Mr. Bialystock."

"Okay by me," I said, and Keith nodded. Though I truly felt my way was better, I was a little nervous about Hunter trying a difference tactic. Hunter was super competitive and wanted the Senior VP job as badly as I did. If the boss preferred his presentation to mine, it could be trouble for me.

The rest of the meeting flew by. Luke wasn't kidding when he said I was a nerd. I lived for this technology stuff, and I had a blast talking about it, writing about it, and preparing to speak about it. As always, we didn't get as much done on the project as I'd hoped. We still had other clients and projects to work on.

"Ugh, all right. I guess we gotta stop for now," I said, glancing up at the clock. I still had tons more work to do, and I was determined to leave the office on time for once. Luke and I had plans to go out, and I couldn't wait to see him.

Hunter rushed off to his office, and I lagged behind to pack up all my stuff.

Big mistake.

Keith lingered behind, too.

"Sooo, umm, Elyse," Keith said nervously, running his fingers through his jet-black hair.

Please don't do it. Please don't ask me out.

"I was wondering, did you maybe wanna stay late tonight to work some more on this security presentation? We could order pizza, or Chinese, or something. I think you and I work really well together. As a team, and well, maybe more."

"Well," I began, busily packing my work bag with the presentation materials. Keith's suggestion would be a dream come true for most women. Working late, alone with an incredibly sexy guy; who knew what could happen? But I already had one dreamy man in my life. The only one I could even think about.

I struggled with what to say as the silence grew awkward. As always, I despised talking about anything personal at the office. I wanted Keith, Hunter—and more importantly, my boss—to think all I ever did was work. They were not to know I had any kind of life whatsoever outside of Wicket Pro. I couldn't tell Keith I had personal plans, but I sure as hell wasn't going to blow off Luke to hang out with another man.

"Umm, I can't tonight, actually." I hoped my obvious hesitation to answer, combined with my gentle brushoff, would be enough to deter him.

"Oh, okay. I get it."

Keith looked dejected, and empathy stabbed at my heart. I was no good at delivering bad news, and I had a horrible time saying no. I knew I needed to stand my ground and get through the next uncomfortable few seconds it would take for me to gather my things and escape the conference room.

I glanced up to see Keith actually *blushing*. He couldn't meet my eyes; he looked so embarrassed, I could hardly bear it. How was he ever going to look me in the eye again? It was now painfully obvious that he had feelings for me. As far as he knew, I was single but simply wasn't into him. All I had to do was say that I was involved with someone, and this would all go away.

I was way too scared to do that.

I'd seen what happens to a woman in the workplace when people thought she was distracted by her home life. At least I didn't have kids. The corporate world despised working mothers. With this promotion on the line, I couldn't cop to having a personal life. But I also couldn't bear Keith's humiliation a second longer.

"I can't tonight, but maybe I can come in a little early on

Monday morning to work on it," I blurted out before I could stop myself.

"Okay," Keith said, literally breathing a sigh of relief. "That sounds great. I'll see you then. If not before."

Keith gazed into my eyes and smiled at me before turning to leave.

Fabulous.

We would meet on Monday morning and not Friday night, but I still had clearly given Keith the wrong idea about us.

CHAPTER 9

$\mathscr{I}$ was practically giddy as I drove over to The Creel Foundation on Friday night. Luke had told me he'd prepared a special song for me, and I could hardly wait to hear him sing again. I hadn't seen him much during the week at the office, but we'd texted a lot and talked on the phone every night. He asked about everything I was working on, patiently listening to me ramble on about all my projects.

In the same way, I inquired briefly about his workday, but then mostly asked about his stage projects. It made me smile to hear him get excited as he told me what he was up to. He was currently hard at work on an audition for an off-Broadway show about pirates. It was a musical comedy thing —his favorite. He wanted the part badly. I hoped with all my heart he would get it.

Miraculously, I found a parking spot on the street. The receptionist was opening the door to leave for the weekend when I came walking up.

"Hi, I'm here to see Luke Rannells?"

"Yes, you must be Elyse! Oh my gosh, I nearly forgot you were coming. I almost locked you out. He's still onstage rehearsing. I can take you down to the auditorium," the young girl offered, starting to head back inside.

"Oh, that's okay. I've been here once before. I know my way."

"Terrific! Nice to have met you. Have a good weekend."

"You too," I said with a smile.

My smile broadened as I walked down the hallway. I could hear Luke singing, and he sounded wonderful. I opened the door to the auditorium and slipped inside quietly. Luke was onstage, rehearsing with a brunette. I figured she must be Susie Peters, the teaching and rehearsal partner he'd told me about.

There was a man sitting in the auditorium; he turned around when he heard the door open. The guy didn't smile, but he offered a quick wave. He wore an expensive suit and looked very important. It wasn't Johnny Creel, though. Johnny was in the news all the time, so I knew what he looked like. Maybe this man was some kind of investor in the place or something.

I took a seat next to him. He still didn't smile, which was a little weird. I hoped I hadn't annoyed him by sitting right next to him. Oh well. Too late to move now. I settled back in my seat to watch Luke rehearse.

My face fell when I looked up at the stage, and a sharp stab of pain pierced me right in the heart.

Luke was passionately kissing the woman onstage.

I knew they were acting and it was just part of the scene, but it was so unexpected—jarring, to see the man I adored making out with somebody else.

The man in the suit leaned over and asked quietly, "See that absolutely gorgeous woman your boyfriend is currently kissing?"

I blinked, shocked by his words. "Yes?"

The guy's face broke into a soft kind of half-smile, and

there was gentle sympathy in his dark brown eyes. "That's my girlfriend."

"Oh," I said, laughing quietly. We looked into each other's eyes briefly, sharing a moment of mutual understanding at how difficult this was for us to watch.

"I know they look pretty hot together up there onstage but trust me. They act like brother and sister when they're not performing."

"That's good to know."

"David Groff," the man said, offering his hand.

I gratefully shook his hand. "Elyse Pippin. Nice to meet you."

"Likewise."

It was funny how David didn't smile, but I found I liked him anyway. It was kind of him to put my mind at ease. Luke and Susie finished up their scene, then they came down to join us.

Susie walked up to me, eyes wide. "Hi," she said, with an exaggerated guilty look, obviously acknowledging the awkward situation we were in. "Sorry you had to meet me for the first time, um, like *this*." She glanced up at the stage where she had gotten hot and heavy with my boyfriend.

I laughed, and said, "Not at all. You must be Susie. I'm very glad to meet you. *Really,*" I insisted with a smile.

Susie shook my hand, her eyes shining with relief. I appreciated her concern for my comfort, and found I liked her already as well.

"I'm glad to meet you too, Elyse. Luke talks about you *all* the time. I mean, like nonstop."

"That's nice," I said, glancing over at Luke.

He walked over to me and ran his fingers through my hair. "Sorry about the timing there. I really thought we'd be done rehearsing by the time you got here. I promise, that is not what I brought you here to see."

He kissed me for emphasis, as if to reassure me there was nothing between him and Susie.

"I understand, Luke. Really. I kiss my co-workers all the time!" It was a joke of course, but I felt a pang of guilt when I remembered how I'd promised to meet with Keith on Monday morning.

Susie laughed and even David chuckled. Luke punched his fist in his palm.

"Why those bird dogs. They better cool their heels. I called dibs on you, see?"

Could he be any more adorable? I laughed and stroked his chin fondly. "Yes, you sure did."

Susie laughed, too, then slipped her arm around David's waist. David seemed a bit high-strung, but I saw him visibly relax when she touched him. They gazed into each other's eyes for a moment, and it was clear that they were very much in love. I trusted Luke of course, but it made me feel better to see that Susie's heart belonged to someone else.

We all looked up as the door to the auditorium opened. A woman with beautiful long red hair cascading down her shoulders entered and walked toward us. I recognized her immediately from the infamous Johnny Creel Apology Video.

Rosemary Sutton.

She smiled at all of us, then she turned to me—the only person in the room she didn't know. I offered my hand.

"Hi, I'm Elyse."

Rosemary met my gaze, and I admired her stunning green eyes. She smiled warmly and shook my hand.

"You must be Rosemary Sutton. Your fame precedes you."

She maintained her smile, but I could see the weariness in her eyes. Luke was right: she was tired of hearing about the video, but that was okay. I wasn't about to bring it up, anyway.

"I hear you've been on *Broadway*!" I exclaimed.

The weary look vanished, and Rosemary's eyes sparkled with the same look of dreamy excitement Luke wore when talking about his theater work.

"Yes, I have," Rosemary said, laughing modestly.

"I saw the *Hairspray* revival twice while it was running. I *loved* it. I must have seen you in the ensemble. Oh, it was a terrific show."

"Thank you so much. I'm glad you enjoyed it. I had such a blast doing that show. It's an experience I'll never forget, that's for sure."

We chatted for a few moments about how exciting it was for her to be on Broadway, and I gushed about how much I loved musical theater. Luke's friends had made me feel welcome already, and I was enjoying meeting the people who were most important to him.

The door swung open once more, and I audibly gasped. Luke, Rosemary, Susie, and David all looked at me questioningly

"Sorry," I said, giggling. "I know it's dumb, but I've never met a celebrity before."

It was *The Johnny Creel*, as he was known in all the gossip rags. He'd been famous long before he met Rosemary, known for his lavish playboy lifestyle. He'd changed his partying, womanizing ways when he fell in love with Rosemary.

Rosemary snorted. "Celebrity. He's just goofy Johnny to us." Her expression softened as she watched Johnny approach us. I could see the love in her eyes.

"Now his fame *really* precedes him," I muttered.

"Everything you read about him is true," Susie announced loudly, making Rosemary giggle.

I stared at Johnny. I couldn't help it. It was bizarre to see him in person.

"I think my girlfriend's a little starstruck over you," Luke observed.

Johnny's eyes opened wide as he turned to me. "Starstruck by li'l ol' *me?*" He placed a hand dramatically over his heart. "I am just a man. A wealthy man. A famous, wealthy man, who's brought joy to the hearts of children and adults alike."

"And a modest man," Rosemary said dryly. "Don't forget modest."

Johnny grinned at Rosemary, then pulled her in for a kiss. He turned back to me, offering his hand. I shook it, still feeling a bit dazed at meeting *The Johnny Creel* in person.

"And you must be the famous Elyse," Johnny Creel said, shaking my hand with enthusiasm. "Luke never shuts up about you. And I mean *ever.*"

"Guilty!" Luke said. "Did I mention she's, like, the smartest woman on the planet?"

"Yes," answered everyone else present, and we all shared a laugh. I felt good all over knowing Luke had talked about me to his closest friends. Then a fresh wave of guilt washed over me. Nobody in my personal or professional circle knew about my relationship with him. I wished I could express to Luke how much I hated hiding him.

Somebody's phone buzzed loudly. Johnny reached into his back pocket and pulled out his cell phone to read a text.

"Shit," he said, then looked over at Luke. "Anthony's mom forgot to pick him up again."

Luke sighed wearily. "Can't say I'm surprised."

"Kristen said he's pretty upset. She got done teaching his class an hour ago. She's got him up front in the reception area."

"Tell her to send him down here. I'll take care of him," Luke said. Johnny nodded and began texting.

"Anthony's my favorite little man," Luke explained to me. "His mom's a drug addict, so he's got it rough."

"Poor guy," I said. My heart ached for the little boy, and for Luke, who looked so sad.

A few moments later, an African-American boy of about ten years old walked in. He looked like he had been crying. I swallowed a lump in my throat and fought my own tears. I felt like rushing over and throwing my arms around him.

Luke did rush over to the kid.

"Hey, dude! Man, I'm so glad you're still here!"

The boy looked up at Luke in surprise.

"You see that pretty blonde girl over there?" Luke asked in a quiet voice but still loud enough for us all to hear. "I really like her. I want to impress her, and I need your help. Can you go up there and sing with me?"

Luke's eyes looked so earnest, playing the part of a lovesick guy trying to win a girl over. He'd already won me over, but Anthony didn't know that.

"I got your back, man," Anthony said firmly. "Let's do this."

Luke nodded. "Hey, guys? We want to sing something for you all if that's okay."

"Of course. I would love to hear you sing," I said, playing along but also meaning every word. Anthony and Luke exchanged conspiratorial looks as if to say "So far, so good."

The two made their way to the stage. Luke found the song that he needed on the sound system, then walked toward Anthony. We all quickly settled into our seats. Susie and David sat to my left, and Rosemary and Johnny sat on my right, giving me the best seat in the middle.

I recognized the song as soon as the music started. It was "When Your Feet Don't Touch the Ground" from the musical *Finding Neverland*. In the show, it was a duet sung by the author, J.M. Barrie, and a young child named Peter. Peter had already lost his father and was faced with having a terminally ill mother.

Anthony sang exquisitely with Luke. The song was lovely and sad and hopeful all at once, and the two voices blended together beautifully.

They finished their song, and all five of us in the audience stood up and applauded wildly. Johnny whistled his approval, and we all walked over to the stage.

I looked up at Luke on the stage and said dreamily, "That was wonderful, Luke. You both sounded so beautiful."

"Thanks," Luke said, meeting my gaze shyly. It was so sweet the way he'd made Anthony feel needed and had given him the opportunity to shine. Like Luke, Anthony came alive onstage. His tears had vanished, and I hoped performing had taken his mind off his troubles for a while.

"You sounded terrific, Anthony! Thank you so much for singing for me."

"You're welcome," he said with a smile.

"Hey li'l man," Johnny said. "Your dad's here to pick you up."

"I'll walk him out," Luke volunteered, and Johnny nodded.

I watched the two of them together. Anthony had been so much happier once Luke took over the situation. He was great with kids. Luke was a wonderful teacher, and I couldn't help thinking he would be a wonderful father.

What if Luke wants kids of his own? Would it be a deal breaker for us?

I was sure I never wanted to have children. It was a decision I'd made long ago. I loved my life the way it was, and I loved my career. This wouldn't be the first time I had faced this problem. My college boyfriend and I had been madly in love, but he wanted a family and I didn't. We parted ways over it, and I didn't ever want to go through that pain again.

It was a worry for another day. Luke and I had just

started dating, and we hardly needed to figure out our future yet. I tried to put the child issue out of my head, but it was hard not to worry about it.

Rosemary, Johnny, Susie, and David were talking and laughing together, clearly in no hurry to leave. My guess was they didn't have specific plans for this Friday night. Neither did Luke and I. We had planned to meet at The Creel Foundation and wing it from there.

Luke came back into the auditorium.

"Okay! I promised Elyse I would sing a song just for her. You guys are welcome to stay if you want. If that's okay with you?" Luke asked, looking at me.

"Of course," I said. I was having fun being with his friends and certainly didn't mind if they hung around for a while.

The five of us settled back into the same seats we had taken earlier, with me getting front and center. A flutter of excitement rippled through me. I couldn't wait to hear Luke sing a song just for me. I hoped it would be something terribly romantic. Though, knowing him, he might choose a comical number to do. Honestly, that was all right, too. Luke always made me laugh; I loved that about him.

Luke walked to center stage. "You know, there are lots of songs that have women's names in them." He sang a few lines of "Oh, Sweet Suzy," directing his attention right at Susie. She laughed heartily. "And then of course, there's ..." With that, he sang a few lines of "Rosemary" to Rosemary. I was a little worried she might be upset by that. It was the same song Johnny had sung to her in the infamous video.

Rosemary laughed, too, her smile reaching all the way to her eyes. It was cool that she had a sense of humor and didn't seem to take herself too seriously.

"Hey!" Johnny yelled out. "Quit serenading my woman!"

Luke stopped singing and stood up straight, his eyes wide. With mock terror, he saluted and said, "Yes, boss!"

We all laughed at that. Luke was a terrific entertainer, and I was proud of him already.

"Unfortunately, there's no song with the name Elyse in it. Unless, you know, you count 'Für Elise.' Even so, I chose a special song for her."

Luke started up the music and headed back to center stage. The music was unfamiliar to me.

"Oh, great song," Susie said quietly.

"I don't think I know it."

"It's 'It All Fades Away' from *The Bridges of Madison County*," Rosemary explained with a smile.

Luke drew in a breath and began to sing. As I had wished, it was an incredibly romantic one. The lyrics told how everything important in the world fades away when I'm with you. Luke gazed into my eyes whenever he sang the word "you." I smiled softly at him, warmth spreading throughout my body. The song was powerful and passionate, and it was such an honor to be singled out like that, especially in front of his friends. Luke made me feel adored and cherished.

The song built to a deep, soaring crescendo, and I got chills hearing Luke's incredible voice. It wasn't only his beautiful voice; it was the passion with which he sang. I wondered if the passion was for performing or for me. It was likely a bit of both, and I loved every second of his performance.

Everyone and everything else faded away for me, too, as I listened to Luke sing. I wiped tears from my eyes as the song ended. I was too overwhelmed to applaud at first. Luke saw my tears and smiled at me.

"If that doesn't get him laid, nothing will," Johnny muttered.

"Johnny!" Rosemary hissed, punching him in the shoulder. She didn't know me well enough to know I wouldn't be offended by something like that.

I looked over at Rosemary and said, "He's not wrong."

She laughed, and so did the others. I got up from my seat and everyone quickly got out of my way so I could go to Luke. He came down from the stage and I pulled him close, wrapping my arms around him.

"Oh, Luke, that was so beautiful."

"I meant every word," he murmured in my ear.

I sighed happily, then pulled back so I could look at him. We gazed into each other's eyes for a moment, then I said, "I was tempted to throw my panties up onstage."

He laughed heartily. "Man, I would *love* that!"

I glanced over to where Rosemary and the rest of his friends were standing, watching us.

"Do you think Rosemary and Susie might want to sing some stuff while we're all here?" I asked.

Luke's eyes glimmered with joy at my suggestion. "I'm sure they would love it. But honey, it's okay if you want to go out. I mean, I know this is supposed to be, like, our date night."

"I don't know about you, but I'm having a blast hanging out here with you and your friends," I told him with a smile.

"Cool," Luke said, unable to hide his huge grin. "Go on, ask them to sing. I'm sure they'll oblige."

Luke and I walked over to where Rosemary, Johnny, Susie, and David were all standing. They had turned around, pretending to talk among themselves. It was kind of cute. I knew they were scoping out Luke's new girlfriend. I got the impression that they approved of me, and they seemed to enjoy seeing Luke look so happy.

"So," I began. "I was wondering if maybe you guys might want to sing something for me while we're all here? I mean, if you're all not too tired from singing and performing all week."

Rosemary smiled at me. There was such kindness in her

pretty green eyes. "I would love that, Elyse." She glanced at Susie.

"Oh yeah, so would I," Susie said, her blue eyes shining.

It had been a long time since I'd hung out with other women, and I found myself wondering if Rosemary and Susie might someday be my friends, too, and not just with Luke. I was close with my family, but I didn't have a lot of friends outside of work. Being with Luke had shown me what I'd been missing out on.

"What kind of song would you like to hear?" Rosemary asked.

"I like funny, upbeat numbers."

Rosemary smiled over at Luke. "Wow, you two really are a good match."

Luke nodded.

"Okay, I got one," Rosemary said, after thinking about it for a moment.

"Perfect," Susie said. "You go first."

Rosemary got the music ready on the sound system, then stood in the center of the stage. I glanced over at Johnny, who was already gazing up at her with adoration. It was still weird for me to be in the same room with *The Johnny Creel*, but he was certainly an approachable celebrity. Down-to-earth and friendly.

Rosemary picked a great song to do for me. It was "Adelaide's Lament" from *Guys and Dolls*. I felt a little starstruck by her as well. After all, she was famous from the viral video, and she had been on Broadway. It was no surprise she did a terrific job with the song, which was a comical number about a woman at the end of her rope because her long-time boyfriend still hadn't proposed.

We all stood and applauded when she finished. Johnny whistled and shouted, "Brava!"

"Was that song a hint?" Johnny teased when Rosemary got

back to her seat. Rosemary smiled slyly, but never gave him an answer. Instead, she leaned over and kissed him.

"Great job, honey," Johnny told her with a smile.

"That was terrific, Rosemary," I said. "Thanks so much."

"My pleasure."

"You'll love this next number, too," David said, as Susie took her place on the stage. "Susannah is a terrific dancer."

David wasn't kidding. Susie *was* terrific. She performed an incredible, energetic song and dance routine. It was "Buenos Aires" from *Evita*. I watched, entranced by her performance. It wouldn't have surprised me in the least if she, too, soon got a role on Broadway. Susie had a fabulous stage presence, and her passion for dance was palpable with every step she took.

David had seemed so cool and reserved, but he was the first to jump out of his seat to give Susie a well-deserved standing ovation when she was done. We all cheered wildly for her.

"She looks so beautiful up there," I said to David. "She's a natural."

"She sure is," David said proudly. "She sure is."

Once again, I thanked my lucky stars that Susie was taken. She was beautiful and sensual, especially when she danced. She could turn anybody's head when she performed, and of course she performed with Luke all the time. I found myself wondering if David was equally relieved now that Luke had a girlfriend.

Luke leaned over to me and said quietly, "I have an idea."

"What?" I asked, curious to know why he was speaking so softly.

"It's totally up to you. I don't want to make you uncomfortable, but ... Do you want to try to sing something with me?"

"Yeah, you should do it!" Johnny said enthusiastically. So

much for keeping Luke's idea quiet so as not to put me on the spot.

"Johnny, don't pressure her," Rosemary gently admonished.

"It's okay, Rosemary." I turned to Luke. "I think it might be kinda fun."

"Really?" Luke asked excitedly. His expression reminded me of when he was acting overexcited but kidding around. He wasn't faking this time. Luke was genuinely excited at the idea of singing with me, which was reason enough to do it.

"Yes. But listen. I've got an okay ear for music and I can hit most of the notes and stuff, but I'm not gonna sound anything like you guys."

"That's okay. We understand." Luke still sounded quite excited. "But you'll do it?"

"Yeah."

Luke's friends clapped and cheered, and I knew they would be a supportive audience for me, even if I was awful.

"What should we do?" Luke asked.

"It should be something where I don't have to sing too much," I said, feeling a bit nervous. "Seriously, I have literally never even stepped on a stage before. Not even for a school play."

"Okay, let me think what we could do," Luke said. "What's a good duet?"

"And it's gotta be something I know pretty well," I said, thinking hard. "I got it! Okay, I got a perfect one. I know all the words, and you can do most of the heavy lifting."

I whispered to Luke, and he laughed out loud. "Yesss! Perfect."

Luke took my hand and helped me to my feet. I was getting more nervous by the moment. I'd given lots of business talks before large audiences, but this was way out of my comfort zone. It was silly, but I felt especially nervous in front of Johnny Creel.

As we walked up toward the stage, I glanced back to Luke's friends. I saw nothing but friendly, supportive faces. I reminded myself that nobody would be scrutinizing my performance. This was just for fun. And with Luke by my side, it *would* be fun.

Luke started up the music and I heard either Rosemary or Susie say, "Great song!"

I had chosen "You and Me (But Mostly Me)" from *The Book of Mormon*. It was a hilarious song where I would play sidekick to Luke. In the show, it's sung by two Mormon missionaries: one who thinks quite highly of himself, Elder Price, and one who is more than happy to play second fiddle to him. I would be Elder Cunningham; my job was to hang on Elder Price's every word. It was perfect for us.

The first time Luke sang the "mostly me" part, he gently but firmly shoved me out of his way. He met my gaze as he sang, making sure I was okay with what he was doing. I pressed my lips together to keep from laughing, and Luke could tell from my expression that I was on board with his plan. We ran with it, Luke boastfully singing about how amazing he was and pushing me away anytime I got close to him. I hammed it up, gazing adoringly at him no matter how many times he brushed me off through song. What I lacked in singing ability, I made up for in humor. I heard the laughter from the small audience of four, and I could see why Luke found performing so addictive.

I did get one note wrong, and I recognized my mistake right away but wasn't sure how to fix it. Luke pointed down, indicating the note should be lower. I switched to the right note, and he gave me a thumbs-up without missing a beat.

We ended our song with a flourish. As we sang the last

note, Luke pushed me out of the way one final time, so he could hog center stage. It was *hilarious*.

Our performance got lots of applause, and I felt a tingle of excitement when I heard Johnny's familiar whistle of approval.

Luke grinned. "Thank you so much for doing this."

"It was really fun," I said, looking into his excited, puppy-dog-like brown eyes.

He leaned over and kissed me, which made the applause and whistles grow louder. We stepped down from the stage and both Rosemary and Susie hugged me warmly. It felt like we were old friends already.

"You guys work great together," Rosemary said.

"That's for sure," Susie agreed. "Your timing is perfect."

"Thanks," I said.

"You hungry?" Luke asked me.

"Starving, now that you mention it." I'd been having too much fun to notice, but it was getting late and I hadn't eaten since lunch.

"You wanna head out?"

"Sure," I told him. "It was so nice meeting you all. Thanks for hanging out with us."

Rosemary and Susie hugged me again, which I loved. Then *Johnny* gave me a hug, which I found exciting. He seemed like such a cool guy, and I admired him for all the work he did for the kids at The Creel Foundation.

David was clearly not the hugger type, but he shook my hand and gave me a sexy half-smile. "Enjoyed meeting you. Hope to see you again," he said.

"Likewise."

Luke slipped his hand around my waist as he led me down the hall.

"Your friends are wonderful, Luke."

"So are you, Elyse. So are you."

* * *

"HOLY FUCK," Luke said as he stared at my car.

I laughed. I'd been dying to show him my red LC 500 Lexus.

"This is yours?" he asked incredulously.

"Yep," I said, opening the passenger door for him. "I know it's crazy to have a car in New York, but I hate being dependent on public transportation. Costs a fortune to park in the garage at work, but to me it's worth it."

I slid into the driver's seat. Luke started playing with the buttons on the dashboard, and I couldn't help but laugh. He was just too cute sometimes.

"This is so cool! You're lucky this thing doesn't get stolen."

"It did once. I was lucky to get it back. Where do you want to go for dinner?"

"Surprise me," Luke said, fiddling with the radio buttons. He found a rock station he liked and started playing drums on my dashboard. I laughed again and shook my head as I started to drive. He was all keyed up, probably from the adrenaline of performing.

I could think of all kinds of delightful things he could do with that energy.

"I love this song!" Luke exclaimed as "Uptown Girl" by Billy Joel started playing. "This song makes me think of you. You are my beautiful Uptown Girl."

"Cool. I like that almost as much as Nerd."

Luke sang the entire song along with the radio, looking at me the whole time. When the song was over, I glanced at him.

"I love to hear you sing, Luke."

"Yeah? Well, I love the way you look at me when I sing."

I reached over and ran my hand through his soft brown hair. He smiled.

CHAPTER 10

I'd had such a great time on the weekend with Luke, I hated to see it end. Already, I found myself fantasizing about what it might be like to live with him. It was crazy how fast our relationship was progressing. He was such an important part of my life now, and it was hard to believe we'd only been together for such a short time. It was a big deal for me to consider living with somebody else.

Though I'd looked forward to coming back to work as usual on Monday, I was dreading being alone with Keith. We met in the conference room early to continue work on the Wicket SecurePro project.

"Good morning," Keith said, his blue eyes lighting up when he saw me. He truly was a ridiculously handsome man. It was possible that I might have given him a shot if it weren't for Luke. But Luke was my boyfriend, and I had never cared for a man as much as I did for him. With his vivacious and entertaining personality, every other guy seemed boring in comparison.

"Good morning," I said. "I came up with a few more ideas for the campaign that I wanted to go over with you."

I figured it best to get right down to work. We were totally alone on the tenth floor, but we were still here on business. Hopefully, he would get the hint.

We were on the same page as far as strategy was concerned, and our brainstorming session went well, but the way Keith kept looking at me the whole time put me on edge.

"I think we came up with some good stuff here," I told Keith as we wrapped up our work session. Our co-workers had starting filing into the building. The conference room door was shut, but anybody glancing in through the glass door could see we were hard at work. "I think there's a lot here to convince Hunter that we're on the right track. It's best to have a united front when we show Mr. Bialystock our final presentation."

"Agreed," Keith said. Relief flooded through me as he started packing up his things. Then he added, "Elyse, can I ask you something?"

No, no, no I wanted to scream.

"Would you maybe want to go out for a drink or something soon? You know, outside of work?"

My heart thudded with anxiety. Keith had taken a risk and put himself out there. I didn't know how to turn him down without embarrassing him.

"Uh, well, I don't know. I'm super busy with work."

"I know," Keith said with a smile. "We both have the same job. Hell, we're both such workaholics, we could go out on a date and talk about nothing but work without boring each other."

I laughed nervously. He wasn't wrong.

"I—I don't think so," I finally managed to say.

"I really like you," Keith said, then nervously ran his fingers through his hair. "In case you can't tell."

"You don't really even know me."

"We work sixty hours a week together. Sure I do."

"No, you know how I am at work. You don't know a thing about what I'm really like."

"I know you're insanely smart," he said, his blue eyes softening as he looked at me. "And not just book smart. You've got an incredible business sense, and you know how to sell anything to anybody. I know you're sweet and kind, and you never have a bad word to say about anybody."

I swallowed hard. Brushing him off gently wasn't working.

"And you like showtunes."

"What?" I asked, stunned. How the hell did he know that?

"You hum them sometimes," Keith said with a smile. "I can usually tell what Broadway show you probably saw over the weekend by what you're humming on Monday morning."

I stared at him. "I—I never realized I did that."

"I know you try to keep up this front that you're all-business all the time, but I know what a wonderful woman you are. You're amazing."

Keith's words were so sweet, I hardly knew what to say. My heart ached for him. He'd clearly harbored these feelings for me for a while, and I knew it was miserable to have a crush on someone who didn't feel the same way.

I have a boyfriend. That was all I needed to say.

I couldn't say it. Not now. I was still Work Elyse. The one whose life completely revolved around work, as far as my co-workers knew. I especially needed Mr. Bialystock to believe I was one-hundred-percent focused on the company, at least until the promotion was decided. As far as he, Hunter, and Keith knew, I did not have a personal life.

"You're so sweet, Keith. Really. I—I—I just don't think I really think about you that way," I said finally.

Keith looked dejected, then nodded. "I understand. But maybe someday you might start thinking of me that way."

There was still hope in his eyes as he spoke. "Maybe we could just go out for a drink, just once, and see how it goes?"

I picked up my things and hurried toward the door, opening it so Keith couldn't say anything more without being overheard.

"Just promise me you'll think about it?" Keith asked.

"Think about what?" Luke said.

I gasped as I nearly ran into him. "Sorry! I didn't see you there."

"It's okay, Miss," Luke said, brown eyes sparkling. I prayed he couldn't see the guilt in my eyes.

"Oh hey, Elyse?" Hunter called from down the hall. "Keith, too, for that matter. Mr. Bialystock wants an update on Wicket SecurePro. Can the three of us meet sometime today to discuss it?"

Luke smiled at me, then hurried off so I could get back to work.

My chest physically hurt from the guilt I felt looking at Luke. He had proudly showed me off to all his friends. He sang a love song to me in front of them, for God's sake. And yet in my world, nobody knew we were together.

I felt terrible for not telling people about him. I remembered Luke's defensiveness on our first date. I hoped he didn't think I was ashamed of him. On the contrary, it would be wonderful if we could go public at work with our relationship soon.

As it turned out, the meeting with Mr. Bialystock went quite well, at least for me. I was dying to share my good news with Luke, but I wanted to tell him in person. He was always so supportive of me, and I knew he would be almost as excited as I was.

I didn't have any reason to go down to the second floor, but I casually wandered down there anyway. I couldn't help but smile with pride when I saw Luke sitting in his office. He was on the phone, looking busy.

He caught sight of me in the hallway and grinned. Luke quickly wrapped up his conversation and left his office to join me. I glanced around nervously, not wanting anyone to see us. I gestured for him to follow me, and I slipped into the stairwell.

Before I even knew what was happening, Luke's lips were on mine. He kissed me passionately, pushing me against the wall. After allowing myself to indulge in his affections for a few all-too-brief seconds, I pushed him away.

"Behave," I told him breathlessly, only half-meaning it. Having a love affair at work—risking being caught and all that—was exciting. Even so, I didn't want to get caught.

"Guess what, guess what, guess what?"

"What? What? What?" Luke asked, matching my enthusiasm already. He was just too wonderful.

"I'm going to Finland!"

Luke threw up his hands and did one of those whisper-screams. "Ahhhh!"

I giggled, thrilled that he was happy for me. I knew he would be.

"They picked you to do the presentation? Yay! When do you leave?" His face fell. "I miss you already."

I smiled at him. "It's not for a couple of weeks. And I'll only be gone a week or so."

"That is so cool. Congratulations," he said sincerely, gently stroking my face. "I know how many extra hours you put in on that security presentation dealie."

Yeah. Extra hours alone with Keith.

I stuffed my guilt down deep and tried to focus on being excited about my trip.

"I better get back to work. I just had to tell you my news in person."

"I'm so glad you did," Luke said, then bent down to kiss me. His kisses quickly grew more passionate, and I moaned as his tongue explored my mouth. This kiss wasn't just congratulatory; it felt like foreplay. Like he was about to take me right there. *If only.* I pictured him fucking me hard against the wall while wearing his sexy getup from *Bloody Bloody Andrew Jackson*. That image was quickly becoming my go-to fantasy.

Finally, I forced myself to push him away again. "I said *behave.*"

Luke shot me his sexy grin, knowing full well I didn't want him to behave himself. I slipped out of his grasp and straightened my business suit.

"Ah, yes. Work Elyse. We meet again."

"Good to see you again, Mr. Rannells," I said in my best business voice. "Now, if you'll excuse me, I must attend to my work duties."

Luke saluted me solemnly. I stifled a laugh. I started back up the stairs and paused on the landing. Then I dashed back down, threw my arms around Luke, and kissed him again. His lips shook with muffled laughter.

"Okay! I'm really going now." I rushed back up the steps. Just then, the door to the stairwell below opened, and three people in business attire walked in.

That was close.

CHAPTER 11

$\mathcal{I}$ spent the night at Elyse's place on Friday night, which was awesome. When we were making weekend plans, she had told me in her usual straightforward manner, "Bring a toothbrush. You won't be going home."

"Yes, Ma'am!" I'd responded. Her place was a helluva lot nicer than mine, that was for damned sure. I brought an overnight bag with my stuff, and she emptied out a bedroom drawer for me. It was kinda cool. Like we were already taking the next step in our relationship. I found myself hoping that eventually I could move in with her. I had never lived with a woman before. Up until now, I had never wanted to.

Since I hadn't had a class to teach on Saturday, we got to sleep in and spend the whole day together. She made me an incredible breakfast, and then we had wild sex on the dining room table. As in the kitchen, we did it in full view of the open windows. I loved having sex with her on hard surfaces. I could penetrate her so deeply when she was on her back, which was incredibly pleasurable for both of us. If it was uncomfortable for her, she never complained.

We were getting ready to spend Saturday night hanging out with Johnny and the rest of the theater crew. It was so cool the way Elyse fit right in with my friends from the moment they met.

The day after I'd introduced Elyse to my friends at the foundation, I'd arrived there to find Rosemary and Susie greeting me with their arms folded.

"Shit, what did I do now?" I'd asked.

"We need to talk to you about Elyse," Rosemary said, and Susie had nodded grimly.

"Okayyy," I said warily.

"We love her," Rosemary stated firmly.

"Yup. We sure do, so you better not screw this up, Rannells," Susie warned.

"Right. If you ever break up, you know we'll choose her over you, right?" Rosemary told me, her green eyes twinkling with mischief.

I laughed. "Understood."

"Seriously," Rosemary said with a laugh. "She's amazing."

"You don't have to tell me that." I was fully aware of how incredible my girlfriend was, but it felt good to hear others say the same.

Susie glanced up at the stage, and then back at me. "She gets it, you know? What we do here."

I met Susie's gaze and smiled. She and I were very close and had spent a lot of time sharing our hopes and dreams together. Her last boyfriend had belittled her ambitions, and she was incredibly grateful to have a supportive man in her life now. David truly understood her in a way no one else ever had. Susie had told me many times how much she wished I would find a woman who understood me the same way. We both knew I had found her in Elyse.

"She really does," Rosemary agreed. "The way she went up

there onstage with you and just went with it? That was incredible."

I laughed. "Yeah, it really was." That had even surprised me. It was brave of her, and I would never forget the way I'd felt when Elyse stepped into my special, magical world of the theater. Sharing it with her was, well, I didn't have the words to describe how utterly fucking cool it had been of her.

"I can't believe we're going to hang out at Johnny Creel's place tonight," Elyse said excitedly, snapping me back to the present. I chuckled as she primped in front of her bedroom mirror.

"I still don't get the big deal. It's just Johnny."

"To you, maybe. For me, he's the guy who was in all the papers, and *Inside Edition*, and all that. Rich, famous playboy *The Johnny Creel!*"

"That was BR—Before Rosemary. He's not like that anymore."

"I know. He really does seem like a nice guy," she said, grabbing her purse.

"Yup."

David was sending his limo for us so we could arrive at Johnny's place in style. It was mainly so we could both drink and not worry about cracking up Elyse's gorgeous car. I'd mentioned to Susie that we were gonna take a cab, but she was having none of it.

* * *

"HEY, COME ON IN," Rosemary said, greeting us warmly at the door.

"Wow, your place is beautiful," Elyse exclaimed after hugging Rosemary. Johnny and Rosemary lived in an incredible penthouse in Chelsea. It offered a panoramic view of the city, which was especially gorgeous at night.

"Thanks. I'm spoiled rotten living in a place like this."

Rosemary led us into another room where David, Susie, and Johnny himself were lounging.

"Whoa," Elyse said taking in the room. It looked like a restaurant, with a long wooden bar and barstools, as well as a few tables and chairs. Johnny grinned at us, lifting his beer by way of greeting.

"Right?" I asked, eyes wide. "I about fainted when I first saw this place. I don't know why Johnny ever leaves the house."

David nodded in our direction, then sipped his scotch.

"Check it out," Rosemary said excitedly, running behind the bar. She gestured at the four beer taps. "Johnny got some great local microbrews on tap, just for you. Luke said that's what you like to drink."

"Oh, that's so sweet. Thank you!"

"My pleasure," Johnny said. He turned to me and David. "Gentlemen, shall we retire to the other room to play billiards?"

Elyse, Rosemary, and Susie laughed at Johnny's faux rich-guy imitation.

"Indeed we shall," I said, pushing my nose up with my finger.

"First, what's your pleasure?" Rosemary asked.

"This is an important decision." I went over and surveyed the taps, scrutinizing them carefully. "Let us see." I closed my eyes and then touched each tap with my finger. "Eeeny, meeny, miney—"

"You are impossible," Elyse huffed, then came over pointed to one of the beers. She never tired of teasing me about my taste in beer. "Try this pilsner. You'll like it."

Rosemary poured my beer.

"Thank ye, miss!" I took a sip. It was delicious, smooth and malty.

I kissed Elyse, then asked quietly, "You okay hanging out here with the girls?"

"Of course," she said with a smile. I searched her face and could see she meant it. I didn't want to abandon her if she wasn't comfortable, but she seemed to like being with Rosemary and Susie.

"Cool."

I joined Johnny and David in the other room so we could shoot some pool.

"You play me, David plays the winner. Sound good?" Johnny asked.

"Poifect," I said.

We began playing, and Johnny quickly started kicking my ass.

"No fair. You get to practice all the time," I whined. "I wish *I* had a pool table."

"Practice won't help. You just suck," Johnny informed me.

"I do not."

Johnny sank another ball in response.

"Son of a bitch," I muttered while Johnny chuckled.

"So how are things with Elyse?" David asked. He sipped his scotch as we watched Johnny wipe the floor with me, billiards-wise.

"Amazing. Awesome. Perfect."

"How's the sex?" Johnny asked bluntly.

"Dude," David admonished. "That's his *girl*." He glanced toward the other room, even though there was no way the girls could hear us.

"Come on, you know you want to know," Johnny said.

While I was single, David and Johnny were always asking about who I was hooking up with. I'd told them about some of my one-night stands and the occasional fling with an actress I was working with. Plus, I *may* have embellished the number of women I was with. Johnny and David certainly were not aware of my pre-Elyse sex drought.

I grinned, trying to think of a respectful way to describe my terrific sex life with Elyse. I'd had no problem going into explicit detail about those nameless, faceless and, occasionally *fictitious* women, but Elyse was different. I was serious about her.

"She's ... *enthusiastic*," I said finally.

"Really," Johnny said with great interest. David arched an eyebrow but was too reserved and polite to comment.

"She's just so *into it*, you know what I mean? It's like I never have to beg her, because she's usually ready to go. She loves sex, and she's not shy about it. It's awesome."

"Nice," Johnny said, wiggling his eyebrows.

"And she's adventurous, too. So far we've done it on the kitchen floor and the dining room table. We're kinda making our way through her apartment."

"*Very* nice," Johnny said, and David cocked a half-smile.

I felt a tad guilty for talking about our sex life, but I figured the women probably talked like that, too. Susie certainly did. David was calm and cool most of the time, but she said he was incredible in bed. He was a fashion designer, and one time he had tied her up with his own custom-designed ties when he had sex with her in his office.

"It's not only great sex, though. Elyse is amazing." I leaned on my pool cue and let out a happy sigh. Johnny had demolished me in the game, but I didn't care. "Rosemary and Susie are always telling me how cool you guys are when it comes to their theater stuff. You go see them in all their shows, you're a shoulder to cry on when things are going rough, stuff like that. Elyse is like that, too, you know? She just gets it."

"That's wonderful, Luke," David said sincerely.

"It really is, dude," Johnny said. "Just don't let her watch you play pool. She'll lose all respect for you."

I flipped Johnny off, then grabbed my beer. "I hope she's having fun with Rosemary and Susie."

"I'm sure she is. They love her to death," Johnny said, and David nodded.

* * *

I SETTLED in with Rosemary and Susie in the living room. They were drinking wine while I enjoyed my delicious microbrew.

"You gals hungry?" Rosemary asked.

"A little," I said, and Susie nodded.

"Our cook, Stephanie, put together lots of snacky stuff for us, like brie and crackers and stuff. And she made some chicken wings for the menfolk," Rosemary said.

"Oooh, chicken wings," I exclaimed. Just then, the cook came through with a large tray of delicious-smelling food. She was about to walk past us toward the other room, when Rosemary stopped her.

"Hold up a second. Thanks!" Rosemary took the tray from her and brought it over to me. "Help yourself. You get first pick before the guys."

I smiled at her and gratefully filled a small plate with chicken wings. It was nice not having to pretend I was a brie and wine kind of girl around Rosemary and Susie.

"Thanks," I said to Stephanie, and she smiled before heading off to feed the guys.

"How's work going?" Rosemary asked. "Any news on that promotion yet?"

"Luke told you about that?" I asked, surprised Luke had mentioned it, and touched that Rosemary had remembered.

"Of course. I told you he talks about you *all the time*," Susie said with a smile.

"So, you want to be Senior Vice President of International ..." Rosemary laughed. "Okay, help me out here."

I laughed too. "Senior Vice President of Worldwide Sales Strategy and Operations."

"Yeah, that," Rosemary said.

Stephanie walked through the living room and into the kitchen, then quickly returned with a large tray of cheese and crackers for us. After Rosemary and Susie filled their plates, they turned their attention back to me.

"That sounds really exciting," Susie said.

"Oh, it is. I mean, I love what I do now, but this would be such a huge step up. I get along great with my co-workers, but it's tough having to compromise all the time. If I get the Senior VP job, then I'll be in charge. Don't get me wrong, I'd still listen to my co-workers and get their input and ideas on strategy and all, but I'd get to make the final call."

"Nice," Susie said before taking a sip of wine.

"I'd get to travel a lot on business, too, if I get the promotion."

"To places like Finland," Rosemary said with a smile.

"He told you about that too?" I asked.

Both women nodded.

"He's said you're leaving next week and he'll be miserable without you. But he's excited for you," Rosemary said.

"He's really proud of you, Elyse," Susie said, and I could see warmth in her eyes. It seemed to make her quite happy that Luke and I were together.

"I'm proud of him, too," I said, feeling the familiar rush of guilt. My co-workers all knew Luke, or at least they knew *of* him. They knew him as the guy who fixed everything. Luke was so much more than that, and I wished I could brag to everybody about him the way he clearly did about me.

"A toast!" Rosemary said, lifting her glass. "Here's hoping Elyse gets her well-deserved promotion!"

Susie eagerly lifted her wine glass, and I toasted them with my beer.

"Thanks, you guys. That means a lot to me." We drank, and then I asked Rosemary, "So, what have you been up to? I guess your schedule has eased up a bit since the show ended."

Luke had mentioned that Broadway's revival of *Hairspray* hadn't run as long as Rosemary had hoped, but the reviews had been good, and it was a wonderful experience for her. Luke said she'd taken it well, all things considered, when the news had broken that the show was closing. I figured it was safe to ask her about it.

"You would think that, wouldn't you?" Rosemary said with a laugh. "Things have still been pretty crazy. I'm going on a bunch of auditions, for both on- and off-Broadway shows, which is good, but exhausting. I've also got a heavy course load at NYU. Believe me, I'm thrilled to have the chance to get my theater degree, but I'll be glad when I'm done, you know?"

"Of course," I said, munching on a chicken wing. "That'll be so exciting when you graduate. Just think, you'll be able to focus only on auditions then."

Rosemary nodded excitedly. "Exactly."

"What about you?" I asked Susie. "How are your auditions going?"

Susie's expression fell, and Rosemary looked at her with sympathy. I had a bad feeling I had put my foot in my mouth.

"I—I'm sorry. Should I not ask about that?" I mentally kicked myself. Luke had told me that Susie had been struggling with her auditions. At one point, she'd pushed herself so hard, she had collapsed from exhaustion. How could I have forgotten that?

"Oh no, not at all," Susie said kindly, reaching over and squeezing my hand. "Of course you can ask. Will give me a chance to vent if nothing else."

"Of course," I told her. "What are friends for?"

Susie's eyes softened, and she smiled when she looked at me. It was the first time I had officially called myself her friend and not just an acquaintance because I was Luke's girlfriend.

"Exactly," Rosemary said. We both looked at Susie, ready for her to unburden herself to us.

"I feel like," Susie began, then stopped. Tears welled up in her eyes, and my heart ached with empathy for her. "I haven't gotten cast in anything yet. I mean, I do shows at The Creel Foundation, which is wonderful and rewarding, but it's not the same thing, you know what I mean?"

"Yeah," I told her, nodding in understanding.

"I want to get cast in something on my own merit, and not because it's part of my job. I mean, Luke and I decide on the casting for all the shows."

"I understand what you mean. Sometimes you just need the validation that comes with being cast in something outside of work."

"Yes, exactly! It's just a slump, I guess. It's not the first time it's happened. You just feel like you're never gonna get cast in anything, ever again."

"I know how that feels," Rosemary said. "We've all been there. You will get cast in something, but it's tough when you're in a bad place. I promise it will get better, but I know how much it hurts in the meantime."

Susie wiped her eyes with a napkin and nodded gratefully at her.

"Susie, I'm hardly an expert on these things, but I've seen

you perform, and I think you're incredible," I gushed, meaning every word. "Your dancing, your stage presence—I think you're amazing! I go to Broadway shows all the time, and there's really no difference in the Broadway stars I see there and what I see when you perform. You're so good, girl. I mean it. Talent like yours can't go unnoticed forever."

Susie squeezed my hand again. "Thanks, Elyse. I needed to hear that. The other night at the foundation with you and Luke was so much fun. I needed that too, you know? To just play around onstage and have fun with it. With no pressure."

"It was fun," I said happily, remembering being onstage with Luke.

"We were all really impressed with you, Elyse," Rosemary said. "It was so cool of you to just get up there onstage and have fun. I can't tell you what it means to people like us," she said, nodding at Susie, "when our significant others take an interest in what we do. Johnny's great about that. He'll get up onstage and sing with us from time to time. He's actually pretty musical. Plays the guitar and all that."

"I can't see David doing that," I observed wryly. He seemed like a nice guy but wound pretty tight.

Susie laughed. "Oh, he's a horrible singer and he knows it. But he's more supportive of me than anyone I've ever known. He's amazing. I can be the quintessential temperamental artist, believe me, and he's incredibly patient. David quietly listens and supports me, no matter what."

"He did sing that one time," Rosemary said.

"Yes, he sure did," Susie said softly. "When I was particularly down, he sang "You'll Never Walk Alone" to remind me of how much support I have all around me. He can't sing well, but he still sang in front of all my friends."

"It was beautiful," Rosemary said.

I nodded. "I get chills when Luke sings. Honest to God, *chills*. He's amazing."

"Luke is incredible," Susie said. "I love working with him. Not only is he a terrific performer, but he's been my shoulder to cry on, too, that's for sure. And I can't tell you how happy I am that he found you. He really does talk about you all the time, and he gets so excited when he knows he's going to see you soon. I know when he has plans with you. I don't even have to ask. I can see it in his eyes. He's just so happy."

"I see it, too," Rosemary said.

Then *I* started tearing up. "Oh, you guys. You're the best."

I fanned my eyes, laughing softly at my own emotions.

"True friends are hard to come by," Rosemary said, lifting her glass. "To the three of us."

We clinked glasses and drank to true friendship.

CHAPTER 12

I asked Elyse to come to my floor as soon as she got a chance. I had exciting news to share with her, and I wanted to tell her in person. It was safer for her to come to see me than the other way around. None of her co-workers had any reason to come to the second floor as far as I knew, so we could hopefully talk privately.

No such luck.

Roger and Manny burst into my office, both grinning from ear to ear. I should have expected it from them. After all, it was August sixth, and time was up on the bet we'd made. Little did they know, I had won the stupid bet easily, since Elyse and I had had sex on our first date. Not that I would ever tell the guys. I was prepared to take my lumps and move on with my life.

"Heyyyyy, Twinkletoes," Roger said, striding into the room. "Guess what today is?"

"Yeah, yeah, yeah," I grumbled, realizing this was gonna be harder than I'd thought.

"Time to pay the pipers, man," Manny said cockily.

I swallowed hard, knowing I would have to suffer the

humiliation of them thinking I'd lost, and lost badly. It was maddening, since Elyse and I had had sex more times than I could count.

If they only knew.

I pictured Elyse's lovely face and warm laugh, and remembered what was important. She was the most beautiful, exciting woman I'd ever met, and every day I was falling more crazily in love with her.

I chuckled to myself, amused that I'd realized I was in love with Elyse at the same moment these goons stood here thinking she wouldn't give me the time of day.

"You lost *bad,* man. She never even looked your way, did she?" Manny gloated.

I bit the inside of my cheek. No, she didn't dare look at me when we were in the office because she knew she would start laughing if she did. I often found any excuse I could to go to the tenth floor, and I was forever trying to crack her up. I made faces at her if she happened to glance my way, or I quietly sang the girliest showtunes I could think of; songs like "I Feel Pretty" from *West Side Story.* I knew her co-workers were looking at me like I was insane, which only made it funnier.

"Nope, she never did. I couldn't break the Ice Queen," I said with a sigh. I felt guilty for talking about her like that, but I was trying to protect her. Elyse's focus right now was on her promotion, and I knew how much she wanted everyone at work to think she *was* an Ice Queen. No personal life, strictly business.

"So pay up already," Roger said in his most menacing voice, leaning across my desk like some mobster collecting his due.

I snorted. Roger looked like he could break you in half with one arm tied behind his back, but he wouldn't hurt a fly.

"Come on, dude," Roger whined, changing tactics right quick. "I got no cash for lunch today. Gimme gimme."

"I'll stop at an ATM at lunch," I said, waving him off. Elyse was due here any minute, and I needed to get rid of these idiots. They'd get super suspicious if they saw her anywhere near me.

Suddenly, Elyse appeared at my door. My eyes opened wide, and Roger and Manny turned around to see what I was looking at. Man, Elyse was *quick.* She slipped out of sight just as they turned to look.

"I'll pay up later. I promised. Now go away. I'm busy."

"Poor little Lukey," Roger said, shaking his head. "She would have been a great lay."

I winced. It felt weird talking about Elyse like this.

"Hey, maybe I should take a shot at it. Whaddya say?" Manny asked. "Double or nothin' says I can bag her in three weeks or less."

I swallowed, fighting the urge to lunge across my desk and grab Manny by the collar for even suggesting he try to mess with my girl. Of course, I knew that was insane. Manny had no idea she was my girl, and he was only trying to finish a childish game I had started.

It suddenly dawned on me what a dick move it had been to bet on Elyse in the first place. What the hell had I been thinking? Now that I really knew her, it was horrible to think of betting on her sex life. She didn't deserve to be treated like that. No woman did.

It was funny. Knowing Elyse, she would have been fine with hooking up once, as long as it was a safe sex partner. Even so, it would have been wrong to use her like that. What if she was the type who found sex deeply emotional? She could have gotten seriously hurt in the process.

What the hell was wrong with me?

"I'm in," Roger announced. "Double or nothing. Two

hundred bucks says Manny can fuck Very Important Blonde Lady in under a month."

I felt sick to my stomach.

"No way. Just forget the whole thing," I said irritably. I was madder at myself than anything else.

"Jeez, lack of sex makes you so bitchy," Manny huffed.

"He's right. You need to get you some, and *quick*," Roger agreed.

"I'll be sure to get right on that. No more bets."

"Fine. Be a pussy. See if I care," Manny said, shrugging. "Then you gots to pay up, Nightingale."

"I told you. ATM. At lunch. Now *go away*, or I'll make you clean the bathroom in the men's gym locker room."

Both men grimaced. "That's what I thought. Out." It was good to be the boss sometimes.

I got up and locked the door behind them, just in case. I'd been in such a good mood earlier, too. Even though I felt super guilty about the whole thing, it was embarrassing to have the guys think I hadn't gotten anywhere with Elyse. How great would it have been if I'd been able to tell the truth? That Elyse and I had had mind-blowing sex on our first date, then did it again on the floor of her kitchen on our second?

I grabbed my cell phone and angrily punched speed dial number one.

"Hey, is everything okay?" Elyse asked immediately upon answering. She sounded worried; I had asked her to come see me right away, but she didn't know why.

I leaned back in my chair and smiled, feeling my bad mood evaporate into thin air. Hearing her sweet voice calmed me, and it was a terrific reminder that there was more than just great sex to our relationship.

Renewed excitement and energy rippled through me just

thinking about the reason I had needed to talk to Elyse in the first place.

"Yeah, babe. Everything is perfect." The only thing better than getting fantastic news was having somebody you loved to share it with. "I got the part."

Elyse gasped. "That pirate thing? The music comedy show?"

"Yep, that's the one."

"Ahhhhh," she said in a whisper-yell. "I want to scream but I can't!"

I pictured her sitting in her office while talking to me. She was probably trying to keep her expression neutral, but inside I knew she was bursting.

"I'm so happy for you! Oh Luke, I know how much you wanted that part. From what you described, it sounds perfect for you. Catchy songs and lots of humor. You're gonna be so incredible."

I grinned. This was a big deal, and it felt good knowing Elyse understood how important it was. This off-Broadway show, called *Pirated*, featured three main pirate characters, and I was one of them. If things went well, there was always a possibility the show could actually make it to Broadway.

"If I wasn't leaving for Finland tomorrow, we would *so* be having celebration sex."

"Dammit!"

Elyse laughed. I was gonna miss her like crazy for the week she'd be gone, but I was thrilled she had this amazing opportunity to represent Wicket Pro for the Finland company. I was so goddamned proud of her.

"I'm like out-of-my-mind excited about this show," I said, "but I can't help but feel bad for Susie."

"Oh, you're right." I could hear the concern in her voice. "It's got to be hard for her to see other people having so much success. When are you gonna tell her?"

"She already knows. Believe me, I wanted to tell you first, but she was with me at the foundation last night when I got the call."

"Oh. How did she take it?"

"Well, she's happy for me, of course. She's helped me rehearse for it and all that."

"Yeah, I remember," Elyse said dryly. Susie and I were rehearsing *Pirated* when Elyse first laid eyes on her. God, that had been awkward. Elyse had been a good sport about it, though.

"Yeah," I said. "I'm sure she wanted me to get the part, but it has to hurt. I just wish there was something I could do to make her feel better. She's so goddamn *good*. I don't know why she keeps getting overlooked."

"You're a good friend, Luke." Elyse sounded sincere, and not mad or jealous. Thank goodness. I was incredibly lucky that she, Susie, and Rosemary had really hit it off. They had become close friends over the last few weeks. "Maybe I'll give her a call."

"That's nice of you. I'm sure she would like that. She'd never want to rain on my parade by telling me she was feeling down. Christ, she took it so hard when Rosemary got that part on Broadway."

"I'll call her. I'll make sure she's okay."

"Thanks, baby. You're the best. I mean it."

"I gotta go for now, but we have to make sure we see each other sometime today, before I leave for my trip," Elyse said.

"Definitely. Getting harder all the time around here, but I'll make it happen."

* * *

I HUNG up the phone feeling practically giddy. I was excited for Luke, and it warmed my heart to think of how happy he

129

must be, going about his day, thinking about the amazing opportunity of being in an off-Broadway show. Still, my heart ached for Susie. She'd already been feeling left behind. Like she was the only one who was still going nowhere in her career.

I opened up a document on my computer that needed some basic edits as I dialed her number. I could get some work done while I talked to Susie on the phone. She was probably working at the foundation, but she shouldn't have a class right now because it was a school day for her kids.

"Hey, what's up, Elyse?" Susie said cheerfully when she answered the phone. It made me smile to know she had my number programmed into her phone. We had become fast friends, just like Luke and I had fallen into a relationship quickly after our first date.

"Hey, girl. I know you've heard the news about Luke and the pirate show."

"Yes!" Susie gushed. "I'm so excited for him."

"I know you are, sweetie. But I wanna know how you're really feeling."

"What do you mean?"

"I know you're happy for him, but I'm sure it still hurts."

Susie was quiet for a moment. I hoped she wasn't hurt or embarrassed that I knew she was jealous of my boyfriend's success. All I wanted was for her to know she could confide in me.

"Ugh," she said at last. "I guess Luke told you how I collapsed from exhaustion after Rosemary got a part on Broadway. I feel like such an idiot."

"You're not an idiot, Susie. You're passionate about what you do."

Susie laughed softly. "That's what David says."

"You get upset because you care. I know I'm gonna be devastated if Hunter or Keith get the promotion instead of me, and they're just my co-workers. I don't know if it would be better or worse if it was a friend who got the job instead of me. I don't know how I would feel."

"You want the truth?"

"Yes. And I promise not to tell Luke whatever you say. This is just between us."

Susie paused for a moment. "The truth is I'm jealous as all hell. I am happy for him. I wanted him to get the part. I really, truly did. But it hurts." I heard the quaver in her voice and it broke my heart. "I feel like everybody around me is getting all these great roles, and I haven't landed a thing since I set foot in New York. Every time this happens, it makes me wonder what's wrong with me, and I question whether I'll ever be good enough."

"I understand," I said softly.

"And I feel so envious of people like Rosemary and Luke, and a teeny part of me doesn't want to hear about their successes because it's too painful. And then I hate myself for being a terrible friend."

"You're not a terrible friend. Not in any way. Your reaction is totally normal. It hurts because you care about your craft so much, and you feel conflicted about it because you *are* a good friend."

"You're so sweet to say that, Elyse."

"Well, I mean it. And I want you to know you can talk to me anytime. It might be easier for you to talk to somebody outside the theater business, you know?"

"Oh, you are so right. I mean, the last thing I want to do is dump all over Luke and Rosemary, and ruin their excitement by making it into a pity party for me."

I laughed. "I hear ya. Well, I'm prepared to throw a pity party for you if that helps. You're good at what you do, Susie. Like *really* good. You should give yourself a little time to hurt and feel sorry for yourself, and then move on toward your

131

next audition. It's gonna happen for you, Susie. I know it. And all this struggle will be worth it."

"Thank you so much. This was the pep talk I needed," Susie said, and she did sound like she felt better. It made me happy that I could cheer her up a bit.

"Doesn't David give you pep talks like this?"

Susie laughed. "David is a man of few words. But that's okay. He has his own wonderful way of taking care of me. I texted him the good news about Luke last night when we found out he got the part. I told David how wonderful it was for Luke and all that. But David knew better. When I came home last night, he didn't say a word. He just wrapped his arms around me and held me tight."

"That is so sweet," I said, picturing David's gentle brown eyes. He might not be an overly emotional guy, but he loved Susie with all his heart.

"Yeah, it really was. One of the many things I love about him. I don't have to tell him how I'm feeling. He gets it. He knows."

"That's so cool."

"I better let you go. I'm sure you have a million things to do before your trip tomorrow."

I felt like squealing at the mere mention of my business trip. I could hardly wait.

"Yeah, I certainly do."

"Thanks so much for calling me. It means more than you know."

"You're welcome, sweetie. Call me anytime, okay?"

"Thanks. Have a safe trip!"

"Thanks. Take care," I told her.

Later in the afternoon, I texted Luke to meet me in the usual stairwell. Not exactly a romantic place to see him one last time before my trip, but I didn't know what else to do.

Luke had a class to teach tonight, and I was leaving early in the morning.

I waited nervously in the stairwell, afraid of getting caught with him. The last thing I needed was my company thinking I wasn't one-hundred-percent committed to my job now, with the Senior VP job on the line. It would be especially awful if they knew I had a boyfriend *at work*. Talk about a distraction.

The door swung open and I gasped, startled. Luke grinned at me, and I could see the excitement in his eyes.

"Oh, Luke," I said, rushing over to kiss him. "I'm so happy you got the part!"

"Me too," he said, looking all lit up inside. He stroked my face with his finger. "I'm gonna miss you so much."

"I'll miss you, too."

"Knock 'em dead, babe. You're gonna be great," Luke said, and I could see the pride in his eyes.

I pulled him toward me and held onto him until I started feeling nervous again about somebody walking in on us. I reluctantly pulled away.

Luke gazed into my eyes. "Elyse, I ..." My heart skipped a beat. I was pretty sure he was trying to say he loved me. "I ... I'm really gonna miss you."

I felt a little disappointed, but it was okay. In most relationships, a month was too soon for "I love yous." Even so, for us, the moment felt right. I thought about saying it myself, but maybe it was best to wait until I came back.

"I'll miss you, too," I said, pulling him in for another kiss.

Just then, the stairwell door opened and my boss, Mr. Bialystock walked in.

CHAPTER 13

My alarm woke me up at 6am. It took me a moment to remember what day it was. Then, with a jolt of excitement, I realized it was time to get ready to go to Finland. I'd taken a shower last night so I could get to the airport extra early. My big presentation for the Presko Group, the largest clothing retailer in Finland, was scheduled for tomorrow. I would go over my notes about Wicket Pro's hyperconvergence technology while I was on the plane, but there was no need. I knew the presentation cold, and I knew everything there was to know about our products. I was totally prepared for any questions the CEO of the Presko Group might have.

If my presentation went well and I landed this tech contract with them, my chances of getting the Senior VP job would go up exponentially. I had to ensure things went as smoothly as possible until the job was mine.

Which meant I could not afford to have any more close calls like the one I'd had in the stairwell with Luke yesterday. I'd barely managed to pull away from Luke's embrace before my boss caught us kissing. I shuddered to think what would happen if he knew I was having a love affair with the head of maintenance in our building. Mr. Bialystock shot me a kind of weird look, but he seemed normal for the rest of the day, so I was fairly sure I was in the clear.

I picked up my cell phone to put it in my purse and saw I had a voice mail message from Luke. A flicker of anxiety rippled through me. He had called at 11:30pm last night while I was asleep. Luke never called that late on a week-night, and I feared something might be wrong.

I pressed the button to hear the message and burst out laughing when I heard Luke's voice loudly singing "Finland/Fisch Schlapping Dance" from *Spamalot*. I couldn't believe I'd forgotten all about that song. In the show, the narrator talks about England, but the cast mishears him and launches into a song all about Finland instead.

I played the message three times while I finished packing my luggage. By the third time, I teared up a little. It was so sweet and thoughtful of him.

While I would miss Luke terribly, I was rather excited about going on this adventure all by myself.

* * *

THE EIGHT-AND-A-HALF-HOUR FLIGHT to Finland had been fairly smooth. I made my big presentation for the Presko Group CEO, Vice President, and Head of Operations yesterday after having had a full day to recover from my jet lag. The people at Presko were terrific and seemed quite eager to learn what our company had to offer. I felt good about my presentation. After spending a few hours touring the clothing retailer's headquarters and answering lots of questions about our hyperconvergence technology, I'd had the rest of the day to wander around Helsinki. I did a hop-on bus tour where I could get off the bus whenever I came across something I wanted to explore. So far, I'd visited Senate Square, the Helsinki Olympic Stadium, and the famous Temppeliaukio Church.

I missed Luke, but I had enjoyed sightseeing alone. I loved going on adventures like this on my own, all the while knowing Luke would be genuinely interested in learning all about my trip. That was what made Luke so perfect. He never got angry or possessive if I was too busy to see him when I had a deadline. He was supportive of my work life. I hated having to hide my relationship with him, but I was glad to have my technology sales work as something that was all mine. Luke was every bit as passionate about his own work, and it was a good thing our work lives were so different. I thought about Susie a lot and could imagine how painful it would be if both Luke and I had the same job. Of course, we would still celebrate each other's successes, but life would be a lot more complicated.

My phone rang at exactly 4pm my time, which was 11pm for Luke in New York.

"Hey, baby," I said when I answered.

"What's wrong?" Luke asked immediately. I smiled weakly. I'd said two words and he already knew something was up.

"I'm in so much pain, I feel like I could throw up."

"Christ, Elyse," Luke said, sounding panicked. "What's the matter? Are you sick? You might want to go to the hospital, just in case—"

"It's all right, Luke. It's just my time of the month. Nothing unusual."

"Shit. I wish I was there with you, sweetie. I could lie down and at least rub your belly or something."

I closed my eyes and smiled, thinking how soothing that would be.

"At least I have my Get Well bear with me."

"Do you really?" Luke asked, sounding amused.

"Yes, I do. It's nowhere near as good as snuggling with you, but it's better than nothing." I glanced at the bear Luke had given me. He was resting on the pillow next to me, where I wished Luke was right now.

"I'm so sorry this had to happen now. I hope it doesn't ruin your trip."

"Thank God it didn't start getting really bad until after I gave the big presentation. I'll still be here a few more days to answer questions and set them up with some demos, but the most important part is over."

"How did it go?"

I told him all about my presentation. I also told Luke about my day trip, exploring Helsinki. Then Luke told me all about the pirate show, as rehearsals had started already. It was wonderful talking to him, and it helped take my mind off the pain for a while.

"You sound tired, Geek," I told him.

"Yeah, I am. It can be rough working all day and then going to rehearsals in the evening. Susie's taking over my classes for now."

Poor Susie. That was salt in the wound. Taking on extra classes so Luke could work on a show. Susie was a fiercely loyal friend, so I was sure she didn't mind helping Luke, but still. Taking on all the extra work, which included her having to play the role of Willy Wonka in the show with the kids, would be tough. I made a mental note to check in with her again when I got home.

"You sound tired too, Nerd," Luke said, sounding worried. "When was the last time you went to the doctor?"

"It's been a while," I admitted.

"I want you to promise me you'll go get checked out when you get back to the States, okay? Your pain meds aren't cutting it, and you need to make sure there isn't something else wrong. Promise me!" Luke demanded.

"Okay, I promise. I miss you so much, Luke."

"I miss you, too. Come back home to me."

My heart ached when he said that. Being with Luke did feel like home for me. But what if he truly felt he needed children in his life to complete our family?

"I will, baby," I said. We said our goodnights and hung up the phone.

I lay in bed, now in both physical and emotional pain. I'd kept putting off my discussion with Luke about having children someday because I was terrified that it would mean the end of us. I wanted to cry just thinking about it. My sister-in-law was due to give birth any day now, and I feared it might get Luke thinking about the future.

I'd gone over and over the child issue a million times in my head. I kept trying to convince myself that perhaps there was some way I could handle having children if it meant keeping Luke in my life. No matter how many times I tried to talk myself into it, the idea of having kids filled me with dread. I didn't dislike children, I just did not want to have any of my own.

I loved my work life. It was who I was. It seemed no matter how involved a father might be in his child's life, it was almost always the mother who did most of the work. And it was usually the woman's career that suffered, even if she was lucky enough to afford childcare. I'd seen the scenario play out a million times during my career. Women who had to leave work early to tend to a sick child, or had to stop several times a day to pump breastmilk. And mothers in the workplace could be a serious liability to a company's bottom line.

It was a cold, cruel, and ruthlessly unfair fact of life.

Many times I had seen mothers at work struggle. Smart,

motivated, incredibly valuable women having to split their time between work and family life. I admired their incredible work ethic, but never wanted to be a working mother myself.

I thought about Luke and how passionate he was about his career. Would he be able to give it up to have a family?

Anger surged through me, because I knew he would never have to make such a sacrifice. He would be off working on a show, and I would have to be the one to leave work early. I shuddered to think of how quickly Hunter and Keith could swoop in and take over all my work, my projects.

No.

I did not want to have kids. There was nothing wrong with being a stay-at-home mother, a working mother, or anything in between. *But it was not the right path for me.*

Tears slipped down my face, and I moaned out loud from the searing pain in my belly and the agonized ache in my heart. I wondered if I could bear the pain of breaking up with Luke over this. God, how I would miss his humor and laughter and light.

I grabbed my Get Well bear and clutched him to my chest. I was in too much pain to think clearly, so I just held onto the bear and let my tears fall on him.

CHAPTER 14

On Sunday, I got back from my trip and collapsed from exhaustion. Things were crazy busy at work and though my boss had told me I could have the day off on Monday, I didn't want to take it off. I never missed work unless I absolutely had to. There was too much going on, and I didn't want to miss anything. I had enjoyed my time in Finland, but I was looking forward to getting back to my office.

Work wasn't the only thing I had missed. I hadn't seen Luke in far too long, and I could hardly wait to hold him in my arms again. I'd been tied up in back-to-back meetings all morning as my team caught me up on everything that had happened while I was away, and I filled them in on the details of my dealings with the Presko Group.

Early in the afternoon Luke and I tried to meet up in the stairwell, but there were too many people around. It was frustrating not being able to see him when we were right there in the same building. It was my own fault for being so stubborn. Hopefully the secrecy wouldn't have to last much longer. Once Mr. Bialystock announced who would receive the promotion, I could relax a bit. If I became Senior VP and once I got settled into the job, I could loosen my self-inflicted constraints and finally go public about my relationship with Luke. If I didn't get the job, I'd be devastated, but at least there would be no reason to keep things secret anymore.

On second thought, though … If I didn't get the promotion, wouldn't it mean I'd have to work extra hard to eventually advance in the company? Would it reflect badly on me and my future with Wicket Pro if they thought my personal life would interfere with my professional one?

I groaned irritably and shook my head as if to shake off my obsessive thoughts. It would be a relief once this damned promotion business was settled one way or another; the wait was killing me. I forced myself to focus on my work, starting with the emails that had piled up in my absence. It didn't take me long to get wrapped up in work, which was a perfect distraction from worrying about the Senior VP job.

My heart leapt when I heard a familiar voice from the hallway. *Luke.* I wanted nothing more than to sprint out of my office and run into his arms. I got up from my desk and peered out into the hall. Luke was talking to Roger.

"I thought you said the wiring issue was on twelve," Roger said.

"What are you, my mama checkin' up on me?" Luke said. "I'm on my way. Gimme a damn—"

Luke caught sight of me and stopped mid-sentence. We gazed longingly at each other from across the room. Luke was so close to me, and yet still so far away. There were so many people around, that we both knew it was impossible to reunite yet.

Roger chuckled, and I heard him mutter to Luke, "Let it go, man. She's waaaaay outta your league. It's not happening with her."

Luke tore his gaze away from me and turned to Roger. "Don't you have a fuse to fix?"

"What're you, my mama?" Roger teased.

"No, I'm your boss," Luke said sternly.

"Okay, okay. I'm on it, Twinkletoes." He punched Luke in the shoulder before finally walking away.

I was about to at least walk closer to him when Keith came out of nowhere. To my horror, he walked right up to Luke. It was bizarre to see the two men standing side by side. My secret lover and the guy who wouldn't stop hitting on me.

"I'm sorry, please forgive me. I'm blanking on your name," Keith said.

"Luke," he said with a smile.

"Luke, right! Sorry. The microwave in our break room is on the fritz. Food seems to get only partially heated up, and sometimes it won't heat at all. It's like the timer works and counts down but nothing's happening. Do you think you could send somebody to take a look?"

"Sure thing," Luke said. "We'll check it, but most likely we'll have to put in an order for a new one."

"Great, thanks!"

The moment we got rid of Keith, Hunter headed toward me. "Elyse, got a question for you."

Luke and I exchanged a brief, frustrated glance, both knowing it was hopeless.

I sat at home alone that night. Luke had rehearsal, and there was no way he could bail on it. Johnny was quite flexible when it came to Luke's hours at the foundation, and teachers were constantly filling in for each other due to auditions, shows, and other scheduling conflicts. Had he been scheduled to teach tonight, he could have easily begged off, but *Pirated* was an incredible opportunity for him, and he didn't want to do anything to mess it up.

I understood completely, the same way he understood my crazy work schedule. Still, I missed him like crazy and I was horny as all hell. Times like this, I used to call Brad to relieve my sexual tension. That was completely out of the question now, as I happened to have a boyfriend I adored.

I have a problem, I texted Luke. *I am in desperate need of sexual servicing. I miss you.*

He didn't answer right away, but I knew it was only because he was busy with rehearsal. I texted him again a little while later.

I need you, Luke.

Luke answered me back shortly after that.

Be over after rehearsal. Then he added, *As soon as humanly possible.*

I smiled.

It was nearly 11pm by the time Luke got to my place. I rushed to the door, dressed in a new lacy red negligee, when I heard him knock.

We drew in simultaneous deep gasps when we saw each other. Luke's eyes grew wide when he caught sight of me in my fancy lingerie, and he looked positively delectable in tight black jeans and a black button-down shirt. He still had on his stage makeup, complete with dark eyeliner, looking almost as sexy as he did in the emo-rock Andrew Jackson getup that was the subject of my favorite sexual fantasies.

"Good *God,* Elyse," Luke said as he looked me up and down. I bit my lip and smiled, pleased I had gotten the reaction I wanted.

"I missed you so much," I said, finally throwing my arms around him like I'd been dying to do since I got back home.

Luke ran his fingers through my hair as we shared a delicious reunion kiss. His mouth still on mine, he gently pushed me into my apartment and kicked the door closed behind him.

"I was going crazy without you, baby," Luke said before reaching under my legs and lifting me off my feet.

"Me too," I said breathlessly. I slipped my hand inside his shirt, moaning softly as I felt his hard, muscular chest. "I need you."

He carried me into the bedroom, threw me onto the bed, and climbed on top of me. Oh, how I'd waited for this moment since my plane landed in New York. It was already better than my numerous fantasies. Luke had a wild look of sexual desperation in his eyes. Those *eyes*. It was *such* a turn-on when he wore stage makeup. He looked so handsome, and it was a reminder that my lover was a fabulously talented actor. Hell, it almost felt like I was being ravished by a real pirate. Having sex with an actor involved lots of role playing, even if Luke wasn't aware of it.

"Elyse, oh God, Elyse," Luke said as he went to work pulling off my negligee. I fumbled desperately with his belt buckle, trying to free him from his clothing as quickly as possible.

The instant we were both naked, Luke plunged right into me. I threw my head back and screamed out loud. Not only had it been two weeks since I'd had sex, but I'd spent the last several hours fantasizing about being with him, and I felt ready to explode. The burst of sheer ecstasy when Luke rammed into me was even more powerful than I had imagined.

I opened my legs wider so he could penetrate me as deeply as possible. He made deliciously sexual noises, grunting and groaning as he pounded me harder and harder. The bed itself made sensual sounds, the headboard banging into the wall, the box spring squeaking with the motion of our frenetic lovemaking. The delightful tingling sensation between my legs was so intense that this was already the most pleasurable sexual experience of my life. And I hadn't even *come* yet.

Just as I was inwardly marveling at Luke's stamina, he slowed down a bit. Breathlessly, he said, "I gotta chill out a bit, or I'm not gonna make it."

Equally breathless, I smiled and ran my fingers through his hair. "I know. It's been a while for both of us. It's okay, baby." The way Luke had pounded me, it wouldn't have taken me much longer to reach orgasm, but it still might take me longer than him. Maybe a tad too long.

"No, it's not okay. I gotta take care of you, Elyse. I promised to sexually service you," Luke said, with a sexy arched eyebrow. A fresh wave of arousal rippled through me. I didn't know what it was about the black eyeliner, but it pushed my libido into overdrive.

Luke pulled out of me. Before I could protest, his head was between my legs, his warm tongue stroking my most sensitive spot. The pleasure was so sharp and intense, I couldn't even scream.

"Oh, Luke. Luke, oh Luke," I moaned as I placed my hands on his head. I closed my eyes and surrendered to the sheer ecstasy of the movement of his head, matching the waves of tingling bliss. "Luke, Luke, oh my darling, Luke ..."

My breath came in gasps as I felt a powerful climax build inside me. A forceful explosion of ultimate pleasure suddenly relieved two weeks' worth of sexual frustration.

I let out a long cry of release as Luke gave me an orgasm that rocked me to my very core. As the waves of pleasure finally began to subside, I gently pushed his head away.

Luke climbed back up to face me. I gazed weakly into his eyes, feeling more satisfied than I ever had felt in my life. "Now, *that* was the sexual servicing I desperately needed.

Come to me, baby," I said, opening my legs for him. "I need you to feel as amazing as I do right now."

Luke slid his swollen cock back inside me. My vagina still tingled delightfully with the aftershocks from my powerful orgasm, and his hard shaft gliding in and out of me felt *wonderful.* He quickly picked up speed, and I knew his need must be desperate by now. We resumed the perfect rhythm as before, Luke groaning, the bed squeaking. It was fascinating to watch his handsome face contorted with pleasure as his orgasm began.

"Elyse," he groaned. *"Elyse,"* was all he could say as he closed his eyes and forcefully came inside me. Again, I imagined he was a sexy pirate having his way with me. It was exciting and fun.

When he opened his sweet brown eyes he was no pirate. He was Luke Rannells, the man I adored with all my heart. He caught his breath for a moment, and then said, "I'm so glad you're home, Elyse."

I smiled up at him and gently ran my fingers through his hair. Even though he said it right after having an orgasm, the soft way he spoke made me know in my heart it wasn't just the sex he had missed.

We lay there for a while, tired and happy.

"Have I ever told you how sexy you look in your stage makeup?" I asked him.

"Really? I thought it might look weird. People don't realize how heavy it is until they see you up close. I meant to wash it off, but I was in too much of a rush to come see you."

I traced his face with my finger, then gently touched the spot above his left eye. "I love it. Especially the eyeliner. You wanna know what my absolute favorite sexual fantasy is?"

Luke's eyes opened wide. "Of course I want to know!"

"It's you ..." I began, "dressed up as Andrew Jackson. Well, not because you're being Andrew Jackson. You know, the whole murdering Indians thing is hardly a turn-on. I mean you dressed like you were in those pictures you showed me. In those tight black jeans, your hair all dark and wild, and the black eyeliner around your eyes."

Luke stared at me, fascinated.

I drew in a breath, getting aroused all over again just thinking about it. "My fantasy is you, dressed like that, just fucking me hard against the wall."

"*Damn*," he said, looking enthralled with the idea. "You've put a lot of thought into this, haven't you?"

"Ever since you first showed me those pictures," I said, then murmured in his ear. "That image helped me to satisfy own needs while I was in Finland."

"*Daaaamn*," he said again. "That is good to know."

I smiled and snuggled up close to him. "I missed you like crazy. And not just your beautiful body."

We lay there, holding each other tight. It was the perfect moment.

Until I heard snoring.

I was irritated at first. We could finally spend time together, and he fell asleep? I sat up to look at him. He made a muffled, sleepy sound and started snoring again.

I laughed softly. I couldn't help it. Luke looked utterly adorable. All worn out, black eyeliner smearing. I knew he hadn't meant to fall asleep right after being intimate with me. But he'd been working an awful lot lately, what with putting in a full day at his day job and then going to rehearsal.

Still keyed up from having terrific sex, I wasn't ready to go to sleep yet. I put the TV on low for a while and let Luke rest. He woke up a little while later, looking quite disoriented.

"You fell asleep," I told him with a smirk.

"I did?" he asked groggily, rubbing his eyes and smearing his makeup even worse. "Shit. Oh, shit, Elyse. I'm so sorry."

Luke sat up and looked into my eyes, utterly repentant. Even if I'd been angry at him, it would have been impossible to stay mad when he looked at me like that.

"It's okay, Luke. Really. I'm not mad," I told him, stroking his cheek tenderly. "You're working yourself too hard. You're exhausted, honey."

Luke nodded. Then he said, "I love you, Elyse."

I smiled. It was easy for me to say it back.

"I love you too, Geek. Now let's get some rest. You go get washed up. You can use my cold cream."

Luke chuckled, glancing at his fingers, black from smearing his makeup.

"Brush your teeth and all that, and then come back and hold me. That's all I need from you."

"Sounds perfect," he said. "I love you so much, Elyse. So very much."

CHAPTER 15

*M*y sister-in-law gave birth to my nephew, Zach, just a few days after my return from Finland. I'd been excited ever since my brother had announced they were expecting. I always knew Leo would be a terrific dad, and this was the first grandchild for my parents. It was an exciting time for all of us, but I was a nervous wreck as Luke and I drove over to my brother's house to meet the new arrival.

I was terrified that being around a newborn would bring up questions I wasn't sure I wanted the answers to.

"You okay?" Luke asked. I'd been uncharacteristically quiet on the drive to the suburbs of New Jersey. "Are you nervous about me meeting your family?"

I glanced over at him, and he looked quite concerned.

"No, of course I'm not! Luke, they're gonna love you. No question about that," I said with a smile.

Everyone in my family had a terrific sense of humor, and I was sure they would get a big kick out of Luke's goofy manner. It was extremely rare for me to bring a man home to meet my family, so they knew this was a big deal.

"Cool. I'm sure I'm gonna love them, too," Luke said, sounding relieved. "While we have time here in the car, I need to ask you something."

"Of course I'll marry you, Luke," I said, responding the same way he had on our first date.

"Hmm," Luke said with a sly smile and an arched eyebrow. He seemed fond of the idea of marrying me, which both thrilled and scared me. I loved the idea of being his wife. I only hoped he would still want to be my husband once he found out I didn't want to bear his children. "Well, there is going to be a wedding in our future, just not ours. Not yet, anyway."

Luke scrutinized me for my reaction to his words, and I grinned at him. We were clearly on the same page as far as the marriage issue went. He grinned back, pleased with my reaction.

"Johnny wants us to help him propose to Rosemary."

I squealed with excitement, making Luke laugh. "Oh, he's planning something grand and wonderful, isn't he?"

"Yup."

"I guess he's pretty sure she'll say yes."

"Oh, she'll definitely say yes," Luke said. "And she's gonna cry."

I giggled. "Yes. Yes, she will." I'd been around Rosemary enough to know she always teared up when she was feeling emotional. "Of course I'd be happy to help."

"Johnny's still working it all out, but he plans to get the whole proposal on tape for her for a keepsake."

"That won't upset her, will it? I mean, you told me how that famous video bothers her."

"This video will be just for her to have, not for the public. Besides, it's not the video itself that really bothers Rosemary. She just doesn't want to only be known for having a famous boyfriend."

"And I'm sure she won't want to just be known as Mrs. Johnny Creel."

"Right. But she loves him, and I know she wants to marry him. She has a pretty good sense of humor about the video. She always says she's grateful that it shows off her singing. I mean, yeah, the video went viral because Johnny's famous, but she did get some notoriety in her own right for being a phenomenal singer. Trust me. Johnny knows her well enough to know she will love this proposal."

"Okay, what can we do to help, besides just being there?" I asked.

"If ... hopefully, *when* she says yes, and after she stops crying ..."

"Right," I said with a laugh.

Luke detailed Johnny's plan, which involved music of course, and it sounded terrific. Original and heartfelt and creative. Oh, yes. Rosemary would cry.

"I'm so excited for them both. This will be so much fun!"

"You're cool, Elyse. You're just *cool*," Luke said with a happy grin. I knew exactly how he was feeling. It was the same way I felt when I listened to his rendition of "Finland/Fisch Schlapping Dance," when I left for my trip. It was wonderful having a lover who supported your dreams unconditionally.

"Is David going to sing with us?" I asked, having trouble imagining such a thing.

"Oh, hell no. Susie talked to him about it, but it's too much out of his comfort zone. We want this to be fun for everybody. Instead, he's going to be the one to record it for Rosemary. That way she can have it to show to her grandkids someday."

My heart ached at the mere mention of grandchildren. That was something more Luke would be deprived of if he married me and remained childless. It was so easy to picture

Luke as a goofy grandpa, teasing his grandchildren and playing silly games with them.

We arrived at my brother's house in New Jersey, and I found myself getting excited all over again at meeting my brand-new nephew.

I was still terrified that Luke might bring up the subject of having children, so I did my best to hide my apprehension. After keeping my relationship with him secret at work, the last thing I wanted was for him to think I was nervous about him meeting my family. Quite the contrary; I was looking forward to showing off my handsome and insanely talented boyfriend.

My brother answered the door, proudly holding his newborn baby in his arms.

"Oh my God, isn't he precious?" I exclaimed, but in a whisper because Zach was sleeping.

"He sure is," Luke said. I watched him as he gazed upon the baby's sweet, sleeping form. Luke seemed enthralled, which made my stomach hurt.

Leo nodded. "I'd shake your hand, but ..." He glanced down at his tiny son.

"Excuses, excuses," Luke muttered, and Leo chuckled.

"Come on in," my brother said as he led us to the living room.

Lauren got up from the couch and greeted me with a warm hug. "Good to see you!"

"You too! He's so beautiful, Lauren. Congratulations."

"Thanks," she said with a proud, happy smile. "And you must be Luke."

Luke offered his hand. "And you must be exhausted."

Lauren laughed as she shook Luke's hand. "Yes, I most certainly am."

"I'm hardly an expert, but everybody says the first three months are the hardest," Luke said reassuringly. "I've got two nieces. Both were kinda colicky and nuts there for a while, but they settled down eventually."

"Zach's not too bad, I guess. No colic, but he's not a great sleeper." Lauren glanced at the baby. "Well, not at night, anyway."

It was fairly warm in the room, so Leo took the baby's blanket off him.

"Oh, come *on*," Luke said. "That's just child abuse right there." He shook his head with disgust.

Lauren laughed, getting Luke's joke before the rest of us did. I glanced at Zach and saw he was wearing the New York Yankees onesie I had bought him.

"Yeah, Elyse warned me she's dating a Mets fan," Leo said grimly.

"He's a good guy otherwise. I swear," I insisted.

"If you say so," Leo said. "Do you want to hold him, Elyse?"

"Sure," I said. I wiped my hands with some of the hand sanitizer from the coffee table and then got settled on the couch. Leo carefully placed the baby in my arms. I gazed down at the sweet little guy.

"I'm so glad you're finally here," I said to my nephew. "We've been waiting to meet you."

Zach drew in a deep breath and let out a long sigh. I smiled down at him, then looked up at Leo.

"I can't believe my bratty little brother is a *father*."

"Frightening, isn't it?" Leo said, shaking his head like he couldn't quite believe it himself.

"You guys did good," I said to Leo and Lauren. I looked over at Luke, who was smiling fondly at me holding the baby. I would have given anything in the world to know what was going through his mind. Was he imagining what it would be like to have a child with me?

I marveled at how pink and perfect the baby was. Zach

had the sweetest little nose, and tiny, perfect fingers. It was hard to believe I was holding a brand-new human being in my arms. Times like these, women usually joked about hearing their biological clocks ticking. I still didn't feel that way, not even when holding this precious little miracle in my arms. I loved little Zach already, and imagining hearing his little voice calling me "Aunt Elyse" made me want to tear up with joy. And yet, the mere idea of being stuck at home, dealing with a baby's constant needs instead of being at my exciting workplace filled me with dread.

My God, I would be miserable as a mother. No matter how much I tried to talk myself into it for Luke's sake, I knew it would be a mistake for me to have a child. The harsh truth was that I already knew the child issue was a deal breaker. For *me*.

I held the sleeping baby until he woke up and started to cry.

"Aww, you broke him," Luke told me.

Lauren laughed. "Not at all. He slept for quite a while, and he must be really hungry."

"I'll get him," Leo said and then gently took Zach from me and gave him to Lauren so she could nurse him. I watched as my goofy little brother, the one who had turned farting into an Olympic sport while we were growing up, carefully placed a soft blanket over his wife's shoulder so she could breastfeed comfortably. I was so proud of him.

The four of us shared polite conversation for a while, talking about baby stuff, work stuff, Luke's theater projects, and the like. It was nice spending time with my brother, and I was happy to have at least some of my family meet Luke. I knew my mother would demand a full report from Leo about what he thought of my boyfriend.

"Would you like to hold him, Luke?" Lauren asked once she'd finished feeding Zach. I swallowed hard, as if the question was some kind of litmus test. I held my breath, waiting for Luke's answer.

"Sure," Luke said with a smile. He rinsed his hands with hand sanitizer and accepted the baby from Lauren.

I stared at Luke, hoping to find he was uncomfortable with holding the baby.

The baby looked so tiny in his arms, and he cradled the child like a pro.

"Hey, little man," Luke said to the baby, who was now wide awake and gazing up at him with big blue eyes.

"You're pretty good at this, dude," Leo observed, and I wished I could have told him to shut up.

"My nieces are three and five now, but I remember when they were this tiny."

"He really is good with the baby," Lauren said, giving me a knowing look.

"Yes, he certainly is," I said, trying to ignore the searing pain in my heart. In that moment, I knew for certain I would have to let Luke go if he wanted to raise a family. There was no way I could deprive him of experiencing fatherhood if it was what he wanted.

I drew in a deep breath and forced myself to live in the moment. I wanted to enjoy every moment I had with Luke while I still could.

CHAPTER 16

*A*s I had promised Luke, I scheduled an appointment with my gynecologist. I was long overdue for a doctor visit anyway. Dr. Pratter ordered some tests after we spoke on the phone, so I had gone in for an ultrasound and some blood work about a week ago. At first, my only concern was making the pain go away. After having those tests, I started getting scared that something might be wrong with me. What if it was cervical or ovarian cancer or something?

Today, I would get the results.

Dr. Pratter came into the examination room and smiled at me, which helped me breathe a little better. You don't smile at somebody if you're about to give them horrifying news.

"Okay, Ms. Pippin. I've got the results from your ultrasound, and we've got some important things to discuss here."

"Okay," I said nervously.

In his late fifties or so, Dr. Pratter was a friendly man with a graying mustache and beard. He sat down on the stool next to me so we could talk.

"Your pelvic exam and ultrasound confirmed that you have a fairly advanced case of endometriosis."

I nodded, taking in his words. I'd heard of the disease but didn't know much about it. I *did* know it wasn't cancer. *Thank God.*

"Endometriosis means the tissue that belongs inside the lining of your uterus starts to grow outside of it. It can get wrapped around your ovaries, fallopian tubes, and around the lining of your pelvis, which is what has happened in your case." The doctor's eyes softened as he looked at me. "You must be having terrible pain when you menstruate."

"I am."

"I know we've got you on some pain meds, but I'm going to give you something stronger. It should hopefully help you feel a little better, in the short term at least."

"Oh, that would be wonderful. Thank you so much."

Dr. Pratter scribbled out a prescription and handed it to me. "Again, that's the short-term fix. We need to talk about the long term."

"Are we talking surgery?"

He nodded. "Yes. Eventually you will likely need surgery." Dr. Pratter hesitated for a moment. "This surgery, not right away mind you, but it will most likely involve getting a hysterectomy."

Dr. Pratter eyed me carefully, probably afraid I'd break down into hysterics. I simply nodded, absorbing his words.

"So, again, it wouldn't be right away, but relatively soon. I'm going to put this bluntly. If you plan on having children, you're looking at sooner rather than later, you understand?"

I nodded again.

"And you should know that endometriosis, especially a case as severe as yours, can make it difficult to become pregnant. Again, trying to get pregnant sooner rather than later increases your odds of being a mom before..."

"Before it's too late," I said.

"Yes," Dr. Pratter said, smiling sadly.

I drew in a breath and let it out. I thought about telling Dr. Pratter it was okay. That he needn't look so sad because I wasn't planning on having children anyway. I couldn't bring myself to talk about it. It hurt too much, considering everything I had to lose.

"I know you have a lot to think about. Do you have any questions I can answer for you?"

Dr. Pratter was so sweet and caring, it made me want to cry.

"No, I don't think so. Not at the moment."

I have lots of questions you can't possibly answer, Dr. Pratter.

"Okay. Well, give the new medicine a try the next time you have your cycle, and please don't hesitate to give me a call with any concerns, okay?"

"I will. Thank you."

My head was spinning. Possible infertility. Surgery. It was hard to process everything.

Sitting in New York City traffic on the way back to my apartment gave me lots of time to think things over. What if all this was good news? Surgery would make my pain go away, and then I would have an easy out on the child issue. What if I just told Luke I was infertile, or that I needed to have the surgery right away?

Luke loved me. He might break up with me if I told him I never wanted to have children.

But he would never leave me if I *couldn't* have children for medical reasons.

* * *

I TOOK a drink of ice-cold water to force myself to stay awake. I was working late—very late—in the office. It was nearly midnight, and I still wasn't finished my work. I was finalizing a presentation on virtual networking for a large company in Japan. As with the Finland deal, Hunter, Keith, and I would all develop our own presentations and whoever came up with the best one would make the trip to visit the company. I was out of my mind with excitement about the idea of traveling to Japan, so it was critical that my presentation be perfect. The Presko Group had been impressed with my hyperconvergence presentation and had recently signed a lucrative deal with Wicket Pro because of it. If I nailed the Japanese presentation, the Senior VP job was practically in the bag. To my relief, Mr. Bialystock had promised to decide about the job over the next week or so. The wait would soon be over.

I drew in a deep, exhausted breath. It was like my entire life was at a crossroads. The stress of the job was bad enough, but the crushing anxiety of the whole child issue with Luke was far worse. I felt like the next week would determine the course of both my professional and personal lives forever. Once the promotion issue was settled one way or another, I knew it would be time to have The Talk with Luke. We'd already hinted and joked about marriage, but we both knew we weren't kidding around. We were crazy in love and wanted to spend the rest of our lives together. We couldn't possibly decide about marriage until we'd talked about having kids. I owed it to Luke to have a conversation about the vital issue.

An *honest* conversation.

After obsessing about it for days, I knew there was no way in hell I could ever lie to Luke about my health issues. Telling him I couldn't get pregnant because of my endometriosis, guilting him into staying with me and robbing him of a chance to be a dad would be a horrible thing to do. Besides, he might suggest adoption or a surrogate or—

I let out a frustrated breath, knowing it was useless to speculate. I'd talk to Luke and have my answers soon enough. First things first. Finish the Japanese presentation.

My phone buzzed with yet another text from Luke. He was up late worrying about me. He wasn't crazy about me being in this huge office building all alone late at night, and he kept telling me to go home and get some rest. I kept saying I would leave soon, and yet the hours continued to pass.

Are you STILL at work??

I glanced at the clock. It was nearly 2am.

Yes. I texted back.

Good.

I stared at the phone, trying to make sense of his meaning. Luke had been begging me to go home for hours. So why would ...

I gasped when a dark figure suddenly appeared at the door. In my exhausted, bleary-eyed state it took me several seconds to recognize him. It was Luke.

Dressed as emo punk-rock Andrew Jackson, complete with tight black jeans and the sexy black eyeliner that made me crazy with desire.

I put my hand on my heart, still trying to recover from my initial fright.

"Luke, what the hell?"

Luke shot me a grin that was part Luke Rannells and part punk rock star. It was so damned hot.

"I figured maybe this would get you to finally leave work."

I took my time looking him up and down. Dressed like this, Luke was my hottest sexual fantasy come to life. I could hardly believe my eyes. I was wide awake now. In my mind, he was already fucking me hard against the wall with only his pants unzipped and the rest of him still in that scorching hot rock-star getup.

"If that doesn't make me quit working, nothing will." To hell with the Japanese presentation. I was about two seconds away from sweeping my desk clean and letting him take me right then and there.

"Cool," Luke said with a sexy smile, still in character.

I stood up. The presentation was ninety-nine-percent done anyway. The rest could wait until Monday morning. I went over to Luke and threw my arms around him.

"Thank you for coming all the way down here."

Luke sexily narrowed his eyes. "I came here because I know you need me." He spoke forcefully and in character. It was *so hot.*

"Yes, I certainly do need you," I said huskily, looking up into his eyes.

Luke grabbed the collar of my blouse and pulled me up toward him roughly, then kissed me with raw passion and desire. He pushed me against the wall, and I felt like I would lose my mind if he didn't get inside me immediately. The moment he stepped into the doorway I had planned to go home with him right away. But what if we didn't have to go home? We couldn't do this in my office ... could we?

"Oh, baby," I moaned, slipping my hand inside his black shirt to feel those hard muscles. Luke pinned me harder against the wall, which elicited another moan from me.

"There's no one else in the building, you know," Luke said, his eyes full of searing desire. He almost seemed dangerous in that moment. It was a safe, exciting kind of danger, since I knew he was a terrific actor.

"Are you sure?" I asked.

Luke nodded, and I saw a hint of gentleness in his eyes, letting me know this was okay.

"I need you so bad," I said sensually. "I've been working so much, and I'm so *tense.*"

Luke gripped me roughly by the shoulders. He fixed his

steely glare on me. "That's why I'm here. To relieve all your tension."

I gasped. Luke even *sounded* different. His look and sound and feel, the way he touched me. He was deeply in character as a punk rock star, about to give one of his groupies the ride of her life.

Without taking his eyes off mine, he began unbuttoning my blouse. Slowly, methodically, one agonizing button at a time. I suddenly felt shy in the most deliciously sensual way, as if this achingly gorgeous man was about to see my naked body for the first time. He finally reached the last button and then jerked off my blouse, making me gasp again. After expertly unclasping my bra, he whipped it off me with a snap.

Luke took a step back, lowering his eyes to my naked breasts. I felt completely and utterly exposed, and aroused beyond belief. He pressed his huge hands on my breasts, squeezing them tight.

"Hmmm," he said with approval. Luke dropped his hands down to my skirt, yanking it down with my pantyhose and underwear with one quick move.

Luke's breath visibly caught in his throat, and it was thrilling to see him drop the smooth act if only for an instant. *Oh, yes. He's every bit as turned on as I am.* He stared deeply into my eyes and slowly began unzipping his pants.

"Oh, God," I whispered with breathless anticipation.

He arched an eyebrow and nodded slightly, as if telling me to get ready. He pulled his pants down just enough to free his cock. I loved that he remembered exactly how I had described my fantasy; him fully dressed as he fucked me. His brown eyes still boring into mine, he slipped his right hand under my knee and pulled up my leg, spreading me open wide.

Luke cockily narrowed his eyes and then slammed

into me.

I threw my head back against the wall and screamed out loud. I hoped to God there was nobody in the building, because my cry of passion rang out loud and clear.

Luke rammed his cock in and out of me, driving me half-insane with pleasure. I was so turned on, I could hardly see straight. The pleasure between my legs was so intense, it nearly hurt.

"Oh, God, oh God," I wailed as emo-Luke fucked me hard against the wall, making my wildest sexual fantasy come true. I'd lost count of how many times I had touched myself in Finland while conjuring this very image. This mind-blowing, exhilarating sexual experience that *was actually happening.*

"Look at me," Luke growled.

I opened my eyes and was instantly grateful that I had. Luke's sneer was fierce, arousing me even more. He looked like a cocky rock star, pleased with his own sexual prowess, knowing he was giving a horny groupie what she needed.

"You like that, don't you?" Luke asked with another cocky sneer, pounding me even harder against the wall.

"Yes, oh God, yes," I cried. As the agonizingly pleasurable sensations grew more intense between my legs, I knew the experience couldn't possibly last much longer. I took a quick glance around my office, wanting to remember every second of this sexual encounter. The diplomas and awards on my office wall were shaking with the force of Luke's thrusts, in rhythm with our frantic sexual activity.

At last I looked back at Luke, his eyes still intently on me.

"This is it baby," he told me with another cocky sneer. "I'm gonna give you everything you need, girl."

All I could do was moan louder when Luke shifted his body ever so slightly. He knew the exact spot to pound hard, to get me to come.

I started screaming the moment my orgasm began and didn't stop until I went limp from the force of my climax. My breath came in heavy gasps as I tried to recover my sanity.

Luke pressed his hands against the wall and pumped in and out of me, faster and faster, until he finally groaned with his own release. The two of us panted for a moment. He grabbed my face and kissed me once more with great force. Then he pulled out of me and zipped up his pants. He took a step back and looked me up and down.

"You can get dressed now," Luke said, still in rock-star mode.

I put my underwear and blouse and skirt back on while he watched. When I glanced back up at his face, his lips curled into a sexy sneer again. He looked exactly the way he had in my favorite picture of him from *Bloody Bloody Andrew Jackson*. Hot. So, so, hot.

Luke walked over to my desk and plopped into my office chair. He grinned widely and opened his arms for me. The bad boy rock star was gone, and I had my sweet, charming Luke again.

I sat in his lap and he enveloped me in his huge arms, making me feel warm and cherished. *Loved.* Sexual role playing was a lot of fun, but in the end, it was the real Luke I wanted.

I lay back in his arms and gazed up at him. "Oh, Luke, that was *so* exciting."

He smiled at me. "Was it everything you hoped it would be?"

"Yes, God yes. Boy, it's fun dating an actor," I said biting my lip, relishing the delicious tingling between my legs.

"I can be anybody you want, baby," he told me as he stroked me.

"Hmmm, that is good to know." I thought of all the fun we

could have in the bedroom playing different roles. "Still, my favorite lover is Luke Rannells."

He bent and kissed me gently, and I wrapped my arms around his neck. I loved that he could be wild and daring during sex, but tender and sweet afterward. Perfect. He was simply perfect.

"So, now I have a story to tell," I said.

"What do you mean?" Luke asked as he looked into my eyes, still stroking my hair.

"Well, Susie and Rosemary and I got to talking not too long ago, after having lots of wine and beer ..."

Luke chuckled softly, nodding.

"And we were talking about the most exciting sex we'd ever had. Rosemary told me about a time she and Johnny had sex in the middle of the stage back in D.C. And Susie and David did it in his office here in New York."

"He tied her up with his own neckties," Luke said, and I could see the amusement in his eyes.

"Yeah, he did," I said with a laugh. "And now I have an *amazing* sex story to tell them. I mean, if it's okay with you."

"Are you kidding? Rent a billboard."

I laughed again, enjoying the prideful look in his eyes. Luke *should* be proud after what he had just done to me.

We rested in my chair for a while, enjoying being together. I felt safe and warm and cherished lying in Luke's arms.

Luke tenderly stroked my cheek. "Elyse, you know I want you to get this promotion as much as you do. But promise me once you get it, you'll slow down a little. Just a little. I know you're a workaholic, and that's okay. But I don't want you pushing yourself too hard and ruining your health. No job is worth that."

"I know," I said, swallowing hard, thinking of my recent doctor visit.

LINDA FAUSNET

"You need to take care of yourself, okay?" Luke said, sounding worried. "I want you around for a long, long time."

I nodded. "I'll take it easy soon. I promise. We're supposed to find out about the job in a week or so."

Luke bent and kissed me again. I gazed into his sweet brown eyes, marveling at how different he was from the character he had been moments ago.

"Ready to go home?" he asked.

"Yes."

I got up from the chair and held out my hand to help him stand. Luke towered over me when he stood.

"Thank you for tonight," I whispered to him.

Luke caressed my cheek. "Any time, my love. Any time."

I gathered up my belongings and was soon ready to go. Luke put a protective hand on my back as he led me out the door.

I let out a deep, happy sigh. Exhausted, I was more than ready to go home and fall asleep in Luke's arms.

CHAPTER 17

*R*oger and Manny came busting into my office not twenty minutes after I arrived on Monday morning. Manny shut the door behind him, which I figured was not a good sign.

They both stared at me for a moment.

"What's with you two idiots?"

"You really weren't gonna tell us?" Roger asked, wide-eyed.

"Tell you what?" I asked, getting a little annoyed. I was busy and not in the mood for guessing games.

"That you're screwing Elyse Pippin!" Roger said.

"What?" I asked as a sick feeling settled the pit of my stomach. "What are you talking about?"

Deny it, deny it, deny it, I told myself. At least until Elyse gets her promotion, she really didn't need anybody knowing about our relationship. I wondered who she might have told that couldn't keep a secret.

"We're talking about how you *fucked* her in her office!" Manny practically yelled.

It took me several seconds to fully process what he was saying. No. It couldn't be. No.

No ...

"H—how did you know about that?" I asked, terrified to know the answer. Somebody must have been in the building. Dear God, please don't let it have been one of her co-workers. If it was one of the cleaning people or one of my maintenance guys, I could probably shut them up before they told anybody else.

Manny and Roger just chuckled.

"*How did you know?*" I roared, jumping up from my desk. Both men took a step back. They'd known me for years, but I don't think they'd ever heard me yell before. I was a theater guy, and I knew how to project my voice when needed.

Manny looked almost afraid to speak. Finally, he said, "From the video, man."

"Video," I said weakly. "What...video?"

"Charlie over in security was skimming over the security tapes from the weekend, and he saw it. Sent the whole thing to me on my cell phone, see?" Manny said. He held up his phone, and I caught a glimpse of myself banging Elyse against the wall in her office. I was fully clothed, but her breasts were on full display.

Feeling like I was about to throw up, I shoved the phone away, as if I could make the video disappear.

"Manny, you can't show this video to *anybody*, you hear me?" I pleaded.

He didn't say anything, but he looked guilty.

"You already did."

"Well, yeah. Just to a couple of guys, you know. Like him, of course," Manny nodded toward Roger. I let out a breath. Okay, so maybe nobody really knew about this yet. I could still stop this thing from spreading like a horrible disease throughout the building.

"I know Charlie showed some people," Roger hesitantly volunteered. I whipped my head to look at him and he took a step back. They both stared at me like I had lost my mind.

"Dude, you're like the hero of the office. What's the big deal?" Manny asked.

"*Elyse*," I told him. "Elyse is the big deal. Did you watch the whole video?"

"Well, yeah. I mean we stopped watching when she put her clothes back on."

The thought that Manny and Roger had seen Elyse naked made my stomach hurt. It wasn't their fault, but it was a horrific violation of her privacy.

"Watch the rest," I said as I stormed past them. Seeing the way I had held Elyse in my arms for a long time after we had sex would at least make them understand that I had real feelings for her. That this wasn't just some cheap office fling, and it had nothing to do with our idiotic bet. Not that it mattered what they thought, anyway. All that mattered was that nobody else saw the video.

And that Elyse never, ever found out it existed.

I hated keeping secrets from her, but the humiliation would be too much for her. No. I had to protect her from this.

I sprinted out of my office to find Charlie.

I burst into his office to find him nonchalantly munching on a donut. He was a tall, rather heavyset guy with a beard and mustache. Charlie was a good guy. We'd always had each other's backs around here, and I knew I could count on him.

He grinned widely when he saw me. "Well, well, well ..."

I was in no mood to be praised for my sexual escapades.

"Charlie, you gotta stop showing people the video."

He picked up his cell phone, and I fought the urge to close my eyes. I didn't even want to think about how much of Elyse's body he had seen.

169

"Are you kidding? I should charge people to see this!"

"I mean it, Charlie. *Do not show anyone this video*, do you hear me?"

"Sorry, man. I didn't think you'd be upset. It was pretty impressive. I mean, bravo man. You clearly know your way around a woman."

I felt the tiniest prickle of pride, and I hated myself for it. Anyone who had seen the video knew I made Elyse come and come *hard*.

Jesus, what in the fuck was wrong with me?

"Please, Charlie. I am begging you not to show it to anyone."

"Okay, okay. I promise," Charlie said, looking at me curiously. He could see the desperation in my eyes. "Can I ask why?"

"Because it would hurt her very, very badly."

His expression softened, and he nodded. It had seemed like all fun and games to him until now, but he could see how much pain this could cause Elyse.

"Please, Charlie. She doesn't deserve this."

"I hear ya, man. You can count on me. I won't tell anybody else."

I let out a deep breath. "Thank God. As long as nobody up at Wicket Pro finds out."

Charlie's eyes opened wide. "Uh … um … well …"

A fresh wave of nausea and dread washed over me.

"Please, please, please tell me you didn't. Please tell me you didn't tell any of her co-workers."

"Well, it's just that my cousin works up there. That's how I got this job."

"Who's your cousin?"

"Hunter Higgins."

I closed my eyes, feeling like all the air had been sucked out of my body.

CHAPTER 18

*H*unter was eying me strangely as I filled my water bottle in the break room.

"What?" I asked him.

"Nothing. Did you have a good weekend?" he asked. I could see amusement in his eyes. It was a tad disconcerting, but I didn't have time to ponder what he was up to. "It was busy. Had to work late to put the finishing touches on the Japanese presentation."

Hunter chuckled for some reason.

"How was your weekend?" I asked, before taking a sip of water.

"Uneventful. I didn't do anything exciting." He raised an eyebrow.

I nearly ran into Mr. Bialystock in the hallway in my rush to get back to work.

"Oh, sorry! Almost drenched you," I said, clutching my water bottle to my chest.

"Uh … uh … That's okay," my boss stammered. I could have sworn I saw him blush. What was with everybody today?

"Will you, uh, be ready for the presentation at eleven this morning?" Mr. Bialystock asked, avoiding eye contact.

"Absolutely. I put in a lot of extra hours this weekend, and I think you'll be happy with what I came up with."

His blush deepened. Seriously, what the hell?

"Okay, sounds good. See you at the meeting." He rushed off down the hall, still not really looking at me.

I was starting to wonder if something was wrong.

Oh, no.

Between Hunter's cockiness and Mr. Bialystock's refusal to meet my gaze, I began to wonder if Hunter had already gotten the promotion, and my boss didn't know how to tell me.

Until I knew anything for sure, the job was still up for grabs. I got down to work, reviewing my presentation to make sure it was perfect. I was so engrossed in my work, I didn't notice Keith in the doorway at first.

I gasped when I finally saw him standing there.

"Sorry, Elyse. I didn't mean to scare you."

There was a deep sadness in Keith's eyes I had never seen before.

"Hey, are you okay?" I asked softly. He looked so down, I was afraid he was going to tell me someone close to him had died.

"Yeah. Can I talk to you for a minute?"

"Of course," I said, still worried about him. He might be my competition for the job, but he was still a good friend. "What's up?"

Keith closed my office door behind him and sat across from me.

"Elyse, do you know about ... Are you aware there's ..." Keith began as he studied my face.

I watched his sad expression, waiting for him to say whatever was on his mind.

"Look, Elyse, I don't want to get into your personal business here," he said nervously, running his hand through his jet-black hair.

My heart sank. I hoped he wasn't going to ask me out again. He was so sweet, and I couldn't bear the idea of hurting him.

"But you should know there's a ... a ... rumor going around about you."

"What?" I asked. I couldn't begin to imagine what it could be. I was so guarded about my personal life.

"Some asshole made a bet with his friends that he could ..." Keith's face colored slightly. "That he could sleep with you. He bet money and everything."

"Why would anybody do that?"

"I don't know," he said, and I could hear the anger in his voice. "You deserve so much better than that, Elyse. I wanted you to know before you got any more involved ... I—I—I mean before you get involved with this guy."

"Who is he?"

"The head of maintenance," Keith said, watching my expression carefully. "Luke Rannells."

"What?" I asked, my voice barely a whisper.

ELYSE BURST INTO MY OFFICE. I could see the pain in her beautiful blue eyes.

Oh God. It's too late. She knows.

"Did you make a bet you could get me to sleep with you?" she asked, her eyes wide.

I blinked, letting her words sink in for a moment. Was that the only thing she knew about?

"Well ... Well—" I stammered, totally unprepared for her question.

"You did, didn't you?" she said, her eyes pleading with me to tell her she was wrong. I briefly considered lying to her, but I knew it was a bad idea. I didn't know how she found out about the bet. Had Roger or Manny told her? It didn't matter. Most of my maintenance guys were aware of it, and any one of them might confirm it if Elyse asked. Besides, I had hurt Elyse enough. Lying to her would make everything worse.

"I did. I admit it. And it was a totally stupid thing to do. But that was before—"

"Is that why you asked me out in first place?"

"No—no. Not exactly. I—I just …" I wasn't even sure how to answer that truthfully. It was part of the reason. But I had also asked her out because I had been intrigued by her and wanted to get to know her better.

"That *is* why you asked me out," she said, sounding like she was confirming the truth to herself. "So you could fuck me and brag to all your friends and make some money on the deal."

I hadn't fully realized how horrible the bet was until that moment. Elyse was right. That was exactly why I had made the bet. Out of stupid pride and the hope I could swagger into work one day and tell the guys how I'd bagged her. I was so much in love with her now, the mere idea of doing that filled me with revulsion.

"Elyse, look," I stood up at my desk so I could get closer to her.

She backed away, fury flashing in her eyes. She made it perfectly clear I'd better not touch her.

"It was a stupid, childish bet, Elyse. I can't even begin to tell you how sorry I am that I did it. Honest to God, Elyse. I'd pretty much forgotten all about it until now. I swear to you, I never told a single soul about our relationship. My theater friends—*our* theater friends are the only ones who knew. I never told anybody we work with about us."

Elyse's eyes bored into mine, as if she were searching for the truth. I was dying to ask her how she found out, but I knew better.

"I guess one of the guys must have opened their damn mouth about the bet, but I swear to God I never told them we were together. And I sure as hell never told them that we were having sex."

But they know anyway. Lots of people know. Dear God.

"I let them think I lost the bet. I paid them off and let them humiliate me on a daily basis, but I never told them about you and me. At first, I wanted to win the bet. But everything changed when we went out on our first date. It changed for both of us. You know that."

Elyse's expression softened briefly, then hardened again.

"And I put out on the first date," she said angrily. "You expect me to believe you didn't tell all your friends?"

"I don't blame you one bit for not believing me. I wouldn't either. But it's the truth. I never breathed a word."

"And you had sex with me in my office on Friday, and I'm supposed to believe you never told anyone about that either?"

I suddenly flashed on the video clip on Manny's phone. Me fucking Elyse while she was completely naked and vulnerable. Roger, Manny, Charlie, Hunter, and who knew how many other guys had seen it.

Oh, my sweet, Elyse. I'm so sorry.

"No, I never told anyone. I would never do that," I told her, looking into her eyes, imploring her to believe me.

"It doesn't even matter. Everybody seems to know about this stupid bet, and everybody's talking about it. Keith heard the rumor, and he took me aside and told me because he actually seems to care about my feelings."

My heart ached. Keith Foster, the super hot guy who seemed to really care for Elyse was coming to her rescue just as I let her down.

"Hunter and even my boss are acting really weird, so they clearly know about it."

Good Christ. Some asshole must have shown Mr. Bialystock the video. If this ended up costing Elyse her promotion, I would never, ever forgive myself.

"Everybody's talking about me behind my back. Goddamnit, Luke!" she yelled.

I had never heard her raise her voice in anger before.

Then her eyes filled with tears. I had never seen her cry before, either. Elyse's tears spilled over, letting me know how deeply I had hurt her.

"How could you do this to me?" she whispered.

A small sob escaped her throat. She quickly wiped her tears away, then rushed out of my office.

Elyse would do what she always did at work. Put on a brave face no matter how much pain she was enduring. I pictured her struggling to keep her expression neutral while sitting at her desk. Pretending like I hadn't just ripped out her heart.

I put my head in my hands, wracking my brain trying to figure out how I could possibly fix this mess. I knew I couldn't go after Elyse. Having her co-workers see me with her would

make everything ten times worse.

I heard my office door open. I jerked my head up, hoping Elyse had come back to allow me more time to explain.

No such luck. Roger and Manny entered quietly and shut the door behind them.

"So, you're ... dating her?" Manny asked tentatively.

"I *love* her," I told him.

Roger sighed. "Dude, why didn't you just tell us? We'd

have had your back, man. You know that. We never would have told anybody if we'd known she was your girl."

I nodded. I wanted to be mad at Roger and Manny so I'd have somebody else to blame for this disaster. I couldn't blame them, though. As much as I hated to admit it, I would have done the same thing they did. If I'd gotten my hands on a sex video featuring a naked female Very Important Person, I would have shown it to every guy I knew. I closed my eyes, thinking of my beautiful, sweet girlfriend. Christ, I would never spread gossip again as long as I lived. Now I understood that there was a real person behind every juicy secret.

"I know. I didn't tell anybody here. I went out with her to try to win the bet," I said, finally admitting the truth out loud. "But we just hit it off right away. She's perfect for me. I mean, *perfect.*"

Roger nodded, and I knew he understood. I'd been at his wedding two years ago when he married the love of his life.

"Now she thinks I was just using her to win the bet. She'll never trust me again, and I don't blame her. God this is bad, this is so bad. Elyse is very protective of her private life. You have no idea. This whole thing is killing her."

Manny and Roger looked at me somberly as I spoke. We loved to tease and torment each other, but when the chips were down, they really did have my back.

"You know how we all thought she was this uptight hard-ass executive with no life outside of work? She's nothing like that. She's amazing. She's sweet and kind, and she supports me in ways I never thought possible." I struggled to find the right words to express how much she meant to me. "Elyse just gets me, you know what I mean?"

Both men nodded, and they seemed to understand, even though I wasn't exactly eloquent.

"There's this promotion she's been busting her ass for. I mean, that's why she was here 'til all hours on Friday night in the first place. It's this really important job for Wicket Pro. Senior Vice President of Worldwide Sales Strategy and Operations."

Manny whistled, sounding impressed. "Wow. That does sound important."

"It means everything to her. This whole mess could cost her the promotion. Her career means as much to her as mine does to me."

Roger and Manny nodded again, knowing damned well I was talking about theater and not my job as head of maintenance.

I covered my face with my hands, moaning with anguish for Elyse. "Her co-workers saw the video and her boss did, too. She'll never forgive me if I fucked up her career. I'll never forgive *myself.*"

"Dude, there must be something we can do," Roger said, sounding determined.

"I don't know what to do. I thought about talking to her boss. Explaining that she was just trying to get her work done and it was my idea to fool around in the office. I'm scared to death it might make things worse for her, though. We always worked so hard to keep our relationship a secret. I know she doesn't want me going anywhere near the tenth floor right now."

I sat back in my chair, feeling lost and utterly hopeless.

CHAPTER 19

I sat at my desk, doing my best to get ready for my presentation later this morning. My chest physically hurt every time I thought about what Luke had done. It made me wonder what other secrets he had been keeping from me all this time. It was unbelievably frustrating that I had managed to keep our relationship a secret, only to have it explode into hot office gossip mere days before the promotion was decided.

Clearly, everyone at Wicket Pro was now aware of my love affair with the head of maintenance. That part wasn't too bad, I supposed. It wasn't like either of us were married and were cheating. It was painful enough that Luke had bet he could get me into bed, but it was humiliating that everyone in the damned building seemed to know about it. It made me look like a naive fool who'd been taken advantage of sexually by a man.

A naive fool was not exactly the ideal choice to be negotiating worldwide technology deals as Senior Vice President of Worldwide Sales Strategy and Operations.

Goddamn him.

If I lost out on this promotion because of Luke and the cruel bet …

I swallowed hard against the lump forming in my throat. Obsessing over the promotion could only distract me for so long from thinking about how deeply his betrayal had hurt me. The pain washed over me. I trusted him. I *loved* him. Had he told me the truth about keeping our relationship a secret? Or had he bragged to his co-workers about how I slept with him on our first date? The idea of my private sex life being discussed openly behind my back infuriated and embarrassed me. I wondered how much he had collected when he won the bet. How much was my body worth to him?

I gasped when I saw a large man standing in my doorway.

"I'm sorry, Ms. Pippin. I didn't mean to scare ya!" he said, his soft brown eyes opening wide. Though we'd never been formally introduced, I knew who he was. "I'm Roger. I, uh, work with Luke."

He said those last few words hesitantly, knowing he was walking a dangerous line by mentioning Luke's name.

I nodded, narrowing my eyes. "I know," I said flatly. I was pretty sure Roger had been in on the bet.

"I wonder if I might have just a quick minute of your time?"

He seemed so earnest, I didn't have the heart to tell him no. I nodded, and he shut the door.

Roger sat in the chair across from me.

"I know you're really upset right now, and I don't blame you. I … Well … I can't even imagine what you're going through right now," he said, wincing a bit.

"I just wanted the chance to explain a few things to you. I've known Luke for years, and he would never do anything to hurt anybody on purpose. That's not who he is."

I looked into Roger's eyes, desperately wanting to believe

him. That wasn't the Luke I knew, either. My Luke was the guy who supported my dreams, the one who cared deeply for the kids he worked with, and the one who was a good and loyal friend and lover. I wanted—*needed*—to believe that was the real Luke Rannells.

"We did make a dumb bet with Luke about you, and it was a stupid, childish thing to do. Both Manny and I egged him on about it. It was really disrespectful to you, and I'm really sorry."

I nodded, finding it easy to forgive Roger. He seemed to genuinely care that his actions had hurt me, and he clearly cared enough about Luke to come to his defense.

"Ms. Pippin—"

"You can call me Elyse."

Roger smiled, seeming relieved I wasn't quite as angry anymore.

"Elyse. I swear to you, Luke never breathed a word to us that you two were dating. We had no idea. All this time we been bustin' his ba— I mean, we been givin' him a hard time that he'd been gettin' nowhere with you because you were out of his league. Which you *clearly* are."

That coaxed a small smile out of me. Roger was nice, and he was telling me everything I wanted to hear. That Luke had done a dumb thing, but it hadn't been done with malicious intent. That he hadn't been telling everyone about our private sex life.

"Luke says you're up for a really important promotion, and he's down there in his office tearin' his hair out, worryin' that he might have screwed it up for you. He wants to know if there's anything he can do to help. Luke wanted to maybe talk to your boss and explain everything, but he didn't want to do anything without your permission. So, just know he's willing to do anything and everything he can to make this up to you, and to make sure you get the job you worked so hard for."

"Thank you, Roger. I appreciate you coming to talk with me."

He smiled. "And let me know if there's anything I can do. I know everything seems bad right now, but these things always blow over. In time, everybody will forget all about the stupid video and just move on with their lives."

Terror seized my heart. I replayed Roger's words back in my head, trying to make sense of them.

"Video? What video?"

Roger's horrified expression told me everything I needed to know. I slowly lifted my eyes to the security camera in the hallway outside my office.

I drew in a deep shuddering breath, unable to speak or even move.

No. This can't be happening. This has to be some kind of nightmare.

"Y—you mean, you didn't know there was a … a …" Roger stammered, but I could barely hear him through the haze of my thoughts spinning out of control.

Hunter's snide attitude this morning. Keith's tender concern. Mr. Bialystock blushing, unable to look me in the eye.

They had all watched a video of me completely naked, having sex with Luke.

Violent nausea rose up in me so fast, I barely had time to cover my mouth before running out of my office. I raced to the bathroom, which was mercifully vacant, and emptied the contents of my stomach, mostly into the toilet. I retched so hard, my stomach and throat muscles hurt.

After a few moments there was a soft knock on the stall door.

"Are you all right?" came a gentle female voice with a hint of an Hispanic accent.

Shakily, I got to my feet. I tentatively opened the door to find Crista, a young woman in her twenties. She was one of our cleaning ladies.

"I—I'm sorry," I stammered, tears spilling from my eyes. "I'm afraid I made kind of a mess in there."

"Don't you worry about that," Crista said, her brown eyes widening. "Are you okay?"

"N—not really."

"I'll take care of the bathroom. You just take care of yourself, okay?" she said, and her sweet concern made me want to cry harder. Crista looked kind of horrified at my expression, and she knew something was terribly wrong.

"Th—thank you. I—I—I better go," I said, rushing to the sink to splash some water on my face.

This cannot be happening to me.

* * *

ROGER CAME INTO MY OFFICE. He didn't look so good. He almost looked pale, if that was possible for a guy as dark-skinned as he was. He sat in the chair across from me.

"Luke, I really screwed up. Like *really* screwed up."

I sighed heavily. I was already incredibly stressed and in no mood to deal with another crisis today. Still, Roger was a good guy and I wouldn't let him down. I had his back like he always had mine.

"It's okay, man. Whatever it is, I got you covered. Management doesn't need to know. What'd you break?"

"Elyse's heart," Roger said somberly.

"What?"

"I went up to ten to see her. I wanted to tell her how bad you felt about the bet and everything."

"Okay," I said, holding my breath.

"Christ, Luke. I thought she knew about the video ..."

"Oh, God!" I said, jumping up in a panic. "You told her."

"God, I am so sorry, Luke. I knew she must be going through hell, and I was trying to make her feel better."

"What did she say? What did she do?" I asked him in desperation. *Please tell me she's okay.*

"I ... Well, I'm pretty sure she ran to the bathroom and got sick."

"Oh, my God," I said, rushing past Roger and out the door.

I had to find her.

Waiting for the elevator was excruciating, but I knew if I ran up eight flights of stairs, I'd be so out of breath, I wouldn't even be able to talk. I had no idea what to do once I got to Elyse's floor, anyway. She must be feeling utterly humiliated and wouldn't be happy about being seen in public with me. She might scream at me to go away, and who could blame her?

Why now? Why in the hell did this have to happen now? If Mr. Bialystock had made a goddamned decision about who would get his job already, maybe this wouldn't be so bad.

Or maybe it would have made it worse. What if Elyse had gotten the job, and then had to resign in disgrace because of what we'd done on office property?

I wracked my brain, trying to come up with something, *anything* to fix this for her. But what could I possibly do?

When I finally got to the tenth floor, I made my way toward Elyse's office. I still had absolutely no idea what to do or say once I got there. I drew in a deep breath as I hesitantly peered into her office.

It was empty.

"Well, well, well. Look who's here."

I turned around to see Hunter smirking at me.

"Where is she?"

"Figured you should know. Considering you've been—"

"*Where ... is ... she?*" I demanded in a quiet yet threatening tone. I wanted to yell at the top of my theater voice and then punch Hunter in his smarmy face. I'd have done it, too, if not for Elyse. Causing a scene at her workplace could only hurt her career more.

"She went home," came a male voice from down the hall.

It was Keith. He walked up to us and shot me a look of utter disgust.

"She did?" I asked in astonishment. Elyse never went home early. Never.

"Guess I'll have to do my presentation on the Japanese company instead of her," Hunter said with a grin.

Rage flooded my body, and it took every ounce of restraint I could summon to keep from knocking him out cold. Lucky for him, he walked down the hallway. Whistling.

You goddamned bastard.

Keith stared at me. "Do you have any idea how lucky you were to be with her?"

He shook his head and walked away.

"Yes," I whispered to the empty hallway.

* * *

I DROVE MYSELF HOME, crying so hard I could barely see the road. I kept reliving this waking nightmare over and over in my mind, still thinking *this cannot be happening.*

I tried to convince myself maybe the video wasn't too bad. That it might have been grainy or hard to see, but I knew I was lying to myself. I'd been in the security room, once, when I first started working there, and I remembered the bank of screens on the wall. The pictures on them were crystal clear.

Then I began imagining the worst. Thinking of all those security guys in there watching, laughing, and reveling in their voyeurism. And then sharing the video with everyone they knew.

Roger and Manny had seen it. So had Hunter, Keith, and Mr. Bialystock. And those were only the ones I knew about.

Trying to convince myself the video probably hadn't shown too much of me also proved fruitless. Sure, Luke had remained fully dressed, but he had stripped me completely naked. I recalled how Luke had grabbed my naked breasts and had even taken a full step back to look at me, which had probably provided a clear view of my totally nude body. I remembered a time not so long ago when I had thought the idea of being watched was exciting. Having sex with Luke in the kitchen, in full view of the window, had been thrilling. The cold reality of being caught in the act felt horrifying, not exciting.

I sobbed louder as I drove, knowing I would never get over this humiliation as long as I lived. All my co-workers and countless other strange men had seen me in my most vulnerable moments. They had watched me having sex. They had seen me have an orgasm. My most private sexual fantasy had become public display.

My career and reputation had been destroyed in a matter of moments.

I could hardly bear the pain when I thought of Luke's betrayal. Now the entire building knew he had made a sexual bet about me, and that he'd had his way with me up against the wall of my office. I felt used and violated and utterly alone.

I didn't know who to turn to, as Luke had been my closest confidant. I was close with Leo, but I wasn't sure this was something I wanted to discuss with my brother. My sister Angelica and I got along great and had a lot of fun together, but we didn't have the kind of intimate relationship where we shared our deepest secrets.

Wobbling on shaky legs, I managed to make it up to my apartment. I still felt sick to my stomach, but I had nothing left to throw up anymore. I rinsed my mouth with mouthwash and then drank some cold water in an effort to calm down. I had a bunch of missed calls from Luke, but there was no way in hell I was calling him back. I supposed we'd have to talk again at some point, but I was in no mood to hear his voice right now.

My tears started to flow again, and a feeling of crushing loneliness washed over me. And then I remembered I wasn't alone. At least not yet. If Luke and I broke up for good, I might lose Susie and Rosemary in the process, but they were still my friends for now. I could talk to them. They would understand.

I dialed Susie's number first. We'd had lots of heartfelt conversations about her professional struggles, and I knew she would understand how devastated I was about my job.

"Oh my God, Elyse, what's wrong?" Susie asked, her voice filled with concern when I called her, crying.

I did my best to steady myself, then somehow managed to get the whole sordid story out of my system. The horrible bet, the video of us having sex being circulated throughout the office, and that I would never get the promotion and could even lose my job.

"Elyse honey, I'm so sorry," Susie said. "I can't even begin to imagine what you're going through right now."

I wiped my eyes and began to calm down a little. Susie was such a wonderful friend, and I could hear the compassion in her voice. It felt good to know she cared.

"I don't understand what Luke could have been thinking," she told me. "That is so unlike him!"

"I don't know what to think about him anymore. Do you think he does this kind of thing all the time? You've known him longer than I have. Did he used to sleep around a lot before me? Wait, you don't have to answer that. I know he's your friend, too, and all."

"He is, but I'm still mad as hell at him. I'm as confused as you. I can tell you he would have the occasional fling with an actress or whatever, but I wouldn't say he really slept around that much."

"I wouldn't even care if he was with a bunch of women before me. As long as he was faithful since we've been together. Now I can't help but wonder if he made sex bets like this all the time. I mean, is that the kind of person he is?"

"Ugh, I hope not," Susie said, sounding almost as disappointed in Luke as I was. "I want to believe this was just some dumb thing he did one time, you know?"

"I want to believe that, too. The alternative is just too awful," I said, feeling my heart break all over again. "But what if he really did all this on purpose? What if he came to my office and had sex with me to prove he'd won the bet?"

Susie paused for a moment, and I wondered what she was thinking.

"If he did, then he's not the person I thought he was," she said at last, her voice full of sorrow.

I suddenly felt very tired. "I think I'm gonna go lie down for a while. Could you do me a favor?"

"Of course. Anything!"

"Can you tell Rosemary about everything that happened? She's such a good friend, and I want her to know. I don't have the energy to rehash the whole thing."

"Sure, I can do that. And please tell me if there's anything

I can do. If you want to talk, Rosemary and I can come over any time, day or night. We're here for you, okay?"

"Thanks. Thanks so much, Susie. That means a lot to me. You have no idea. Whatever happens with Luke, I don't want to lose you guys, too." Saying it out loud made me start to cry again.

"Hey," Susie said firmly. "There's more to our friendship than some stupid, *and I do mean stupid*, man, you hear me?"

"Thank you, Susie."

"Try to get some rest," she told me in a soothing voice.

CHAPTER 20

$\mathcal{I}$ tried to give Elyse space, but it was killing me not to see her. I left a bunch of voice mail messages, doing my best to explain that the bet was just a one-time, stupid thing I'd done, and that having sex with her at work had nothing to do with it. I told her the security guy was a friend of mine and wouldn't show the video to anybody else, and only a handful of people had seen it. I tried to express how sorry I was and begged her to tell me what I could do to help. I even told her I would hand in my resignation if that was what she wanted.

So far, she hadn't responded to any of my messages, and I had no idea if she had even listened to them. Rosemary and Susie were pretty tight with her, so I got as much information from Johnny and David as I could. They both told me the same thing; Elyse was still devastated, and I'd better steer clear of Rosemary and Susie. They were both furious with me. I also sent Roger and Manny on regular missions to the tenth floor to check on her. They stole glances into her office throughout the week, and always came back with the same report: she looked sad.

Roger, Manny, and Charlie were amazingly supportive of me. They could see how much I loved Elyse, and they were pulling for me to patch things up with her. They also felt terrible for their role in what went down. The video wasn't some entertaining porno clip for them anymore. Now they understood how deeply it had hurt an innocent woman.

Toward the end of the week, I finally got up the nerve to call Susie.

"Hi," she said curtly.

The conversation would have been much easier in person. Susie knew me so well, all I would have had to do was look her in the eye and she would know I was being sincere. Trouble was, I rarely got a chance to see her these days because I was so busy with rehearsals instead of teaching with her at the foundation.

"I didn't do any of this to hurt Elyse, and I would give anything and everything I have if I could just take it back," I said, cutting right to the chase.

"Luke, why would you make a bet like that?" she asked, sounding more exasperated than angry with me.

"Because I was being an idiot. I know it was wrong to do it, but I didn't even know her at the time. I asked her out, partly because I wanted to win the bet and partly because I was into her. She probably told you we had sex on our first date, and even then, I knew I would never tell anybody at work about it. Elyse and I just clicked right away, and I knew she was the woman of my dreams."

"She is perfect for you, Luke," Susie said, her voice softening. There was no denying that Elyse and I were meant for each other. Even now.

"I *never* told *anybody* at work about sleeping with her, and I never planned to. I let the guys think they won the bet, and that was the end of it. Elyse didn't want anyone at work to know anything about her personal life, and I respected that. I swear to God, Susie. Nobody knew. And I came to her office that night hoping to get her to quit working and come home with me. I hadn't planned on having sex with her there. It just kinda happened. I never even thought about the security camera. You gotta believe me!"

Susie paused for a long time. "What you're saying makes sense." She paused again, for a much longer time. I held my breath. "I do believe you. Elyse is afraid you used her to win a bet, that you planned this whole thing, but no. You wouldn't do that, Luke."

"No, I wouldn't!" I exclaimed, feeling elated that somebody finally believed me. "Not to her. Not to anyone."

"I know."

"Can you help Elyse understand that? Please?"

Susie went silent again. "I'll do what I can."

"Thank you, thank you, thank you!"

I hung up feeling lighter and more optimistic than I had in a long time. I knew the next phone call I had to make was to Rosemary. And this time, it wasn't for my own selfish reasons in getting her to help me with Elyse. Rosemary didn't know it, but Johnny was planning on proposing to her this weekend. I'd talked it over with Johnny, and he still wanted me to be there. The last thing I wanted was for there to be weirdness between me and Rosemary on her big day. Saturday would be all about her and Johnny, not me and my petty drama.

I called Rosemary, and our conversation pretty much mirrored the one I'd had with Susie. In the end, I thought Rosemary had believed me. At least she wasn't furious with me anymore. If nothing else, I was sure she would be okay with me helping with Johnny's big proposal.

I waited until Friday to go see Elyse, hoping she would have talked to Rosemary and Susie by then. I was nervous about visiting her at work and wondered if I should have warned her I was coming. She might be embarrassed about being seen with me, considering how horrifyingly public our relationship had become.

From out in the hallway, I could see into her office without her seeing me. I watched her for a few moments. Elyse was hard at work and visibly stressed. There was an exhaustion in her face that hadn't been there before. She always worked hard, but she used to be so excited about her work, just like I felt when I was onstage. It hurt to see how upset she was.

I went over to her office and stood in the doorway.

"Hey," I said softly.

Elyse looked up, giving me an even closer look at the sorrow in her eyes. She seemed relieved, though not necessarily happy, to see it was me. It made me wonder if her co-workers had been giving her a hard time. My money was on Hunter being the biggest jerk about this whole thing. I clenched my fists just thinking about it.

"What do you want?"

"I wanted to see if you're all right."

"No, I'm not all right," she said, and I heard the catch in her voice. Elyse stared at her computer, no doubt working on something very important. She let out a deep, weary sigh and then looked up at me. "All those years. Everything I've worked for. It's all been for nothing. Now I'm just the girl who had sex in her office. That's all I am now, and that's all I'll ever be known for."

Tears filled her eyes, and it hurt to look at her.

"I'm so sorry," I told her, knowing the words were inadequate.

"I know you are," she said gently. "I'm not even sure how much of this is your fault, or if I'm just—" Elyse's tears spilled over, and she quickly grabbed a tissue and wiped her eyes. "I can't do this now, Luke. Please."

I nodded. I knew how hard she was struggling to keep from breaking down at work, which was the last thing she wanted to do. Elyse never let herself be human at the office, and she wasn't about to start now.

Elyse pulled a compact mirror out of her purse and inspected her eyes. She powdered her face, doing her best to look like she wasn't falling apart inside. She took a deep breath, and I watched as she visibly pulled herself together. It reminded me of how I got into character before a show.

"I'm not ready to talk about this yet," she told me in a stronger, more confident voice. I could still see a hint of sadness in her eyes, but for the most part, she was Work Elyse now.

"I understand," I said.

I walked away, pinning all my hopes on reconciling with Elyse on that critical word: yet.

* * *

I FELT nauseous as I pulled up at the curb outside The Creel Foundation on Saturday night. My emotions were still raw, and I wasn't ready to see Luke. Even so, I was not about to let my friends down.

Susie had contacted me yesterday about Johnny's proposal. We'd all met to rehearse our parts several weeks ago, but that was before everything had happened with Luke.

Sweetie, we'll all understand if you're not up for being there. God knows Rosemary would understand, Susie had told me via her text.

That was sweet of her, but Rosemary was so dear to me, I wouldn't have missed this important moment in her life for anything.

Johnny greeted me at the door with a warm, comforting

hug. I wasn't starstruck by him anymore. He was goofy Johnny to me now, too, and I absolutely adored him.

"Thanks so much for coming, Elyse."

"My pleasure, Johnny. I'm honored to be here!" A ripple of excitement went through me when I imagined Rosemary's expression when Johnny proposed. I was genuinely glad to bear witness to the happy occasion.

"He's here," Johnny said gently.

I nodded.

"But you don't have to talk to him if you're not ready. I mean, I know we're kinda throwing you two together here."

"Don't you worry about that. This is about you and Rosemary."

"Thanks. I gotta go get ready. You can head on back to the auditorium. Susie and David are here too," Johnny said reassuringly.

"Okay, great. See you in there. Good luck!" I said, squeezing his hand. Johnny grinned at me, and I relished the look of boyish excitement on his face.

I walked into the auditorium and saw Luke right away. He looked so handsome in his black shirt and pants. It was hard not to rush over and throw my arms around him.

"Hey, girl," Susie said, hurrying over to me and giving me a big hug. "Okay, let's everybody get up onstage in our places. Rosemary should be here soon."

Susie, Luke, and I headed toward the stage. David nodded his greeting at me as I walked past, and I smiled at him. He had the same look of worry on his face that Johnny had had a moment ago. I was touched by their concern. I was lucky to have so many wonderful new friends in my life.

It was hard for me to stand close to Luke, but I did my best to focus on the job at hand.

"This is gonna be so great," Susie said happily.

"Oh, I know. I can't wait to see her face," I said.

195

"I know!" Susie let out a squeal of excitement, then straightened out her expression. "Okay! Poker faces. Rosemary will be here any minute, and we don't want to give anything away."

Luke put on an exaggerated serious expression, and I laughed. I couldn't help it. It was a reflex. Nobody could make me laugh the way he did.

This is about Rosemary, I reminded myself. Now was not the time to deal with Luke.

The door to the auditorium opened and Rosemary walked in. She smiled and walked toward the stage.

"Hey, we having a party up there?" she asked.

Not yet, but soon we'll have lots to celebrate.

"We're just playing around," Susie told her. "Come on up."

Rosemary headed up the steps to join us onstage. It wasn't uncommon for us to sing together onstage, goofing around and enjoying the magical playground Johnny had built to honor Rosemary and her love of theater. There was simply no better way to propose to her than right here onstage.

My stomach fluttered with excitement. It was almost time.

Susie and I chatted with Rosemary about what we might like to sing, trying to kill some time before Johnny's arrival. David sat in the front row of the auditorium, ready to record the main event.

"Rosemaryyyyyyy," came Johnny's booming voice from offstage.

Rosemary glanced in the direction of his voice. She laughed softly, and I could see the happiness in her eyes. I'd been concerned about Johnny singing the same song from the infamous viral video, but he had reassured me it would be fine. He was right. Rosemary wasn't the slightest bit upset.

She was visibly charmed, waiting expectantly for her favorite guy to emerge from backstage.

She gasped when she saw him wearing a gorgeous black tuxedo. I had to chuckle. Johnny nearly always dressed casually in blue jeans, and it was funny to see him all decked out. He looked handsome with that mischievous glint his warm, gray eyes.

Rosemary covered her mouth in shock. Obviously, she'd figured out what was going on.

"Rosemaryyyyy," Johnny continued, and then dropped to one knee. Rosemary was already crying. He sang on about there being music in the sound of her name. Last time, Johnny had changed the song's wording from asking if she would marry J. Pierrepont Finch, the character from in *How to Succeed in Business Without Really Trying,* to "will you forgive Jonathan Thomas Creel?" This time, Johnny held out the ring, looked into Rosemary's beautiful green eyes, and asked, "Will you marry Jonathan Thomas Creel?"

Rosemary's response was a choked sob, making us all laugh gently.

"Was that a yes?" Johnny asked.

"Yes," she managed to say, and then she held out her hand for Johnny to slip the ring on her finger. Just as she had in the video, she took his hand and helped him to his feet.

Johnny smiled and then dipped his head to kiss her. We all went crazy with applause. Luke looked at me, and I couldn't help but share a sad smile with him. Though we were both hurting, we were overjoyed for our friends.

Luke walked over to the sound system to cue up the music for Phase 2 of Johnny's proposal. Johnny grinned at Susie and me, and we eagerly took our places onstage.

The two of us began to sing "Diamonds Are a Girl's Best Friend" from the musical *Gentleman Prefer Blondes.* Our version was closer to the sillier Carol Channing one, rather than Marilyn Monroe's more sultry rendition.

Rosemary threw back her head and laughed, wiping the tears from her eyes. My heart felt light just looking at her. She was so *happy*, and I loved being a part of her joy. Susie and I had practiced our song a lot, and I thought she could tell. It was our way of showing Rosemary how much we cared about her. She giggled as we sang, and happily played along by holding up her lovely ring each time we mentioned diamonds.

It wasn't the most romantic of songs—basically, it said diamonds are more valuable than men, and we focused our attention on Johnny any time we sang a line about how lousy men could be. But it was humorous, which was what we were going for.

I stole a glance at Luke while I sang, and he smiled proudly as he watched me perform. We ended our performance with an over-the-top kick-line dance, and everyone applauded loudly when we were done. Everyone except David, who was busy recording the whole event with his phone.

"No, *you* guys are my best friends," Rosemary said, walking over to us. She held out her arms and she, Susie, and I shared a warm hug. Susie and I laughed when we saw Rosemary had started crying again.

"Rosemary!" Johnny said in a loud, commanding voice.

Rosemary looked up at him with surprise, while Susie and I quickly rushed over to him so we could do our parts for Phase 3.

Once again, Luke started up the music and Johnny launched into an absolutely hysterical, over-the-top rendition of "Never Getting Rid of Me" from the musical *Waitress*. Susie and I sang backup, and it was nearly impossible to keep a straight face. Luke played the lovesick guy's boss, yelling at him to get back to work instead of wooing the girl. It was good to see Luke get so into the part. I knew he was having fun.

I accidentally caught his eye and couldn't help but smile. I was proud of him, like I always was when I saw him perform.

Rosemary played along beautifully, knowing all of Dawn's lines in the song as she tries to rebuff her overenthusiastic suitor. We all collapsed into laughter when the song was over, and Rosemary rushed over to embrace her husband-to-be.

"Oh, Johnny this was so wonderful."

He grinned at her and then kissed her.

She gazed at him fondly and sang a few lines of "You'll Never Get Away from Me" from *Gypsy.* We all laughed again. It was such a warm, wonderful moment for all of us. To be surrounded by such love and friendship.

"I don't ever want to be rid of you, Johnny. I'm more than happy to be stuck with you for life," Rosemary said affectionately, tracing Johnny's lips with her finger. "Thank you so much. Thank you all!"

She spun around to look at us, her eyes tearing up again. She turned back to Johnny and serenaded him with the song "Gimme, Gimme" from *Thoroughly Modern Millie.* It was a sweet, romantic song about wanting that thing called love, and wanting a happy ever after.

I found myself tearing up as I watched Rosemary sing to the love of her life. It was especially sweet, since *Thoroughly Modern Millie* was the first show Johnny had ever seen Rosemary in.

Johnny and Rosemary shared a tender kiss when she finished her song. It was lovely.

"That was beautiful, baby," Johnny told her without a trace of his usual silliness. A sense of peace settled over me, seeing how much in love they were. They were both such dear friends to me, and I wished them a lifetime of joy.

"David got this all on tape, honey," Johnny said, pointing at David. "But this is just for you, okay? I have no intention of having another video go viral. I just wanted you to have it."

"That was a wonderful idea, Johnny," Rosemary said, eyes shining. She waved her thanks at David in the front row.

A loud popping noise startled us, and we all turned to see Luke pouring champagne.

"Oh, Johnny. You really thought of everything," Rosemary said dreamily.

We all sat on the stage to toast the happy couple. David came up to join us, kissing Susie before settling down beside her. It amused me to see David sitting on the floor in his fancy suit. He always dressed to the nines. It was hard to imagine what he might look like in blue jeans.

Johnny sat on the floor, too, in his expensive tux. Luke took a seat between Johnny and Susie, so as not to separate the two couples, and so I wouldn't have to sit next to him. I appreciated his respecting that I still needed some space, but it made me sad not to be cuddled up next to him.

Where I belonged.

Or did I?

My mind was still a mess, and I didn't know what to think. Rosemary and Susie had both had long conversations with Luke and had both separately come to the same conclusion: they believed the sex bet was just a stupid, one-time mistake and that Luke hadn't meant to hurt me.

Deep in my heart, I believed it too. I knew I needed to have a long talk with Luke, too, to sort everything out. Even if everything was okay as far as the work disaster, I was still worried that Luke wanted to have a family. That there might still be no hope for a future with him.

I shook off my thoughts. This was Rosemary's night, and I needed to focus on her.

"To the most wonderful couple I know," Luke said, hoisting his glass. "Good luck to ya, you crazy kids!"

We all clinked glasses and toasted the happy couple.

"I love celebrating your engagement here," I said, looking around the stage. "It's just so perfect."

"It is perfect," Luke said, looking at me and making my stomach flutter. I still loved him. That was the only thing I was sure of right now. He gazed at me for a moment, then turned to look at Rosemary. "Reminds me of the party we had for Ryan and Jack."

"Yeah," Rosemary said with a smile. "I was thinking the same thing."

"Who are they?" I asked.

"Oh, Ryan is a dear friend of mine from back in D.C. I miss him so much!" she said. Johnny smiled, and I was surprised that he seemed fine with her gushing about another man.

"Jack is his fiancé," Rosemary said.

Oh. That explained Johnny's utter lack of jealousy.

"Jack's a Marine, and he'd been deployed for a long time," Johnny told me. "Rosemary planned a surprise reunion between Ryan and Jack. Right here onstage."

"Oh, that is so cool," I said.

"It was. Oh, it was so sweet," Rosemary said, tearing up with emotion.

I laughed. "Look at you, cryin' just thinking about it. You must have been a mess when it happened."

"She was," said both Susie and Johnny. Rosemary laughed, as did the rest of us.

"They're really great guys," Luke said. "That was an unforgettable day. Mainly because David actually sang for us."

"Is that so?" I asked, though I already knew.

"Yes. I did sing. Once. Now let us never speak of it again." David's voice was stern, but his eyes betrayed his amusement. He gently nudged Susie and said quietly, "Tell them your good news."

"No, not now," Susie said in a low voice. "This is Rosemary's night."

"What good news?" Rosemary asked excitedly. "Tell me, tell me, tell me!"

Susie laughed. "Okay. I got a part in a show."

Rosemary and I both screamed with excitement. That made David laugh, which was no easy feat. I saw the happiness in his eyes, and I knew he was overjoyed for Susie.

"Was it the dancing role you really wanted?" Rosemary asked.

"Yes."

Rosemary and I screamed again, making all the men laugh. We both jumped up to hug her. David stood, then helped Susie to her feet so we could descend upon her.

I'd lost count of how many conversations I'd had with Susie about her struggles, and I couldn't have been more thrilled for her.

Johnny screamed, mimicking us, and jogged over to give Susie a hug. Luke came over too and kissed her on the cheek.

"Congratulations. Nobody deserves this more than you," Luke said, his eyes shining.

He really is a good man.

"Thanks, Luke. I couldn't have done it without your help. I mean it."

"Aww, garsh," Luke said, feigning modesty.

"What a perfect night," Rosemary said, looking at Johnny. "We got engaged. Susie got a part. Now, if Elyse can just get her promotion, we'll be all set."

I smiled at her. "I guess anything's possible." I wasn't

holding out much hope for getting the job, but it wasn't over until my boss made his decision.

I bent down and picked up my champagne glass. "To Susie and her exciting new adventure!"

We all raised a glass, and my spirits lifted again to see Susie so excited. Looking from her happy face to Rosemary's equally joyful expression made me feel good all over.

Eventually, the party wound down and it was time to leave. Rosemary took me aside privately for a moment.

"Elyse, I can't tell you how much it means to me that you came here tonight." She smiled sadly. "I broke up with Johnny once, and it was horrible. I don't know what I'd do if I had to watch a proposal and have some obnoxiously happy couple in my face."

I laughed. "You're not obnoxious. You're *adorable.*" I glanced over at Johnny. "He looks so cute in that tux!"

"Yeah, he sure does," Rosemary said, looking at her intended with love and affection.

"I wouldn't have missed this for anything, Rosemary. Congratulations," I said, giving her one more hug before I left.

I said my goodbyes to everyone else and headed toward the door.

"I'll walk you out, Elyse," Luke said.

A hushed silence fell over the group.

"Is that all right, Elyse?" Johnny asked uncertainly. "Because I can walk you out if ..."

He glanced over at Luke. This whole situation was awkward for everyone, and I appreciated that nobody seemed to take sides.

"Yes, it's okay," I lied. I wasn't ready to be alone with Luke, but I wasn't about to make a scene during such a happy occasion.

I dropped my smile the second we were alone in the hallway. I was angry that Luke had cornered me. Until now, he'd kept a respectable distance, waiting for me to make the first move.

"Elyse, are we ever going to talk about this?" Luke asked wearily.

"Now is not the time," I said, hurrying down the hallway. "I came here tonight for Rosemary and Johnny. Not for you."

"I know. But we did what we came to do. We were there for our friends. That doesn't mean we can't talk now."

I let out a weary breath, knowing I wasn't really angry with Luke anymore. I was stressed out and scared, both about my future at work and my future with him.

"Look, Mr. Bialystock is supposed to tell us, *finally,* who gets the job this week. I need to concentrate on that right now. I've got enough distractions, enough strikes against me. Please, let me get through this one thing at a time."

Luke nodded sadly. "Okay. If that's what you want."

No, it's not what I want. I want you to tell me you're sorry you made that cruel bet, and that you want to spend the rest of your life with me. Childfree.

"It is," I forced myself to say.

"I miss you," Luke said simply when we got to my car.

"I miss you too, Luke."

I caught a glimmer of hope in his eyes when I said it.

CHAPTER 21

I'd been working almost four straight hours, and I needed a brain break. It felt good to keep busy, though. When I got into the zone, it helped me forget the undercurrent of squirmy humiliation I endured constantly at the office, nowadays. I let out a deep sigh. God, I hated feeling this way at work. I used to be so excited to be here; energized and alive, excited by Wicket Pro's new technological advancements, and thrilled at the chance to come up with creative ways to sell our products to new clients.

Now I was embarrassed all the time. I couldn't even look anyone in the eye anymore. I felt violated by the video, angry that so many people had seen it. I couldn't really blame my co-workers for looking at it. I had done a stupid, reckless thing at the office, perhaps permanently screwing up my career.

Sipping from my water bottle, I checked the news on the Internet. I usually took a break every few hours to scan the headlines. I clicked on one of my regular national news sites and was horrified by what I saw.

The headline read "Another singing video from Johnny Creel. Now he's engaged!"

I gasped. I scanned the headlines: they briefly recounted the events of the video proposal we'd all done. Sure enough, the video itself was embedded in the article. I watched the thirty-second clip, featuring Johnny in his tux getting down on one knee and proposing. Another link at the bottom of the article promised to show the video in its entirety.

How could this have happened?

As far as I knew, David and Rosemary were the only ones who had a copy of it. I wondered if Rosemary's phone had been hacked.

The thought made me sick to my stomach. *Dear God, what if Johnny and Rosemary had taken intimate photos with her phone camera?* It had happened to a lot of celebrities.

I clicked around to a bunch of other websites. Thankfully, there was no mention of any other private discoveries concerning Rosemary. Unfortunately, every one of them carried the news of Johnny Creel's engagement.

My heart ached for Rosemary. I grabbed my phone and dialed her number. I didn't want to be the one to break the news to her if she didn't already know the video had been released, but I also didn't want her to find out about it from some stranger on the street. She didn't answer her phone.

Since it was weekday, she was probably either at school or rehearsing at the foundation. I wracked my brain, trying to figure out how I could possibly reach her. I couldn't bear the idea of her happiness being so short-lived.

I didn't want some awful video stealing her joy the way my scandalous video had ruined my job for me.

Somehow, I had to get ahold of Rosemary before it was too late.

* * *

I WAS BRIEFING Roger and Manny on the jobs I wanted them to do this afternoon when Elyse burst into my office. The three of us looked at her in surprise.

"Uh … uh," Elyse stammered as she looked at Roger and Manny. Her face turned bright red, and she turned her head away from them. She was clearly painfully aware that both men had seen her naked.

Oh Elyse, I'm so sorry.

Elyse drew in a deep breath and focused on me, trying to block out the presence of the other guys.

"Have you seen the news today?" she asked, looking quite upset.

"No, why? What happened?"

"It's awful. Somehow the video of Johnny's proposal got leaked."

"What? How is that possible?"

"I don't know. All I know is that Rosemary's gonna be devastated. I tried calling her, but she didn't answer. She might not even know about it yet. I'm so worried about her. I don't know what to do."

I gazed at Elyse, feeling a wave of affection wash over me. She was sweet to be concerned about Rosemary, especially with all the stress in her life. Both Roger and Manny looked at her somberly. Now they could see for themselves that Elyse was a warm, wonderful person and not the ice-cold executive we'd all thought she was.

"I'll see if I can get hold of Johnny and see what's going on," I told her.

"Good idea. Let me know if you find out anything, and if there's anything I can do to help."

"I will, Elyse."

She nodded, then rushed out of my office without making eye contact with Roger or Manny.

"God, she couldn't even look at us," Roger said gently.

"This whole thing has been a nightmare for her."

Manny and Roger nodded sadly.

"She used to love coming to work, you know? You gotta be brave and confident in her line of work. If she's this shy around her co-workers ..."

I refused to finish my thought out loud. It was too damned depressing to think Elyse might miss out on her dream job because of me. That would be like me finally getting a huge Broadway audition and blowing it. I knew how much it would hurt, and I hated to think that must be how she felt right now.

I turned to my computer and went to a news website. Sure enough, there was Johnny Creel's engagement news, and not just in the entertainment section. It was one of the main headlines.

"Shit," I muttered. "I gotta call Johnny."

Roger and Manny headed out so I could make my phone call. I hoped to God Rosemary hadn't seen the headlines, and that Johnny could break the news to her gently.

* * *

LUKE CAME to my office not long after I'd settled back down to work.

"Hey," he said as he stood in the doorway. "I talked to Johnny."

"And?" I asked, afraid of what Luke would tell me.

Luke grinned at me. "Rosemary's fine. She's the one who released the video to the media."

"What?"

He laughed, shaking his head. "I know. It's insane. I'm not exactly sure why. Johnny said she did it on the spur of the moment. She asked him first if it was okay, though."

208

"Somehow I don't think he minded," I observed dryly. Johnny Creel loved attention.

"No, I don't think Johnny minded. He did seem a little concerned that she might come to regret it, though. For now, Rosemary's doing fine."

"Good. Thanks for telling me. I feel so much better."

"Me too," Luke said, gazing at me intently.

I had the sudden urge to tell him I loved him. But I fought it, knowing we needed to talk things out first.

"Well, I'll let you get back to work," he said with a sad smile as he reluctantly left.

I stared out into the empty hallway after he'd gone, resisting the powerful temptation to run after him.

Still worried about Rosemary, I texted her. She got back to me a few minutes later and we agreed to meet for drinks after work. I wanted to see for myself that she was okay.

* * *

I WAITED for Rosemary at a table for two at Gypsy's Wine Bar. The moment she walked in the front door, she was accosted by an older woman. At first, I thought the lady must have known her. Then Rosemary laughed and signed her autograph, and I realized the woman was a stranger who simply recognized her. When she lifted her left hand to show her ring to the woman, worry began to gnaw at the pit of my stomach. Notoriety from the latest video had already begun, and I wondered how Rosemary felt about it.

Rosemary's eyes lit up when she saw me. She politely excused herself from her admirer and headed over. She looked lovely, joyful and glowing like a bride-to-be should look. I felt better already.

"I ordered you a Moscato," I said when she took a seat across from me.

"Perfect," Rosemary said with a smile. I stared at her for a moment and she laughed. "I know, I know. You wanna know what the hell I was thinking, right?"

"Damn right I do," I said, shaking my head. "I was worried sick when I first found out the video had been released. I thought you'd be devastated."

"Sorry. I guess I should have given you a heads-up, but it was kind of a last-minute decision."

"That's what Johnny said," I told her.

Her eyes suddenly opened wide. "Oh my God, I didn't even ask you if it was okay to release it! You were in the video, too, after all."

"Oh, it's fine. Believe me, that video going public is fine by me."

Rosemary nodded, looking relieved.

"So what *were* you thinking in releasing Johnny's proposal?"

"I'll tell you exactly what I was thinking," Rosemary said, eyes flashing with excitement.

Her wine arrived, and she thanked our server before continuing.

"*Fuck it.* That's what I was thinking."

"I see," I said with a chuckle, sipping my microbrew.

"I figured I'd heard it all when the first video was released. People said I was using Johnny for his money, and I was an attention whore because of the video. Never mind the fact that to this day I still have no idea who recorded the whole thing and who released it. Somebody in the restaurant, I guess, but it sure as hell wasn't me."

Rosemary took a sip of wine before continuing. "And then, when I landed a role on Broadway, people said the Creels had bought my way into show business. Johnny's father did pay for me to go to NYU to get my theater degree, but I got accepted into the school on my own, and his money had nothing to do with my getting the role on Broadway." She sighed. "At least I'm pretty sure it didn't. I laid down the law with Johnny right away about everything. How I didn't want any special treatment *ever* when it came to my career. You know, except for paying for my school. But lots of people's parents pay for their schooling, right?"

"Mine sure did. My bachelor's degree, anyway. I did the MBA on my own dime, but I was more established by then and could afford it. But sure, nothing wrong with your mom and dad paying for your education."

"Right. And my parents were flat broke, while Johnny's parents were loaded, so why not have them pay for me? Anyway, lots of people attribute any success I have to the Creels rather than my own talent."

"That's awful, Rosemary. And it's total bullshit. Anybody who knows you, knows how hard you've worked to get where you are."

"I have worked hard. I busted my ass in community theater for years and went on tons of auditions since I've been here, while attending school at the same time. The point is, no matter what I do, there will always be some people who'll say that everything I have comes from the Creels and not my own hard work, talent, and ambition."

I nodded, thinking about how unfair that was.

"Look Elyse, my getting engaged to Johnny was gonna be a huge news story whether I wanted it to be or not. Johnny's heir to the Creel fortune, and he used to be a notorious womanizing playboy. His getting married was gonna be a big deal anyway, so I decided to just own it. Get out in front of the story and do it on my terms."

"Wow," I said, impressed not only with her brave decision but also by the confidence in her voice.

"People can say what they want, but I know the truth. I know how much I love the theater, how hard I've worked, and that I've dedicated my life to it. I know where I've been and what I've done to make my own dreams come true."

"That's amazing, Rosemary. Good for you!" I raised my glass and toasted her.

"Thanks," she said with a smile. She took a healthy sip of Moscato. "And don't get me wrong. There are plenty of people who are really wonderful. I get tons of comments online about how much people enjoyed the first video, and now I'm overrun with well-wishes from people. It's so sweet."

She teared up a bit as she spoke. Rosemary had such a tender heart, but she was a lot stronger than she looked. Yes. She would be able to handle whatever was coming her way.

"Like the lady who stopped me when I came in just now. She was adorable! She told me how cute she thought Johnny is, and that I had a nice singing voice. I love that I'm known for my singing voice and my love for Johnny. I know to a lot of people I'll just be Mrs. Creel, but I can live with it. I know my own identity, and that's what counts the most, you know?. I'm so proud of the work Johnny and I do at the foundation, and it's so wonderful to be known for that too, you know?"

"Yeah, you're right. And the video might do wonders for publicity for The Creel Foundation. You could get more donors, more people involved. Get the word out. I'm sure there's lots of kids and parents who don't even know it exists."

"I know," Rosemary said, eyes shining. "I thought about that, too. I'm so lucky the videos featured us singing together, you know? What a great thing to be famous for. It's like these videos are our thing now. If we ever have a baby, we should do a video to announce it."

"Do you want to have kids, Rosemary?" I asked bluntly. I

couldn't help it. The topic had been weighing on my mind for so long, I had to talk to somebody about it.

"Well, yes. Eventually," she looked at me uncertainly. She could see I was upset. "Johnny and I have talked about it, and we decided we want to have a family, but not any time soon. We've both got way too much going on, and there's so much I want to do first. Why? Do you want kids?"

Rosemary asked the question gently, knowing something was wrong by the way I had asked her the same question.

"No. I really don't. I've never wanted to have kids. I'm just so career-oriented and—"

"That's not surprising, Elyse," Rosemary interrupted before I could launch into my well-rehearsed spiel about why I didn't want to have kids. I was so used to people giving me a hard time about the subject, I tended to immediately get defensive.

"Really?"

"Well, yeah. Everybody knows how much you love your job and how hard you've worked on it. You've got lots of ambition to keep moving up the ladder. It's hardly surprising that you wouldn't want to give it all up to have a baby." She sighed. "And let's face it. That's what most women have to do if they want kids. It's not typically the men who stay home with the kids. Or get up with them all night. Or leave work early to take them to doctor appointments."

"Yes! Exactly!" I practically shouted. "You're not gonna lecture me about how I'll change my mind about having kids someday, and I don't know what life is about until I experience the magic of motherhood?"

Rosemary laughed. "Oh, please. Look, I'm sure motherhood is wonderful, but it's not for everybody. I'm sure having kids does give your life meaning, but so do other relationships. Friends, for example?"

She smiled, and some of my anxiety began to ease. Rosemary understood, so was it possible that Luke might, too?

"I think … I think I'm ready to forgive Luke."

"Really? Oh, Elyse, I'm so happy to hear you say that. I didn't want to tell you what to do, or butt in with my advice without you asking. But I really think he's a wonderful man who did a dumb thing with the bet."

"I think so, too," I told her. "And this thing with the video has been just *awful* …" My voice quavered, and Rosemary reached over and grasped my hand in support. "But I know it wasn't Luke's fault. He was just as shocked as I was when it all went down. I just … Rosemary, I'm scared to tell him I don't want to have children. You've seen how he is. He's just so good with kids."

"Yes, he sure is."

"Do you know if he wants a family? Has he ever mentioned it?"

"No, he hasn't. I'm sorry. I have no idea how he feels on the subject."

I nodded and said, "I just figured it's not fair to keep being with him if it's going to be a deal breaker, you know?"

"I understand," she said, squeezing my hand. "Elyse, just know Susie and I will be here for you, no matter what happens."

"Thank you. That means so much to me." I thought for a moment. "Fuck it, huh? I like it. That's a good philosophy."

CHAPTER 22

"Hey asshole," said Jacob, one of my fellow castmates from *Pirated*. "You got a pretty blonde chick out front askin' for you."

"You serious?" I asked, my heart thumping.

Jacob smiled and nodded. "Yup." I'd confided in him that I was having girl trouble, but he didn't know the details. Even so, I knew he was pulling for me to work it out.

I glanced toward the door, wanting to dash out into the street to see Elyse. I looked apprehensively toward the stage where we'd just been rehearsing.

"Go on. Get lost already. We're practically done here anyway. I'll tell 'em you had to split," Jacob said.

"Good deal. Thanks, man."

I grabbed my backpack and headed outside, still dressed as a pirate. In my rush, I nearly ran right past Elyse, who was sitting on the front steps of the building. I slowed my roll, trying to catch my breath. Jittery nervousness tingled in my stomach. Hopefully, we'd finally hash this out and put an end to it. I just hoped it wouldn't put an end to *us*.

Elyse looked up at me and smiled. "You look great."

I chuckled. "Thanks." She always did love seeing me in costume.

I sat down beside her on the steps. Too much time had passed since I'd been this close to her, and it took every ounce of restraint not to pull her into my arms. I had to let her take the lead.

And she surprised the hell out of me by pulling me into *her* arms.

"Oh, Luke," she said, drawing a shaky breath. I could tell she was fighting tears. We held each other for a moment, and I stroked her back soothingly.

"It's okay, Elyse. It's okay," I murmured in her ear. It felt so damned good to hold her again.

Eventually, she let go and faced me.

"Do you swear to me this bet was just a stupid one-time thing you did?"

"Yes," I said, stroking her face and looking intently into her eyes. It was the truth, and I desperately needed her to believe me. "I swear I've never done anything like that before, and I swear I don't have any other secrets from you."

"At first, I was afraid this whole thing was some kind of setup," she said, still speaking in a shaky voice that broke my heart. "Like you wanted us to be caught on camera so you could prove you were having sex with me."

"I would *never* do a thing like that. Not to you. Not to *anybody*."

She gazed deeply into my eyes, as if searching for the truth. I'd meant what I said. The bet was a childish and hurtful thing to do, but the video was horrific. I wouldn't wish that kind of humiliation on somebody I hated, let alone the woman I loved.

"I know you wouldn't," Elyse said at last. "You're not that kind of person."

She let out a deep sigh and let her tense shoulders drop. Then she smiled. "Okay. Now tell me the truth."

"What?"

"Is that why you asked me out in the first place? Because of the bet?"

This time, her tone didn't sound angry or hurt. She sounded curious.

"Honestly? I'm not totally sure."

Elyse laughed softly and nodded.

"I mean, I guess that was part of the reason. I'll tell you one thing; I really was worried about you when I found you in the stairwell that day. I admit, I was headed to the tenth floor to find you, to see if I could flirt my way into getting a date. But when I saw you in so much pain, I felt awful. Especially the way you were hiding it from everybody. I hated to think of you suffering all by yourself. And I swear, Elyse, when I went and bought all that stuff to make you feel better? It wasn't me trying to butter you up so I could pounce on you. I felt so bad. Like I had to do *something* to help."

"See? That's the Luke I know and love," Elyse said softly.

She still loves me.

I stroked her chin, wanting to kiss her. Still, I didn't want to push my luck.

"I stood in the hallway and watched you open the box of stuff I gave you."

"You did?"

"Uh-huh. I was pretty nervous about it. I mean, it was personal, you know, period stuff, and I was afraid you might get offended. Know what you did?"

Elyse shook her head.

"You laughed," I said with a smile. "You laughed when you saw the tea and the chocolate and the pain pills. Then you smiled when you picked up the teddy bear. I'd never seen you smile or laugh before. I didn't know you were capable of it."

"Because you'd only ever seen Work Elyse."

"Yep. And I'll tell you right now: I was intrigued by you. In that moment, I knew there was more to Elyse Pippin than I'd thought. When I asked you out, I guess I was still thinkin' a little about the bet, but I was also thinking I wanted to get to know you better. Does that answer your question?"

"Yes," she said with a smile.

"Now *you* tell *me* the truth."

"What?" she asked, sounding surprised.

"You didn't want to go out with me when I asked, did you?"

Elyse bit her lip, looking guilty. She laughed softly, and said, "I just didn't think we'd have anything in common. I thought going out with you would be uncomfortable. I was wrong. Completely wrong."

Our eyes met, and my urge to kiss her was overwhelming, but I resisted. The tension still hung in the air between us.

"I'm sure you were proud of yourself that you got to have sex with me on the first date. You must have been glad you won the bet."

I'd been right to hold off on kissing her. I wasn't out of the woods yet.

"Yeah, I suppose I was," I said as casually as could. I didn't want to upset her, but I wasn't about to lie to her either. "Okay, yes. I felt a bit cocky that I'd won. But I want to make one thing perfectly clear to you, Elyse. By the end of our first wonderful, perfect date, I'd already decided I wasn't gonna tell anybody I slept with you. You remember how amazing that night was. How we just clicked. We talked about our hopes and our dreams, and you actually asked to hear me sing."

"It was wonderful," she said in a soft, almost wistful voice.

"Yeah. There was no way in hell I was gonna betray you by talking about you with those guys. I let them go on and believe I'd gotten nowhere with you, and I paid the lousy hundred bucks. Each. And I'll be totally honest with you. My plan was to keep the whole thing a secret from you forever. Once we finally went public with our relationship, I was gonna tell Roger and Manny to dummy up, see?"

Elyse laughed, much to my relief.

"I wasn't gonna tell them we'd slept together that soon, and that I'd won. But I planned on telling them to keep their fool mouths shut and never mention the bet to you. I knew you'd be hurt and angry. Understandably so. I didn't want you to find out."

"That makes sense."

"Elyse, I am so, so sorry. I never meant for any of this to happen."

"It's been awful," she said shakily, her tears threatening to spill. "Everything that happened at work. But I know it wasn't your fault."

Elyse put her arms around my neck and pressed her lips to mine. We kissed eagerly, passionately, wanting to make up for lost time. Relief washed over my whole body. We were together again, still in love. *Thank God. Thank God.*

Suddenly, she pulled away.

"Wait, Luke. There's something else we have to discuss before … before we go any further. Or pick up where we left off. Or …" I was shocked by the look of fear in her pretty blue eyes. Something was very, very wrong.

"Baby, what is it?"

Elyse drew in a deep breath. "I, well, after my trip to Finland, I went to see my doctor."

Sheer panic shot through me. *Oh, dear God. She's got cervical cancer. Or ovarian cancer. That's what's been causing her pain. Dear God, no …*

"Oh God, Elyse."

"No, no. It's okay. I'm okay. Really," she reassured me. But she still looked afraid. "I've got endometriosis. It's, well, basically it affects my uterus and stuff like that. And ... and ..."

I held my breath as I watched her struggle to say the rest without completely breaking down.

"And well, I'll eventually have to have surgery. It would be a hysterectomy. It wouldn't have to be done right away, but even before the surgery it would mean it might be really hard for me to get pregnant and ..."

Elyse choked back a sob, her tears falling freely now.

"Oh, honey. It's okay, it's okay," I said, pulling her close so I could wrap my arms around her. "I know we never really talked about it, but is having kids important to you?"

"No," she said, beginning to sob openly. I'd never seen her so upset before. "I don't want to have kids. I've never wanted to have kids."

"Oh," I said, trying to figure out if I'd missed something. "Okay. Well, then why ..."

"Why am I crying like a crazy person?" she asked, dabbing her eyes with a tissue she'd pulled from her pocket.

"Well, yeah, kinda," I said, treading carefully.

"Oh, Luke. You're so wonderful with kids. The kids at the foundation, and the way you held my baby nephew. It's obvious that you were meant to be a father."

"Noooo," I began slowly. "I was meant to be crazy Uncle Luke. The guy who shows up on holidays and special occasions with a bunch of presents for the kids and with a bunch of wacky stories from my acting jobs."

Elyse gazed up at me hopefully. "You mean, you don't want to have kids of your own?"

I considered her question carefully before answering.

"Okay, I know this is gonna sound crazy for such a major decision like having kids, but honestly? I could go either way. I will tell you I'm not one of those guys who've always known they wanted to be a father someday. That's not me. But I have thought a lot about it over the years."

Elyse nodded, hanging on my every word.

"It's funny. When I imagine what it would be like to have kids, I think about bringing them to my shows. You know, them being proud of their dad and all. I imagine them fitting into my world. You know what I don't think much about? Going to all their baseball games and school events. Tucking them in at night. I mean hey, don't get me wrong. I'd love to do those things. That's what good dads do! But I can't picture myself being home to do any of those things. You know what my schedule's like."

She nodded, taking in my whole pirate getup. "Rehearsals all the time when you're in a show. Auditions when you're not."

"Exactly. I would rarely be home. And that's not fair to the kids, and it's certainly not fair to their mother. Even if I married a woman who really wanted to have kids and was ready to do all that stuff. The school events, the bake sales, girl scouts, and everything. Would it be fair to stick her with all that?"

"What are you saying, Luke?" Elyse asked.

"I'm saying I always kinda figured if the woman I loved wanted to have kids, we'd make it work somehow. But if she didn't? Well, that's okay, too."

"Are you sure?"

"Yeah," I said, stroking her face again. "Like I said, it's a weird thing to say, but I'm honestly okay either way on the kid issue."

Elyse covered her mouth, stifling another sob.

"Baby, baby," I said, still trying to decipher her rapidly changing moods.

"I was so scared to talk to you about this, Luke. I've been

dreading it for weeks. I was afraid you really wanted to be a father. That we'd have to break up over it."

Her tears continued to flow.

"Sorry, babe, but you're stuck with me. You can't get rid of me that easily."

"I didn't want to lose you."

"You're not gonna lose me, Elyse."

I put my arm down so I could face her. And kiss her. This time, I felt her whole body relax. And I knew we would be okay.

"Next time, don't spend so much time stressing all alone. Talk to me, okay?"

"I will."

We sat there for a moment, happy to be together. The last thing I wanted to do was upset her when she was in a fragile mood, but I had to ask.

"So, how are things going at work? Are you ... okay?"

Elyse let out a deep, weary sigh. "Well, I've still got a job. So that's something." She paused for quite a while before continuing. "It's been awful, Luke. Just awful. I feel like I've lost all their respect. It's humiliating to think of everything they saw."

She covered her mouth to keep from openly weeping.

"Oh, Elyse, please don't cry," was all I could say. I felt helpless, having no idea how to make this better. It hurt so bad to see her tears.

"Ugh!" she said angrily. "I never used to cry at all, but now it seems that's all I do anymore!"

I watched her fight her emotions, struggling to keep from crying. Maybe that was the problem. She always worked hard, too hard, to keep her emotions in check. Her life sucked right now, and she'd been under too much stress for too long.

"You know what? Forget what I just said. You need a good cry, baby. Come here."

I opened my arms and she sank into them, finally letting loose a torrent of pent-up sorrow and strain. I held her silently and stroked her back.

The door to the rehearsal space opened and Jacob emerged, dressed in his street clothes. He glanced at poor Elyse as she cried into my chest. Shooting me a sympathetic look, he walked down the steps quietly so as not to disturb us.

After a while, Elyse's sobs subsided. She let go of me and wiped her eyes, composing herself.

"You were right," she said, eyes still swollen and red. "I did need that. Okay. I've cried enough. Now it's time for action."

I watched with fascination as Elyse's face transformed into an expression of fierce determination before my very eyes. This was the brave, smart, and ambitious woman I knew and loved with all my heart.

She'd been knocked down, but she was getting back up again, ready to fight.

"Oooh, I like the sound of that," I told her. "What do you have in mind?"

"Well," Elyse said, flipping her blonde hair out of her face. "To quote the wise philosopher Rosemary Sutton, soon-to-be Rosemary Sutton Creel ... *Fuck it!*"

I grinned at Elyse, eager to hear more.

"The way Rosemary handled her own video drama showed me I've been going about this all wrong. It's time for me to quit hiding and just own it. Own it all. At the meeting tomorrow, I'm gonna look them all in the eye and address this thing head-on. Get it out in the open and let the people at Wicket Pro know things are gonna be different from now on. No more Work Elyse and Home Elyse. I realize now that

I need to be the same person all the time. That means going public with our relationship."

"You mean I can tell people you're my steady girl?"

"Yeah."

"Cool."

"I don't know if I still have a shot at the promotion. All I know is I'm not gonna hide anymore."

"I think that's a great idea. It's time people knew the real you. Everybody knows you're smart, but you're also very sweet and so much fun to be with. I've never had anybody laugh with me as much as you do."

Her face lit up in a beautiful smile. "Nobody can make me laugh like you, Luke."

"It's okay for the people you work with to know you have a sense of humor, and that you're a nice person and not an Ice Queen. And it's even okay for them to know you're the kind of girl who likes to get fucked by her boyfriend up against the wall."

She blinked in shock at my blunt statement, but I didn't back down.

"You love sex, Elyse. And that is so *cool!*"

Elyse looked at me for a moment and then burst out laughing.

"Baby, I know how much it sucks that everything was made so public but trust me. The guys you work with are *guys.* I guarantee you they think more highly of you now because of it. Really."

"I don't know about all that. But you're right about one thing." She leaned over and murmured in my ear. "I do love sex."

"Hmmm," I said, then pulled her in for a kiss. She eagerly responded, and we sat for a few minutes making out like horny teenagers.

"You look so hot in this outfit," she said.

"Yeah?"

"Oh yeah."

"Sooo, are you done with role playing now?" I leaned in close, kissing her cheek then brushing my lips against her ear. "Or do you want to get fucked by a pirate?"

Elyse let out a low, sensual moan. My cock stiffened and a smile curved my lips. I was grateful she found my acting sexy.

"Oh, I'm definitely not done with role playing." She bit her lip. "You're such a terrific actor, and there are sooo many delicious possibilities."

Her expression softened, and she tenderly brushed the hair out of my face. "All the same, for tonight I want my sweet boyfriend Luke to make love to me."

I smiled at her. "Yeah. I can do that."

CHAPTER 23

*W*e got back to my place, and I practically threw Luke onto my bed and straddled him. He lay on his back, grinning up at me, loving every minute of it. I started unbuttoning his shirt and ended up nearly ripping it off. I felt like my old self again, and I was glad to be done playing the victim.

I pulled off my blouse and bra, and Luke squeezed and massaged my breasts. I climbed off him so I could pull the rest of my clothes off and he did the same. I straddled him again and slid him inside me.

I threw my head back and cried out, pleasure surging through my body as I rode him. Luke gripped my hips, grunting his approval. Oh, how I had missed that sound. That deep, masculine sound of Luke's sexy voice. I ground myself against him until I could hardly take it anymore.

"I want you on top of me, baby," I said breathlessly. I slid off him and lay flat on my back, spreading my legs wide open.

Luke obliged, pausing for a moment as his cock hovered tantalizingly close to my opening.

"Do it!" I cried.

Luke grinned cockily and rammed into me. I cried out his name as he pounded me harder and harder. I gripped his shoulders and leaned forward, feeling my orgasm build.

"Luke, Luke, oh God ..."

He grinned again and said, "Already?"

"Yes," I managed, panting heavily. "Oh God, I've missed you. Don't stop, baby, don't stop!"

Luke shifted his body slightly, knowing the right spot to push me over the edge. The bed slammed into the wall as he rocked himself in and out of me in the perfect rhythm, giving me the long-overdue orgasm my body desperately needed.

"*Luke!*" I cried as I rode the waves of pure bliss.

He planted his hands on the mattress and rammed into me a few more times until he grunted his own release. I watched his handsome, manly face contort with ultimate pleasure. God, he was beautiful when he came.

Luke let out a long, shuddering breath. "Oh God, I needed that."

"Me too," I said, gazing up at him. "I love you so much, Geek."

"Love you too, Nerd." He bent down and kissed me before collapsing beside me.

We snuggled together for a while, talking softly, happy to be together.

After less than an hour of cuddling we had sex again. Slower, more tender and gentle, it lasted longer, our strongest needs satisfied earlier.

We looked into each other's eyes as we made love and felt that same wonderful connection we'd experienced the first time.

It was so good to be with Luke again. Where I belonged.

We finally fell asleep, exhausted and content.

The next morning, I woke up before Luke. I lay there for

a while, staring at the ceiling. I didn't notice when he woke up.

"You okay?" he asked.

"I'm scared," I told him. Today I was supposed to talk to my co-workers about everything, and I didn't feel as confident as I had yesterday.

"I know. But you got this, Elyse. You really do. It's okay to be scared. You're brave. Brave means being scared and doing it anyway. You. Got. This."

I turned to look at him. His determined expression bolstered my resolve. Luke believed in me. Now it was time to believe in myself.

"Yeah. Yeah, I sure do."

* * *

THOUGH I WAS a nervous wreck all morning, I was determined to go through with my plan. I watched the minutes tick by, excruciatingly slowly, to my 11am meeting. My phone rang at 10:55am, making me jump. It was Luke. Leave it to him to remember it was almost time for my critical meeting.

He didn't even say hello when I answered. Instead, he sang a few lines from "It All Fades Away," the song he had serenaded me with at the foundation.

When he stopped singing, he said firmly, "Now go kick some ass, Uptown Girl."

I broke into a wide smile. "Thanks, Geek."

I thought about how the people closest to me had inspired me to be brave. Susie's courage to keep going back to audition after audition, despite all the rejection and heartbreak; the way Rosemary faced her critics head-on, boldly releasing her video to the media; Luke's love, and the faith he had in me.

Hell yeah, I could do this. I drew in a deep breath, taking a moment to collect myself. I still felt a bit shaky: that wouldn't do. I had to be strong and confident for this to work.

Grabbing my work binder and notebook, I stood up and charged down the hallway. I was surprised to find I felt better already, holding my head up and looking people in the eye as I passed. That was so much better than blushing and averting my eyes.

Hunter and Keith were already in the conference room. Both looked up when I came in. I made a conscious effort to look each one in the eye before I sat down. Hunter eyed me curiously, clearly observing the difference in me already. Keith smiled warmly. He had been so worried about me ever since this happened. He seemed to be the only one who didn't enjoy the salacious gossip. Instead, he cared about what it was doing to me.

Mr. Bialystock came bustling in and put his briefcase down on the conference room table.

"Okay, lady and gents. We've got a lot of ground to cover in this meeting, so let's get down to it."

Do or die time.

"Mr. Bialystock, with your permission, might I say a few words first?"

He looked at me questioningly, and then gestured at me with his hand. "By all means."

I usually came up with some great ideas during our meetings, and he knew it. His confidence in me made this easier. Slightly.

I stood up for emphasis, and all three men, still seated, looked surprised.

"I want to, at long last, address the elephant in the room. I'm sick and tired of stressing out over it, and I want to deal with it once and for all." I made eye contact with each man

229

individually before continuing. "It's time to stop pretending that everyone in this room didn't see a video of me completely naked while having sex with Luke Rannells."

Keith's eyes got wide. Mr. Bialystock's face turned bright red.

"Jesus, Elyse," Hunter muttered. *Hah.* It was easy for him to gossip about me behind my back, but it wasn't so pleasant when he was confronted with the reality of it. The real, human person behind the scandal.

"Sir," I said, specifically addressing my boss. "I know it was a stupid and unprofessional thing to do, but it really was the only time a thing like that has happened. Well, you know, at work at least."

The three guys just stared at me. Oookay. Tough room. Whatever. There was no turning back now.

"For what it's worth, it wasn't some kind of cheap office tryst. Luke Rannells is my boyfriend, and I love him with all my heart."

I saw a hint of a smile on Mr. Bialystock's face. Keith let out a soft sigh and looked down.

"Really?" Hunter scoffed. "The maintenance guy?"

"Yeah," I snapped. "You got a problem with that?" *You elitist fuck.*

Hunter chuckled. "No, Ma'am."

Mr. Bialystock looked annoyed, which worried me. Then I realized he was irritated with Hunter and not me.

"Luke's a fine man, Elyse. Keeps this place running smoothly. Has for years," Mr. Bialystock said. He still looked wildly uncomfortable with this conversation, but overall, so far so good.

"Look, I wanted to address the whole issue so we can all move past it. This hasn't been easy for me. We didn't plan it. It just happened."

"I know, Elyse," Mr. Bialystock said. He seemed sympathetic, which helped. "It was out of character for you."

"Yeahhh, you'd think that, wouldn't you? I've never done *anything* like that in the workplace, and never will again. I promise you that. But it's not as out-of-character as you think."

Mr. Bialystock blushed again, probably worried about what I would say next. He needn't have been concerned. The last thing I wanted to do was make him, or anyone else, uncomfortable. Besides, talking about sexual things in the workplace was treacherous and could cause all kinds of legal problems. Women weren't the only ones who could feel uncomfortable with the topic of sex at work.

"My point is that for my whole career, I've tried to keep my personal life and my home life strictly separate. I wanted everybody to think I was one-hundred-percent dedicated to the job and had nothing going on outside of work. I never told anybody when I was dating someone. I never talked about my weekend plans. I've seen what can happen, especially to women who dare to have a home life and kids. It can destroy their career."

Hunter rolled his eyes.

"I wish I could say you're wrong," Mr. Bialystock said. "But I've seen that happen too."

I thought I saw a hint of regret on his face, and I wondered if he'd ever passed up a woman for a promotion because she was a mother.

"I've tried to create the illusion that I was all work and no play, but it's not true. I'm extremely dedicated to my job, but I do have a life outside of work. I have a boyfriend, as everybody in this goddamn building knows. I have a brand-new nephew whom I adore."

That got a smile out of Mr. Bialystock, who had three boys of his own.

"I have lots of wonderful friends that I hang out with on the weekends. And I'm a microbrew aficionado. I love craft beers. I hate the shitty wine I'm expected to drink at all our work functions when I'm supposed to be all ladylike."

"I like the shitty wine," Mr. Bialystock sniffed. "But I never drink it at work functions because I figure everyone will think I'm a pussy."

I laughed heartily, and so did Keith. Hunter looked annoyed.

"I mean, 'scuse my crude language and all," Mr. Bialystock said. "But maybe I'll start drinkin' wine now. Life's too short, you know?"

"Yes," I agreed.

"You got the Senior VP job, Elyse," he said bluntly.

I rewound his words back in my head, trying to figure out if I'd heard him right.

"What? What?" I asked.

Keith and Hunter both looked at our boss, wide-eyed and open-mouthed.

"I apologize for taking so long to make a decision," he said, making eye contact with each one of us. "You're all highly qualified, but I've long felt that Elyse is the best candidate. She has a strong computer science background, and I've never seen a client ask a tech question she couldn't answer. And she …" he looked at me, addressing me directly instead of in the third person. "You have a natural ability with people. I've seen the way you change your presentation methods mid-talk, just by reading the temperature of the room. You have great business instincts, and you know how to explain highly technical material without talking down to anyone."

"Thank you, sir."

"And you have never once complained about how difficult it's been for you as a female executive, but I want you to know I am aware of how hard you've worked. You deal with men from all different cultures, not to mention some from right here in the U.S., who don't take kindly to a woman explaining technology to them."

"It makes them feel threatened," I said, having lost count of how many times I'd struggled with that issue. The vast majority of the men I interacted with were wonderful, but there were still a lot of them who dismissed me outright because of my gender.

"Yes. And each time you've handled yourself with dignity and grace. I'm sorry I've never told you that before."

"Thank you, sir," I said again, feeling overwhelmed with gratitude. I couldn't seem to find the right words to express how much his praise meant to me.

"And, uh," he drew in a deep breath and let it out. He appeared to be quite sad, suddenly. "I was hemming and hawing over giving you the job, because I was worried about you."

"Why?" I asked. I sat back down so I could look across at him. Whatever he was trying to say wasn't easy for him.

"I had a partner once. Long time ago. Jed Curly. He was a total workaholic. Loved the job, but it was all he did. Up 'til all hours of the night, worked all weekend. Then one day he dropped dead of a heart attack. At work. I was there, and I—"

He swallowed hard and shook his head, clearly not wanting to discuss the horror of watching a good friend die before his very eyes.

"Jed's whole life was his work, and I find that very sad."

Keith and I nodded. To my surprise, so did Hunter. His cocky manner was gone for once.

"I didn't want that for you, Elyse. I was worried your work was a little too important you. That night of the video," he cleared his throat and blushed deeply. "The time stamp said 2am. Two in the morning!"

"I stayed late because I was trying get the Senior VP job."

"I know," he said with smile. "I thought you needed something else in your life. Whether it be kids, or a boyfriend. Hobbies. *Something.* But turns out you're doing just fine."

"I am, sir. I really am. I confess I do work too much, and I likely always will. But I have Luke. And I have siblings, a new nephew and probably more where that came from. And I've made a lot of new friends from knowing Luke. I'm doing well, sir. Quite well."

"Good," he said, looking relieved. "And I know you'll do Wicket Pro proud as Senior Vice President of Worldwide Sales Strategy and Operations."

I wanted to squeal out loud with excitement, but I repressed the urge. I would squeal at Luke later, when I told him the news.

Mr. Bialystock turned to Keith and Hunter. "I think highly of both of you, and there's a lot of room to grow in this company. If you continue to do well, I'm sure you can count on your Senior VP to provide recommendations for promotions and so forth. I urge you to keep that in mind."

He glanced over at me and then back at the guys again. "I consider this whole video matter to be closed."

Keith and Hunter nodded solemnly. Overall, they'd been fairly cool about the whole thing. Well, Hunter had been a bit of a jerk. But the boss had made it clear they were to let the matter drop.

After the meeting, Keith stopped by my office and stood in the doorway. I was elated I'd gotten the promotion and relieved that I'd confronted the video issue at last, but I still felt embarrassed when I looked at him. I wondered if the feeling of shame would ever really go away.

"I'm glad you said all that," Keith told me.

"Really? It was kind of awful. Talking about it like that."

"I know," he said with sympathy. "But I consider you a

really good friend, and I don't want there to be weirdness between us."

"Thanks."

"You coulda told me you had a boyfriend. Maybe I wouldn't have made such a fool of myself pursuing you."

That's when I realized I wasn't the only one feeling humiliated.

"You didn't make a fool of yourself. Really. And you're right. I should have told you. I'm sorry, Keith."

"It's okay. It's funny. Watching the video?"

I swallowed, feeling my face get hot.

"Mostly I was just heartbroken." Keith looked at me with a depth of sorrow I'd never seen in him before. "I just wished it had been me with you."

We looked into each other's eyes for a moment.

Hunter burst into the room, startling me. "Hey, hey, hey Madame Senior VP! Congratulations."

Hunter shook my hand and managed to look halfway sincere. Mostly I figured he was just sucking up.

"And may I say, Elyse, you kinda rock," Hunter said.

"What do you mean?"

"I mean, you're way cooler than I thought you were. And I'm not just saying that because you're my boss now. I gotta admit, you had me fooled. I really thought you were a frigid loser with no life outside of work. No offense."

"Of course. No offense taken." *You imbecile.*

Hunter left, and Keith looked at me.

"For the record, I always knew you were cool," Keith said with a smile. He started to leave and then turned back.

"Elyse, please forgive me, but I gotta ask. What the hell was Luke dressed up as?"

I shrugged and said simply, "President Andrew Jackson."

CHAPTER 24

$\mathcal{I}$t had been several weeks since Elyse took over the Senior VP job, and everything was going well for her. We were open about our relationship at work, which was cool. I was proud to have everybody know she was my girl.

Even so, Elyse still struggled a lot. She did her best to get past the workplace scandal, but things were still uncomfortable for her. Although only a few people had seen the video, Elyse still worried that she'd be forever known as the office whore—her words, not mine—rather than for her intelligence and ambition.

Elyse was talking to Hunter and Keith in the hallway when I came up to the tenth floor. I hung back; I knew it was still awkward for her to be seen with me since our private sex life went public, so I always waited for her to make the first move at work.

It still turned me on to hear her use all those fancy technology words, and she looked so beautiful. She dressed less severely now at work, wearing her pretty blonde hair down at her shoulders instead of up in a tight bun, and she wore more feminine, flowing dresses. She was taking little steps toward being more true to herself in the workplace, and I thought it helped her regain some of her confidence.

"Hey, Geek," she called over to me.

"Hey, Nerd."

"Wanna go to lunch?"

"If you're buyin'," I said with a grin.

She nodded. "Be ready in a second."

Elyse's face turned red, but she went back to talking to her co-workers. God, I hated that she still blushed whenever she and I were in the same room together at work. It was involuntary, and there was nothing she could do but soldier on and pretend it wasn't happening. We were both acutely aware that whenever people saw us together, they would picture me banging her against the wall. I mean, how could they not? You couldn't unsee something like that.

She wrapped up her conversation and smiled warmly as she slid her arm around my waist. I was relieved to know she wasn't ashamed of being with me. It was only the crazy circumstances that made things difficult at work.

We held hands as we walked a few blocks to a nearby sandwich shop we frequented for lunch.

"I'm sorry things are so difficult for you at work," I told her. "I want you to love your job like you used to."

"Oh, I do, Luke. I really do." Elyse's eyes lit up. "It's exciting, it's challenging, and I get to make the final decisions on things according to my vision. I love it! I'm reviewing resumes and getting ready to hire someone to replace me in my old job position, now that I've moved up."

Her face fell. "Trouble is, what's to keep Hunter from telling every new hire in the company about the video? Or even showing it to them? He really might do that. Keith wouldn't."

"Because he has a thing for you," I said.

Elyse looked over at me and said softly, "Yes. He does. I feel bad for him. Honestly, Luke. Even if I wasn't madly in love with you, I wouldn't be interested in him. He's a great guy and all, but I just don't, you know." She shrugged, and I thought, *Thank God.* I trusted Elyse, of course, but Keith was a very attractive man.

"No," she continued. "Keith wouldn't do anything to hurt me. But Hunter, though. I really worry sometimes. And as sweet as Keith is, it's still weird." She winced again, but then shook her head. "Oh well. It's my own stupid hang-up. I'm gonna have to get over it and move on."

I nodded as I held the door to the sandwich shop open for her. We got in line to wait to order our food.

"So, what are we doing tomorrow night?" I asked her.

"I've got Rosemary's bachelorette party tomorrow night, remember?"

"Oh, right," I said with a laugh. "I can't believe you're going to a strip club."

"Me neither. I've never been, but I admit I'm kinda curious," she said, smiling.

"It'll do you good to have a girl's night out."

Elyse had become good friends with Rosemary and Susie, and they always had a blast when they got together.

"I think so, too. I can't do Friday night, but I'm all yours the rest of the weekend. Whatever you want to do."

"Okay, cool."

* * *

I FELT a little nervous showing up at the strip club alone. I'd rather have gone with Rosemary and Susie, but I often worked late, and I didn't want to hold them up.

My anxiety eased a bit when I saw them sitting together, drinking and laughing. Yes. This was going to be fun, like every time we got together. An attractive black lady and two men were sitting with them. I was surprised to see guys at this all-male strip club. Upon closer inspection, one of the men sported military fatigues, and I figured out who they were.

"You made it!" Rosemary cried cheerfully, hoisting her wine in the air.

"Of course I did. I wouldn't miss it." I looked over at the man with brown hair and brown eyes. "Oh my gosh, are you Ryan?"

"Yep," Ryan said, extending his hand. "Nice to meet you, Elyse."

"You too. Rosemary and Susie talk about you all the time."

"And this is Jack," Ryan said, nodding at the cute guy in fatigues next to him.

"Great to meet you, Jack," I said shaking his hand. "I hear you two are newlyweds. Congratulations!"

"Thanks," Ryan said with a smile. I could see the joy in his eyes. He and Jack made an adorable couple.

"Yeah, so this is like a post-nuptial bachelor party for them, too," Rosemary said with a laugh.

"Nice," I said.

"Oh, and Elyse, I'd like you to meet Terry," Rosemary said, smiling at the other woman at the table.

"Hi, Terry," I said, shaking her hand. I loved being introduced to Rosemary's friends. They were such a tight-knit group, and I felt like my own circle of friends continued to expand because of her.

Terry waved a server over and asked, "What are you drinkin', Elyse?"

"Oh, anything you've got on tap is fine. Thanks!"

The server nodded and rushed off to get my drink.

The lights dimmed, and we all watched as the first two guys came out onstage. I found it easy to let loose and have fun with a drink in my hand and surrounded by good friends. We hooted and hollered our approval of the male strippers. Rosemary, Susie, Terry, and I had a grand old time, whistling and yelling until our throats were sore.

Ryan and Jack were more reserved, but they were enjoying the act all the same. They kept murmuring to each other, like they were comparing notes about which guy onstage was the hottest. I had to laugh. I could totally see Luke doing the same thing with me, never mind the fact that he was straight. He just had that kind of sense of humor.

It made me smile when the next song began to play. It was "Uptown Girl," which always made me think of Luke. I found myself wishing he were here with me.

And that's when I realized he *was* here.

I'd know that Luke Rannells strut anywhere.

He was one of the men onstage.

I gasped out loud, and Rosemary and Susie burst out laughing.

"Wh—what in the hell?" I stammered.

"It's payback time, baby!" Rosemary shouted.

"Them boys told me what they did to you, honey," Terry told me. "This is the *least* they can do!"

I stared at the stage and realized I knew every single one of the "male strippers" onstage.

Roger. Manny. Keith. Hunter. And Luke.

My jaw dropped, and I was dimly aware of hearing Johnny's familiar laugh. He'd slipped into a chair next to Rosemary to watch the show.

"You guys knew about this?" I asked Rosemary and Susie.

"Who do you think choreographed their dance?" Susie said with a laugh. She watched proudly as the guys danced onstage.

All five men pointed directly at me each time they sang, or mouthed, the words "Uptown Girl."

Luke came down from the stage and marched toward our table. When he got to me, he pulled off his necktie and wrapped it around my neck, singing to me about being my downtown man.

My eyes filled with tears, and I was laughing and crying at the same time. Luke was *crazy*. And that's why I was crazy in love with him. He provided the spark of insanity my life needed. Grinning, he headed back up to the stage to be with the other guys.

Terry jumped up from her seat and went right up to the stage, waving a dollar bill in her hand. She gleefully stuffed it down Roger's pants. That's when it finally dawned on me that Terry was Roger's wife.

Laughing, Rosemary, Susie, and I all high-fived Terry when she came back to the table.

Luke danced on the stage, hamming it up. The audience loved it. And I loved the way he looked at me and put his hand over his heart in an exaggerated motion every time he sang the part about being in love with an Uptown Girl. I felt like the luckiest girl in the world.

"I can't believe they're actually doing this!" I said, watching in disbelief as my boyfriend and co-workers removed more and more of their clothing. Keith had an *incredible* body. He'd be one hell of a catch for some lucky lady. And Hunter. How in the hell did Luke get *Hunter* to do this?

I turned to Rosemary and asked, "They're not really gonna go all the way, are they?"

"You're damn right they are!" she exclaimed. Then she caught Susie's eye and said, "By the way, they won't show your video ..."

"*If you don't show theirs!*" said Susie and Rosemary in perfect unison. I followed their respective gazes to the back of the room.

241

David was there, recording the entire thing on his cell phone.

"Can he ... Is he allowed to do that?" I asked.

"Oh, honey," Rosemary said. "He's here with Johnny Creel. He can do any damn thing he wants."

Johnny grinned at me, and I understood that he must have laid down a ton of cash to make this whole thing happen.

"Thank you," was all I could say.

He winked playfully at me and then turned his attention back to the stage.

"Wait, do they know they're being recorded?" I asked.

"Yes, they do," Rosemary assured me. "We wouldn't have done it without their permission."

I nodded, then turned back to the stage.

My heart hammered; the song was coming to the end.

Roger, Manny, Keith, Hunter, and Luke were down to their underwear. I glanced back at David to see if he was still recording. I burst out laughing when I saw that he was, but his head was turned so as not to see what was about to happen. Susie laughed uproariously, clapping her hands with glee at her boyfriend's obvious discomfort with male nudity. Johnny, however, didn't seem to have a problem. He sat there grinning at the spectacle before him.

I drew in a deep breath, preparing myself for the finale.

During the final seconds of the song, all five men whipped off their tearaway undergarments in unison, showing *everything*. The crowd of women went wild with screams and applause, and then the stage went dark.

I covered my face, laughing and crying. "You guys are *insane!*" I looked up, taking in all the smiling faces surrounding me. "And I love every last one of ya."

They all laughed with me. Terry leaned over and gave me

a hug, saying, "I hope this makes you feel a little better, honey."

Her sweet gesture made me cry harder. Terry didn't even know me, and yet she was so kind. I couldn't begin to imagine how much time, effort, and money went into pulling off this crazy scheme.

Suddenly, it hit me.

I *did* feel better.

I felt like a huge, physical weight had been lifted off my chest. The crushing humiliation I'd felt for weeks, while not entirely gone, had eased considerably. I could really, truly love my job again.

I could move on.

* * *

WE ALL MET up outside the club. Keith, Hunter, Roger, and Manny grinned at me. I blushed fiercely. I couldn't help it.

"I—I don't know where to look," I confessed with a laugh. The guys laughed with me, and it was wonderful. Everything was going to be okay.

"I can't believe you all did this. I don't know what to say."

"You don't have to say anything, Elyse," Roger said, stepping forward. "I'm really sorry about everything. Had I known you two were involved, I never would have … Well, never mind that. I shouldn't have done that to anybody, no matter who it was. I'm just so glad you got the job anyway."

"Thank you so much, Roger."

Terry smiled proudly. I gave Roger a hug, and I felt his body relax in relief. I'd never realized how bad he'd felt about the whole thing.

I think he was relieved that I'd forgiven him.

"I'm sorry too, Elyse," Manny said. I didn't know him very well, but I gave him a hug anyway.

"Thanks, Manny. That means a lot."

I walked over to Keith. Rosemary and Susie started chatting with Terry and Roger, which made it a little easier for us to step aside for a moment.

"Keith, it was so sweet of you to do this for me," I said, wishing I had more eloquent words.

"I want us to be friends, Elyse. And like I said before, I don't want there to be weirdness between us. I mean, not that this wasn't *weird*, but you know what I mean. I want you to be comfortable around me, despite everything that's happened."

I could see he'd been as embarrassed as I was, but for different reasons. He'd really put himself out there when he asked me out, and now I was his boss.

"Of course we can be friends, Keith. And hey, I hope this isn't too inappropriate coming from your boss, but ..." I leaned over and whispered in his ear. "You sure showed me what I'm missing out on tonight."

Keith laughed, then blushed. "Thanks."

"Thank *you*, Keith." I squeezed his hand.

I walked over to Hunter, having no idea what to say. Fortunately, he spoke first.

"I'm the one who showed Keith—and Mr. Bialystock the video. It was a shit thing to do, and I'm really sorry," Hunter said.

"Oh," I said simply. I wanted to be furious with him, but I couldn't. Not after tonight.

"I know this doesn't make up for everything, but I hope it helps," he said with a smile.

"It does, Hunter. It helps a lot." I looked over at Keith. "Hopefully this means we can relax around each other and have fun at work."

"But not too much fun," Hunter said. "That's what got you in trouble the last time."

I laughed, and it felt good to laugh about it. I hadn't found much humor in the whole nightmare up to this point.

I said my goodbyes and gave hugs to Terry, Rosemary, Susie, and Johnny. Ryan and Jack both hugged me, too, which was sweet. I shook David's hand and thanked him profusely for his help.

"I'll send you the video," he told me. "And then I'm deleting it. Or maybe I'll just burn my phone."

I laughed and patted him on the back. I would guard the video with my life. I didn't want any of those men experiencing what I went through.

Luke walked over to me and I threw my arms around him. He held me tight.

"You're insane," I whispered.

"Yep. And that's why you love me."

"Yes. It is," I said, looking into those adorable brown eyes.

"I just … I had to do *something*. I couldn't stand seeing you so upset. So I thought of the craziest thing I could imagine and went with that."

"How on earth did you get all those guys to do this?"

"It wasn't as hard as you think. They care about you too, Elyse. They were actually pretty happy we found a way to make you feel better."

"Even Hunter?"

"Well, I admit he was a holdout for a while."

I nodded, still stunned that Hunter had gone through with it.

"I convinced him that this might be a way to get in good with the boss," Luke said with a laugh. "But he also felt really bad about sharing the video."

I gazed into Luke's eyes, marveling at how wonderful he was. "Let's go home." I kissed his lips and added, "Maybe you can do that whole striptease thing for me again."

CHAPTER 25

*I*t was past 8pm on a Friday, and I was still sitting at my desk. As always, I was grateful for Luke's understanding of my crazy schedule. Even so, I missed him. The rest of this work could wait until Monday.

I figured I'd better hit the ladies' room before getting on the road. Walking down the hallway, a noise startled me. I stopped in my tracks. I'd thought I was the only one still here. Luke always worried about me being alone in the building at night. It usually didn't bother me, but I was suddenly afraid.

The noise was coming from the restroom where I was headed. I heard the familiar squeak of the cleaning lady's cart, and I felt my whole body relax. I briefly considered using the men's room since nobody was around, then thought the better of it. The cleaning people wouldn't mind if I just used the facilities quickly.

Then I heard singing. The acoustics in the restroom were incredible, and this woman sounded *good*. I mean, like Rosemary and Susie good. I figured I should leave. I certainly didn't want to embarrass the poor woman. I headed back down the hall.

Then I turned back around. I couldn't resist finding out who the mystery singer was.

I slowly opened the ladies room door to find Crista there, mopping the floor and singing. She caught sight of me in the mirror, then gasped and dropped her mop onto the floor.

"Jesus!" she exclaimed in a Spanish accent.

"I'm so sorry! I didn't mean to startle you."

Crista put her hand over her heart. Once she recovered from her fright, her fear turned to embarrassment.

"I'm sorry. I—I didn't know anybody else was still here."

"Oh, don't be sorry. You sounded amazing!" The last thing I wanted was for her to feel ashamed. With a voice like that, she should be proud.

"Oh," she said, dismissing me with a wave.

"I mean it. Have you ever thought about singing professionally?"

Crista refused to look at me. "Oh, no, no, no, no," she insisted as she busily mopped the floor. Then she stopped suddenly and looked at me.

She laughed, and then said, "Only every day of my life."

I bit my lip. "Really. Hmmm. I have some friends I think you should meet …"

FREE NOVELLA

Beloved Reader,

I want to let you know that if you sign up for my email list, you will receive a FREE steamy sports novella that is EXCLUSIVE to my email list subscribers! It's the prequel to the baseball romance series, The Boys of Baltimore.

Thanks so much for spending this time with Luke and Elyse. Sigh...I think Luke might be my favorite hero yet...

I hope you'll continue on with the adventures of Johnny, Rosemary, and the rest of the crew in Book 4 - Finding Her Voice.

Handsome and dreamy, Keith deserves a happy ever after too, wouldn't you say? Crista is another lovely and talented performer who has much to contribute to the theater world...if only she would agree to accept some help in getting there. Find out what they can accomplish together in the next installment of the Wall Street to Broadway series, LOSING HER FEAR.

WAIT! BEFORE YOU GO!

Don't forget to join the email list if you want a FREE, steamy sports romance novella!

Sign up today, and I will send you a **FREE** novella entitled Starting From Zero. The novella is available **exclusively** to Author Linda Fausnet email list subscribers, and it is the prequel to my steamy sports romance series, The Boys of Baltimore Series.

Join the email list so you will always know when I've got a new book out.

I promise not to cram your inbox with too many emails – pinky swear!

You can also keep in touch by:

Following me on Amazon
Following me on Bookbub
Following me on Instagram
Joining my Author Reader's Group on Facebook.

Why Leave a Book Review? I'll give you 3 good reasons.

You can do it in <u>less than a minute</u>! Just choose a star rating from 1 to 5 stars and add a sentence or two on how you felt about the book.

1. Most readers choose the books they read based on the reviews, but <u>only a few readers</u> are kind enough to leave a review.
2. Most readers are not aware of this, but authors live and die by reviews. We really do.
3. It only takes a minute to leave a review, but the impact lasts for the lifetime of the book.

Thank you so very much.

ATTENTION ROMANCE NOVEL FANS!

I hope you'll join my romance novel fan club, Romance Novel Addicts Anonymous, on Facebook, Instagram, Twitter, and Pinterest. Join the email list, and you'll receive WHAT'S YOUR PLEASURE? RNAA'S OFFICIAL GUIDE TO FINDING YOUR NEXT GREAT ROMANCE READ.

www.ingramcontent.com/pod-product-compliance
Lightning Source LLC
Chambersburg PA
CBHW070911180626
46817CB00003B/1015